Ravenwood

ALSO AVAILABLE BY JK ELLEM

Stand Alone Novels
All Other Sins
Audrey Kills Again!

The Ravenwood Seasons
Book 1 Mill Point Road
Book 2 Ravenwood
Book 3 The Sisterhood

The Killing Seasons
Book 1 A Winter's Kill
Book 2 A Spring Kill – coming Spring 2022

No Justice Series
Book 1 No Justice
Book 2 Cold Justice
Book 3 American Justice
Book 3.1 Fast Justice – A Ben Shaw Road Trip Thriller #1
Book 3.2 Sinful Justice – A Ben Shaw Road Trip Thriller #2
Book 3.3 Dark Justice – A Ben Shaw Road Trip Thriller #3
Book 4 Hidden Justice
Book 5 Raw Justice

Deadly Touch Series
Fast Read Deadly Touch

Octagon Trilogy (DystopianThriller Series)
Prequel Soldiers Field
Book 1 Octagon
Book 2 Infernum
Book 3 Sky of Thorns – coming soon

Ravenwood

by JK Ellem

Copyright © by 28th Street Multimedia Group 2021

Ravenwood is a work of fiction. All incidents, dialogue and all characters are products of the author's imagination and are not to be construed as real. Any resemblance to persons living or dead is entirely coincidental.

All rights reserved. In accordance with the U.S. Copyright Act of 1976, the scanning, uploading, and electronic sharing of any part of this book without the written permission of the publisher is unlawful piracy and theft of the author's intellectual property.

No part of this book may be reproduced, stored in a retrieval system or transmitted in any form or by any means, without the prior permission in writing of the publisher, nor to be otherwise circulated in any form of binding or cover other than that in which it is published without a similar condition, including this condition, being imposed on the subsequent purchaser.

Copyrighted Material

"There are many cities, and small towns in America, where quite easily it is statistically unlikely that you'll ever get caught for murder…"
—Thomas K. Hargrove–Murder Accountability Project

Prologue

Flowers of Death from the Garden of Eden

My Dearest Detective Perez,

I believe congratulations are in order regarding your recent, no doubt deserved, promotion. After all, you did catch The Eden Killer.

It has been twelve months now since the atrocities of Mill Point Road, and I still see mention of it in the local news—albeit to a lesser extent with each passing month. Our morbid fascination with death and murder seems to be one of those enduring qualities that make us all human. And yet in those twelve months, as I walk around the town of Ravenwood, I see that very little has indeed changed.

Then there is Mill Point Road itself. I took a stroll up there just the other day and was pleasantly surprised to see that construction of the new house at Number Eight, where Becca Cartwright lives, is nearly finished. Good on her for staying, I say! I would have demolished the previous house too. Some of the townsfolk say that she should have sold it, moved away, like how Zoe and Jason Collins did at Number Ten. I caught a brief glimpse of the new person living in their house while I was there. They certainly look interesting.

I'm so happy to see that Sabine Miller is making a recovery and has moved back into her home at Number Six, minus her husband, of course! I wonder if she will be a changed person, given what she has been through? Rumor has it, she made a deal with the feds, a reduced sentence, and she gets to keep her home in exchange for revealing all the dirty little secrets about her husband's business. Some say that part of her memory is gone forever, that she can't recall much from that fateful night when she, you, and Becca Cartwright confronted The Eden Killer in Becca's own home. Maybe her memory will eventually return. Who knows?

Then there is the wise and ageless Maggie Vickerman at Number Four. It's hard to believe she just turned seventy. One day I overheard Edith Plover, the librarian, say that Maggie has a new, much younger man in her life. Some businessman from Baltimore, apparently. I believe Hank, Maggie's ex-husband, will be released on parole in a few weeks. That should certainly prove interesting.

I couldn't see Paige Hamill about, but I did notice a gleaming, new SUV parked in the driveway of Number Two, with a pink infant car seat in the back. Seems like Scott, her husband, has hit The New York Times *Best-Seller list with his nonfiction crime novel about what happened. There's a huge window display of it in the bookstore in town. Fancy calling it,* Mill Point Road! *How original. I certainly won't be buying it. Dollars to doughnuts, everything he knows about what happened hasn't made it into the book either. Stay tuned for the trashy sequel.*

I also read in the news that your colleague and mentor, Detective Marvin Richards, has recently retired to a cabin in the woods to pursue his passion for fly fishing and be surrounded by his books on philosophy. I'm sorry to also hear about the sudden passing of his wife. To be taken at such a young age! Her funeral was so touching, though, and I particularly enjoyed the eulogy he gave.

I imagine that you still consult with him from time to time, seeking his sage advice and guiding wisdom on the more gruesome cases. Whether or not he has taught you everything that he knows, is yet to be seen—or truly tested.

I hope you accept these flowers. I thought them fitting, black roses. I picked them myself, especially for you from my own garden.

I wish you well in your future endeavors, Detective Perez. And as I conclude this letter, I thought that you should know; The Eden Killer—I taught him everything that he knew…but not everything that I know. As Marvin Richards was your mentor…so I, was The Eden Killer's.

Best Wishes.

Your Admirer.

🐦 Chapter 1 - Taking the Eyes

With a sharp, stabbing motion, he took her left eye first, plucking it clean from its socket.

An eyeball is considered a delicacy in some parts of the world. However, it wasn't to his liking, so he spat it out with a ruffled shiver. Undeterred, he moved next to her right eye and did the same, removing only part of the eyeball this time. Again, he didn't approve of the taste.

Angered, he suddenly attacked her face in an animalistic frenzy, rapidly puncturing her cheeks and nose. Slowly, his anger abated, and he tore bloody ribbons of flesh from the soft hollows of her cheeks and began gulping them down, spattering blood across his neck and chest. The taste was much better, and for a while, he feasted on her, gorging himself well past the point that his hunger subsided, for he knew not when such an abundance of tasty flesh would present itself again.

He regarded her one more time, turning his head one way, then the other, his coal-black eyes glistening in the sunshine. In one fluid motion, he furled his black glossy wings, and with powerful sweeps, lifted effortlessly into the air, climbing higher and higher into the clear blue sky with each feathered pull, leaving the woman and the bonds of gravity behind. Sensing a shift in the breeze, he tilted into a thermal that carried him higher, and for a while, he was content to soar and ride the warm invisible current, his wings outstretched.

Uninterrupted woodland slid past his belly in a green, rippling blur before giving way to roads, barns, farmhouses, fields plowed into neat rows, and quilted squares layered in white. The town loomed ahead, nestled among woodland to the north, a river to the east.

Rolling to the left, the raven began a low circle of the township, riding the cold air for a moment, watching keenly the landscape as it passed under its unfurled wings. Then his shiny black eyes spotted a row of houses on the top of a ridge to the west. His walnut-sized brain was suddenly drawn in that direction, remembering he had found food there, remembering the face of a young man who had shown him kindness, had fed him nuts from his hand.

The raven tilted and rode the breeze toward the ridge. It circled the houses once, unsure as to which house he had sat on the back porch years ago and been fed by the kind man. Finally, he settled for the partially built house, second on the left, where vehicles of all shapes and sizes were clustered out front and where the earth around the house was torn and broken.

Tucking his wings close to his body, the raven plummeted toward the earth, spying a rail on the back porch, hoping to be rewarded again.

🐦 Chapter 2 - Becca

Rebecca Cartwright saw the raven perched on the rail of the back porch, one shiny black eye staring accusingly at her, as though looking past her own eyes and deep into her soul, to the sins that lay hidden there.

The raven's beak and throat hackles were stained red, probably roadkill it had been pecking on, Becca thought.

The shiny eye swiveled once more, the head tilted skyward, and with a sweep of its wings, the raven took flight and was gone.

"Becca!"

Becca turned to see Josh Daniels making his way toward her through skeletal walls of unclad wooden framing, navigating over lumber planks, around dangling electrical conduit, and over power cables that snaked in all directions across the dusty, bare concrete of the ground floor. The sound of hammering, the shrill of circular saws slicing wood, electric drills buzzing, and the occasional yell or swear word floated down from the second-story above her head.

Clad in a cotton shirt with the sleeves rolled up, blue jeans, tan work boots, and a fully laden tool belt around his hips, which swayed as he moved, Josh reminded Becca of a Western movie gunslinger. He was tall, lean, and built with powerful shoulders and tanned arms, with just the right amount of hard muscle honed from a daily diet of swinging heavy tools, lifting planks of raw lumber, and hefting bags of cement on his shoulders. Putting his hands to good hard use. His messy blond hair desperately needed a cut, Becca thought, watching him. But it added a tinge of Viking to his gunslinger look, especially when paired with his intense blue eyes.

Since Becca had decided to raze to the ground her original home on Mill Point Road, leaving nothing except bare dirt, and start again, Josh's role in her life had dramatically increased. The local handyman—eight years her junior—who had previously done odd jobs for her, was now a constant fixture, like the new home that was steadily growing up out of the ground around her. From head contractor, coordinating the various workmen under him on the new home build, to general sounding board, adding a little of his own construction expertise and sage advice, his role was pivotal in bringing to life Becca's vision and design ideas.

"We need to talk," Josh said, unfurling a set of plans on a nearby work bench. Josh ran his finger along the external plan. "We need to shore up the ground here some more, where we excavated a few months back."

"Is there a problem?" Becca asked. As Josh leaned in, she smelled a mix of sawdust, coffee, and the manly spice of physical exertion, which she quite liked.

"Not really. You did want to demolish the original house, including ripping out the slab and footings, as well as removing all traces of the basement, some of which was set below ground level." Josh tapped one finger on the plans where the gradient of the ridgeline dropped away on both sides of Mill Point Road. "So, we had some soil slippage here in this spot after last night's storm. Nothing near the house, but I just want you to be safe."

"Where exactly?"

Josh pointed on the plan. "Here, and here. Nothing major." He looked up at her. "Did you notice the slippage last night?"

Becca glanced up. "Last night?"

Josh frowned. "Yeah." He threw a thumb over his shoulder.

"You left a trail of muddy footprints all the way through the downstairs laundry room. I know you're a stickler for tidiness. That's okay, my crew swept it up this morning before they started laying the tile."

"Sorry," Becca said. "I forgot. I must have too many things on my mind."

Since the new build started six months ago, Josh was a daily constant in her life, giving Becca the distinct feeling he wanted more than just a professional relationship between them. He wasn't pushy or anything and was very respectful and courteous toward her. But he did drop little hints now and then. Like bringing extra for his lunch, only to then coax her outside to where he had laid a rug on the tailgate of his truck so he could share his famous handmade five-inch-thick, pastrami-and-pickle-on-rye sandwiches with her. Or the time when he turned up at her doorstep one evening with a bottle of red wine and a measuring tape so they could discuss the layout of the new kitchen.

These, and other outside-of-work "meetings" seemed to be all clever ploys by him in hopes of securing a casual date under the guise of working on the house. Yet Becca had rebuffed all of his more direct advances. At the moment, just being her builder and friend was enough for her.

Not wanting to live in town in a rental during the build, she opted for a design that incorporated building the separate master wing first so she could live within the build while the rest of the house sprang up around her. The wing comprised of the master bedroom, separate bathroom, a working but not completed kitchen, and laundry room, allowing Becca her privacy while keeping an eye on everything and being on hand for Josh to answer any questions or tackle any immediate problems as they arose. The rest of the house was a work in progress, weatherproofed in some parts but unsecured in others. In the evening, when Josh and his crew finished for the day, Becca would often, with a glass of wine in one hand and her notebook in the other, wander through the rest of the partially finished house, checking on the progress and making notes of any changes or concerns she had.

"Do whatever you need to with the earthworks," Becca said. "I don't want my new house sliding off the ridge in the next downpour."

"Good." Josh scrunched up his face. "Remind me again why you decided not to just sell the place and move on?"

Becca gave a shrug. "I like the location. And...I don't want to keep moving. Plus, the property values have dropped around here, given what happened."

"All the more reason to sell and move on," Josh said, rolling up the plans again. "Well, it's your dime. Just remember, you can't tear down old memories. They tend to last forever." He began walking away and then turned back to Becca. "Speaking of past memories, are you going to the book signing tonight in town?"

Becca didn't want to go, but Paige Hamill had pleaded with her to attend. Reluctantly, Becca had agreed. "Yes, seven p.m., I believe it kicks off."

Josh gave a hopeful grin, and Becca knew what was coming next. "Well, maybe we can go together," he said, "catch a bite to eat after at McKenzies." McKenzies was a new sports bar in Ravenwood, where Josh seemed to frequent a lot.

"Like a date?" Josh added, slowly sauntering back toward her, the larger roofing hammer on his belt slapping against his thigh like an old Colt six-shooter.

Now he really did look like a character out of a spaghetti

Western. "A date?" Becca asked, folding her arms and giving him a questioning look.

His eyes lit up. "Yeah. Maybe I could pick you up?"

"Sorry, Josh. We agreed to keep this strictly business."

The swagger went, and Josh's shoulders slumped.

"But if I see you there at the bookstore, then you can buy me a drink," Becca added, not wanting to hurt his feelings. He was younger than her in more ways than just years.

Josh's face brightened. "Okay…so like a da—"

Becca cut him off. "Not a date. Just a drink."

Josh reluctantly bowed his head in submission. "I heard Scott Hamill is putting on the drinks and some food at the bookstore."

"Then you'll have no excuse," Becca said, before adding, "but, I'll find my own way there."

After Josh was gone, Becca turned and looked back through the unclad framing toward where the laundry room was. That part of the ground floor was still open and exposed to the outside.

Muddy footprints?

🐦 Chapter 3 - Little Lady

Being recently promoted to detective didn't preclude Haley Perez from making traffic stops, especially if the truck she was following for the last mile along the highway outside of Ravenwood had given her an unsettling feeling that made her scalp prickle.

The last time she had such a feeling was twelve months ago as a patrol officer standing on the porch of Becca Cartwright's house up on Mill Point Road, with her handgun drawn.

Perez stood on the sidestep of the truck, her left hand gripping the side mirror strut, her right hand on the butt of her handgun. She peered into the cab at the driver. He was in his late sixties, she guessed, with gray hair, a beard, and a ponytail. He reminded Perez of Willie Nelson, but heavyset with powerful shoulders, not emaciated like Willie. The man's large, rough hands gripped the steering wheel, the skin scaled with age and covered with scars and nicks.

Good. He knew the drill. *Keep your hands where I can see them and don't make any sudden movements.*

"Is there a problem, little lady?"

"Where are you headed, sir?" Perez asked, the prickling of her scalp intensifying.

"Baltimore. I'm just passing through." The man smiled, his eyes like pools of tar, dark and bottomless. "Did I do something wrong? I don't think I was speeding at all." He nodded slowly at Perez, his voice calm, almost hypnotic, like he was trying to bend her mind.

"Can I see your license and registration, sir?" Perez asked, ignoring the spell-like quality of his soft gaze and soothing tone.

A groan came from behind the man, in the sleeper compartment behind the driver's seat. Perez pivoted on the step and caught a glimpse of a head with dark hair and a man's face peeking out from under a blanket.

"That's my cousin," the old man whispered to Perez. "We take turns driving. He drives at night, and I take the day shift." The old man flipped down the sun visor and pulled out some paperwork and handed it to Perez through the open window.

Perez checked the Wyoming license and plates. Everything seemed in order. She handed it back to the old man. "You came from Wyoming?"

The man slid everything back under the visor. "I was up in New Hampshire, drove down through Pennsylvania, little lady."

Perez definitely didn't like how he kept calling her "little lady."

The cell phone on Perez's belt rang. "Stay there," she told the old man before stepping down off the rig and unclipping her cell. "Perez."

"It's Kershaw." Brandon "Fred" Kershaw was her sergeant, one of only two in the Criminal Investigative Division of Hagerstown PD, who supervised the detective pool of twelve, Perez being the youngest, and according to most of her more seasoned colleagues, the least experienced. Females were in short supply in the Hagerstown PD, with Perez being the only female detective on the roster. Kershaw, together with Perez's mentor, the now-retired Detective Marvin Richards, was instrumental in fast-tracking her to junior detective in the CID after The Eden Killer case had concluded.

They called Kershaw "Fred" after Fred Flintstone because, like Fred Flintstone, Kershaw was short, squat, barrel chested with thick arms and neck, and had an unruly mop of dark hair. And like his cartoon namesake, Kershaw could often be heard hollering from one end of the detective's squad room to the other. Kershaw was hard but fair, wanting the best from his cohort of detectives. On Perez's first day after passing her detective's exam, he pulled her aside, telling her that she'd not be granted any special privileges just because she was a woman or despite Perez's fame for catching The Eden Killer. Perez wasn't offended. Far from it. She didn't want it any other way. She just wanted to be treated as an equal. She told him she was eager to learn, and Kershaw told her in return that was all he could ever hope for from his detectives—that, and to catch perps and close cases.

The attention of such a high-profile case was unwanted by Perez, and she shied away from it whenever it came up in conversation, preferring to deflect the accolades and attention to Marvin Richards, who had pulled Perez in on the case when he wanted more resources, and none were forthcoming because of tight budgetary restrictions. For Perez, however, the past was past, and she clearly had her mind on the future, new criminal cases.

"We've got a body up in the Washington Monument State Park," Kershaw said, his deep and gravelly voice in her ear. "The body, a female, is propped up on the monument itself. A couple of hikers called it in. Two patrol officers are at the scene, and a county forensic investigator has just arrived."

Perez glanced back up at the cab of the truck. The old man's elbow was jutting out, his fingers drumming on the doorframe to a tune only he could hear.

"I want you up there, Perez. Make sure the scene is secured."

A body propped up against the massive stone structure that

once acted as a signal station during the Civil War by the Union Army. *Hardly inconspicuous*, Perez thought.

"And Garland is on his way up there."

Great, Perez thought, ending the call. Detective Nate Garland. It was Garland who had argued so vehemently against Perez being promoted to detective. The wiry, three-times-divorced senior detective was the oldest in the CID, with views and opinions about women that seemed to Perez to date back to before the Civil War. He constantly moaned to the other detectives in the squad room about the amount of alimony his ex-wives were extorting from him.

Perez waved up at the truck driver. "You can go, sir."

The fingers stopped tapping, and the arm withdrew inside the cab. She couldn't see his face, but his response floated out through the open window down to her. "Thank you, little lady."

The truck clunked into gear, and it slowly lumbered off the shoulder and began accelerating away with a throaty roar, its twin chrome exhaust stacks pumping plumes of dirty fumes into the air.

Perez scratched her scalp as she made for her SUV.

🐦 Chapter 4 - The Body

All that remained were two bored-out holes where the eyes should have been, giving the body a hollowed-out, ghoulish appearance.

For Haley Perez, the eyes were the epicenter of all life in a person. She looked at the body. What was once a living, breathing human being, was now an empty husk, inert, a thing of waxen skin, lifeless brown hair, and stiff limbs. What Kershaw had said was true. The dead woman sat on the ground, her back against the circular base of the stone monument, its tapered, conical shape rising into the deep-blue sky, where a scatter of shredded clouds slowly shifted overhead. The surrounding ground was dusted with a light fall of snow.

The two dark, gaping holes in the face seemed to be looking directly at Perez, pleading to her, reaching out with pure anguish and total despair. Looking around, Perez couldn't see any sign of Nate Garland.

"The eyes were removed postmortem." A woman who had been crouching next to the body, gathering and bagging samples, stood and turned to Perez. She nodded toward the top of the monument. "By a bird, I'd say."

An intense pair of blue eyes flashed at Perez from behind the face shield the woman was wearing. Though Perez couldn't see much beyond the woman's face mask and full Tyvek suit, with the hood pulled tightly around the woman's pale face, Perez guessed the woman was in her mid-forties.

Perez looked up and saw a raven perched high on the stone

rim of the monument, the bird's neck craned downward, one black eye looking down at her. The raven gave a shake of its head, like a wet dog shedding water, and resumed its staring contest with Perez.

The woman said to Perez, "You can come up here if you like. Just step in my footprints."

Breaking the raven's quizzical stare, Perez stepped carefully up the stone steps, avoiding the yellow evidence markers scattered around the monument's base.

The woman introduced herself as Annabel Chandler, an on-call, part-time county forensic investigator employed by the Office of Chief Medical Examiner or OCME based in Baltimore. The OCME often used self-employed contractors to conduct death investigations on their behalf and paid them a fee for service on a case-by-case basis. The full-time forensic investigators undertook death investigations in the Baltimore city limits, while the on-call investigators covered all other counties in Maryland. Perez had dealt with a few of the on-call investigators and while not given the same standing as the full-time investigators, she always found them to be just as thorough, dedicated, and professional.

"You must be new?" Perez said. "I haven't seen you around."

"I moved here from Boston," Chandler said. "Been here just on two weeks." Chandler squatted down, then pointed to an evidence marker. "The remains of one eye." She pointed near the left leg of the body. "The other is there."

Perez could see a bloody mush in the snow.

"A bird must have pecked them out," Chandler said, looking around. "That may also explain her facial injuries too."

The woman's cheeks were pockmarked with small, bloody stabs. However, it was the rank smell of urine coming from the body that caught Perez's attention. It was normal after death for the bowels and bladder to empty as the body muscles relaxed.

"It's not hers," Chandler said.

"What?" Perez said, confused.

"That smell. It's urine, but it didn't come from her." Crouching down in front of the body, Chandler pulled aside the flap of the jacket to reveal a dark stain across the chest. She looked up at Perez. "Someone urinated *on* her. The stain is too high for it to be her own urine."

"Could it have been an animal?" Perez asked, not wanting to believe what she was hearing. "Like a stray dog?"

Chandler shook her head. "I doubt it. Pet urine has a stronger smell to it. Different hormones, too, that affect the smell."

"Someone actually urinated on her while she lay there dead?"

Chandler got to her feet and made a face that said this wasn't the first time she had seen this happen. "It will be tested for DNA, but it's rare that you can get a result from urine. However, we will be able to confirm if it's male or female urine."

Perez felt her blood beginning to boil. What kind of person urinates on a dead person? "How did she die?" Perez asked. "Was she killed?" As far as she could tell and from her limited forensic experience, cause of death wasn't obvious. The body, apart from the eyes and cheeks, seemed unscathed.

"There are no obvious signs of fatal trauma that I can initially determine." Chandler stood and began placing her samples into a large carry case. "I'll know more once the autopsy is done." She glanced at Perez. "I'll be sending her to Baltimore."

Perez checked her cell phone. No message from Nate Garland. Where was he? Just then someone hollered out to her, and Perez's hopes of not having the wiseass, senior detective trampling all over her were crushed.

"Hey, Perez!"

Perez turned to see Nate Garland walking along the path toward her. Garland was rakish, narrowed faced, with thinning hair. He always looked scruffy, rumpled, and creased, and told everyone his favorite color was brown. Hence the brown suits, brown neckties, and brown shoes he wore. He even wore tan dress shirts, leaving Perez wondering who the hell sold tan dress shirts? Garland reminded Perez of the actor, James Woods, playing the dual role of a narcissistic small-town politician and corrupt cop at the same time, except Garland wasn't acting. That was how he was.

Reaching Perez, Garland glanced at the body. "My, my. What do we have here? One cold, dead stiff. Looks like one of my exes." Garland sniggered and then turned toward Chandler, paying more attention to her butt as she bent over her equipment than he had to the victim. "And one hot body…very much alive," he said, an approving grin on his face.

If Chandler heard the remark, she didn't show it, introducing herself to Garland and telling him what she had already told Perez.

"Any ID on—" Perez started to ask before Garland cut her off with a raised hand.

"No driver's license or credit cards on the victim?" Garland said, cutting in front of Perez as he faced Chandler.

"No ID, purse, cell phone, or jewelry that I can see," Chandler replied. "I can't tell you who she is. Her prints will be taken and entered into the database to see if there's a match. They'll search her more thoroughly once she's there. If they can't ID her, then they'll Photoshop her face, give her eyes, and put her face up on the internet to see if anyone recognizes her."

"You can do that?" Perez asked.

Just then Garland slipped his cell phone out. "Damn it!" He smiled apologetically to Chandler, while totally ignoring Perez. "Sorry. Gotta take this." He moved away, out of earshot.

Chandler nodded at Perez, answering her previous question. "It's rare, but yes. I know we'd just be guessing the color and shape of the eyes, but it's a start, at least. If she's local, and I'm assuming she is, then someone will know her, or someone will soon report her as missing."

"And you're certain someone didn't remove her eyes?"

"As certain as I can be without examining her fully in a lab."

"Will you be performing the autopsy?" Perez asked.

Despite the mask, Perez could tell her question brought a smile to Chandler's face. "God, no. I'm just a humble part-time investigator. I leave that to the staff in Baltimore."

It wasn't much for Perez to go on. An unidentified woman, perhaps in her early twenties, brown hair, average height and build, found dead at the foot of a monument in a state park. Maybe she was killed by someone who wanted her to be found. But she wasn't disfigured by her killer; that came postmortem, by a bird, likely one of the ravens that seemed to proliferate the area.

Perez glanced over at Garland. He was pacing back and forth, his cell phone pressed against his ear, one hand rubbing his forehead, as though he'd suddenly developed a migraine. Part of his conversation floated back to where Perez was standing. "You'll get your money…can't afford it…set your bloodsucking lawyer on me!"

As Chandler began packing up her equipment, Perez walked and knelt down next to the body. "We'll find whoever did this to you," she whispered. "I promise."

"What was that?"

Startled, Perez turned to see Chandler standing right behind her. Despite wearing heavy work boots, Perez had not heard the woman approach. "Just thinking out loud," Perez said, standing before studying the forensic investigator more closely.

Chandler nodded. "I'm going to bag her now," she said. "How can I reach you once I get the results in from Baltimore?" She glanced at Garland, and Perez followed her gaze. Garland had stopped pacing. His face was twisted, and he was snarling into his cell phone like a rabid dog, as though his migraine had now developed into a full-blown brain tumor.

They exchanged cell phone numbers, and Perez was noted down by Chandler as the detective on the file, not Garland.

"Do you live locally?" Perez asked.

Chandler nodded. "Just moved in. Haven't had much time to unpack. Boxes everywhere. I was lucky, though, found a real nice place."

"You bought a property?"

Chandler shook her head. "No, just renting the place for now, until I get settled and know my way around town. The realtor had decided to offer the place as a rental at a massive discount. The property has been for sale for almost a year without much interest, she told me."

"Oh?" Perez said. "Where's that?"

"It's in a gated enclave, high on a ridge just outside of town."

Perez's facial muscles felt like they had just been injected with a massive dose of Botox.

"Spectacular views." Chandler gave a muffled laugh through her face mask. "No way could I afford a place like that normally."

Despite the various layers of clothing Perez was wearing, a chill rippled through her.

"There's just five houses up there, more like mansions,"

Chandler went on, shaking her head in disbelief. "It's called Mill Point Road. I moved into Number Ten." She stared intently at Perez. "Maybe you know the place?"

🐦 Chapter 5 - Dead and Buried

"I can't remember much after I went into Becca's closet to try on shoes," Sabine Miller said to Maggie Vickerman and Becca.

The three of them stood in a quiet corner of the Ravenwood Bookstore, away from the throng of people who had turned up for Scott Hamill's book signing. Paige and Scott were at the signing table near the front of the store, where a line of people were patiently waiting for Scott to autograph their book.

"So, you can't remember being stabbed by The Eden Killer?" Becca asked. To Becca, Sabine looked like she had lost weight despite being super thin previously. Her face was now gaunt, drawn, her hair limp, dry like straw. Gone were the designer clothes, the gold, man-sized watch worn fashionably loose so it slid around her wrist, and the Italian sling-back stilettos wrapped around smooth, tanned feet. Now she wore plain everyday clothes, a plastic Casio on her wrist, scuffed flats on her pale feet, her ankles dotted with nicks where she had cut herself shaving.

Sabine shook her head and a took a sip from her champagne glass. "No, Becca. When I eventually came out of my coma, and I was told what had happened. I couldn't believe it."

Maggie gave a surprised look. "I *still* can't believe it, and who it was."

"Me neither," Sabine agreed. "Who would have thought?"

"And you were saying the judge gave you back your house?" Maggie said. "As part of the plea bargain?"

"I told them I had nothing to do with Mark's investment business," Sabine replied. "I already told them everything I knew, which was very little."

Maggie's eyes narrowed as she regarded Sabine.

Sabine downed the rest of her champagne." I just brought prospective clients to Mark. I had no idea what he did or promised them after that, or where the money went that they had invested."

Becca glanced at Maggie, who didn't seem overly convinced.

Sabine set down her empty glass and turned to Maggie. "I'm really sorry about what happened to you and Hank, to your money. But you must believe me, Maggie, when I tell you, I was as much in the dark as everyone else was."

Maggie's eyes narrowed even farther into thin slits, as though she were suddenly extremely constipated or struggling to find the truth in Sabine's face. Becca believed it was the latter.

"Mark lied to me like he did to everyone else," Sabine said, her tone forlorn. "I'm just as much a victim as you and Hank were."

Becca could see Maggie grip the stem of her glass tighter. Fearing she would smash it into Sabine's pouting mouth, she stepped in. "So, Sabine, what are you doing now?" Becca asked, angling herself slightly between the two women, who seemed to be in a face-off.

Sabine's expression brightened. "Twelve months in jail gave me a lot of time to think, to assess. I've decided to start a wellness business, you know, to guide others like how I have guided myself to becoming a better person." Sabine gave a solemn nod, as though reminding herself. "There's more to life than money or materialistic things."

Maggie nearly choked on her next mouthful of champagne.

Sabine raised an eyebrow at Maggie's snide reaction, and for a split second, Becca thought she caught a glimpse of the Sabine of old.

Sabine smiled and turned to Becca. "I got released just a week ago. When you fall down, you just have to pick yourself up again. I always have."

"So, the Bentley and designer handbags are all gone?" Maggie asked, wiping her lips with a napkin, her tone laced with fake empathy.

A glimmer of hardness gripped the edges of Sabine's eyes and mouth, reminiscent of a look Becca had seen plenty of times before when Sabine was displeased with someone. And just like that—the death stare was gone.

"Correct," Sabine replied. "I have nothing else. Everything Mark and I owned was sold off, the proceeds distributed back to the investors."

"A pittance for what Hank and I had invested," Maggie scoffed into the rim of her champagne glass before draining it. Almost immediately a young, handsome waiter appeared at Maggie's side and smoothly topped off her glass. The young man gave Maggie a lingering smile before gracefully pivoting away and attending to other guests.

"So how is Hank?" Sabine asked with a slight amused expression on her face as she watched the departing waiter.

Maggie's own face shifted into one of disdain. "He'll be released on parole in a few days' time."

"Do you think he'll come back here?" Becca asked.

Maggie shook her head solemnly. "He'll be breaching his parole conditions if he does." Maggie's eyes looked past Becca, her gaze following the young waiter as he threaded his way through the bookstore, topping off glasses as he went. "And if he does show his face"—Maggie sneered, turning her attention back to the two women—"then I'll cut off his balls off and feed them to him." She turned pointedly toward Sabine. "All liars and cheats need to be castrated."

"How much longer do I have to sit here and sign books?"

"I thought you liked all the attention," Paige Hamill whispered out of the corner of her mouth to her whining husband, Scott.

"I much prefer the book signings in New York," Scott said drearily. Another eager fan, a tall, blonde woman clutching a copy of Scott's book shuffled forward in the line that led to the book signing table where Scott was seated with Paige hovering behind him.

Scott's despondent expression suddenly morphed into a warm, welcoming smile as his eyes fell to the blonde woman's ample cleavage, which was compressed into a plunging, low-cut dress.

Paige looked on, amazed at how the woman's two mounds of silicone didn't rupture the dress, which was obviously—and deliberately—two sizes too small.

As Scott opened the book, Paige read over his shoulder the Post-it Note stuck to the title page.

Scott glanced up at the woman. "To Destiny. We were always destined to meet."

Paige felt like puking at such a tacky dedication.

The woman smiled, leaned down, placed both hands on the table and pushed her boobs together with the inside of her elbows. "I've always wanted to meet a best-selling author," she said, batting her heavily massacred lashes.

Scott smiled, then wrote the dedication and autographed the book with a flourish of his pen.

Paige grabbed the book out of Scott's hands before he could return it to the woman, pushing it forcefully into her twin orbs of silicone. "Move along, honey," she said with a dismissive flick of her head. "There's more people waiting."

The woman gave a pouty grin and then slinked away.

For the next ten minutes, Scott signed books until there was a lull in the line.

Paige raised her champagne glass to her lips, then paused. Across the room, her eyes found Sabine Miller, who was standing with Maggie and Becca under a bookcase labeled *Murder*. "I don't buy it for one second," Paige said as she watched Sabine's animated gestures.

"What?" Scott asked, following Paige's gaze. "Sabine's story?"

Paige nodded, taking a mouthful, before swapping out her empty champagne glass for a full one from a tray held by a passing waiter. She took another swig. "Spare me the born-again-guru crap," Paige said. Sabine had already told Paige and Scott about her "new self," as she had put it. How, while inside prison she had decided to become a self-help guru, helping other inmates see the errors of their ways before guiding them on the righteous path of redemption and being a better, caring, and more compassionate person.

"A leopard doesn't change its spots." Paige nodded at Sabine, who had broken away from Maggie and Becca and was moving toward the front door of the bookstore. "Especially one who has been stabbed." Paige turned her attention back to her husband. "A wild animal is even more dangerous when it's been injured."

Scott got up.

"Where are you going?" Paige asked.

"I need to take a break," he replied gruffly. "I'm going to get a drink."

"Wait, Sabine!"

Scott caught up to Sabine in the parking lot, pulling her aside and into the shadows. "Look, if you're hoping to pick up where we left off…" Scott hesitated, and Sabine could see uncertainty, and a little fear, in his eyes.

"Things are different now," Scott continued. "I've got a best seller, and like I said before, I have a new family…Mallory, our baby girl."

To Sabine it was almost as though for a moment Scott had forgotten his own daughter's name.

Scott glanced at the ground, his hands thrust into his pockets. "It's a two-book deal, with a huge advance, just so you know." He looked up at Sabine, more fear clouding his eyes. "Life's good. I'm in a really good place at the moment, and I don't want anything to wreck that."

You pathetic, little fuck, Sabine almost said but didn't. "Of course your life is good, Scott. Because you've been sucking off Paige's rich parents' teats ever since the day you married into that family." Sabine bit her tongue, wanted to say more as anger slowly simmered inside her. God only knew what she had seen in him before. Sabine waved her hand. "Mark is dead, and I've lost everything, including part of my memory. My life is ruined, and my name around here is dirt." Sabine stepped closer, holding back the urge to punch Scott in his whining, little-boy face. "And you really think that after twelve months, after all that has happened to me that my first priority is to come running back to you?"

Scott looked as though he'd been slapped in the face. "Er…well," he stuttered.

"You conceited asshole!" Sabine said, her voice low and even.

Scott's jaw tightened, his eyes flared. "That's a little rich coming from you, of all people!"

"From me!" Sabine threw her head back and laughed. He really was a weak, little man who followed his wife around like a lost puppy. Sabine took a few deep breaths, trying to prevent an outburst. She had promised herself to remain calm and composed this evening. But the reunion of familiar faces with bitter memories was beginning to feel rather tiresome. Sabine locked eyes with Scott again. "Do you really think I wanted to come back here again?" She waved her hand around. "To this town? You have the perfect life, as you say, Scott. But right now, my life is shit! Worse than shit." Sabine shook her head. She felt real pity for him. The new baby was yet another handcuff Paige had clamped around her husband's limp wrist. "I had to come back. I had no choice. All I've got is my house. That's it. I've got nowhere else to go. And when I've sold the place, then I'm gone. I'm going to get as far away as I can from this godforsaken place!"

Some of the fear in Scott's eyes faded.

"So, what happened in the past between us…was just that?" Scott mumbled. "It was…good—great, I mean. But it was just that…in the past. Things are different now." Scott gave Sabine a questioning look, as though trying to coax agreement out of her.

She touched his arm. "I understand," she said soothingly. "Things are different for me, too, now. I've changed. I honestly have. I'm a different person. When I woke up out of that coma, I didn't even recognize the person I once was, who I was in the past." Sabine let out a sigh and tilted her head. "The past is—like you said—the past. We've both moved on." She gave Scott's arm a squeeze. "I'm truly happy for you and Paige. And Mallory seems like such a wonderful"—Sabine paused, searching for the right word—"miracle," she finally said.

Scott's eyes narrowed. "Miracle?" Suddenly, to Sabine, he looked a little pale. *Good.*

"Don't worry, Scott," Sabine said. "Your little secret is safe with me. I didn't come back here to spoil your little family or blackmail you. But it does beg the question, who really is Mallory's father, doesn't it?"

"I am," Scott said in a proud voice. "I'm putting it down to pure luck. Maybe a few of my guys managed to get through. It can happen."

"Maybe you're right." Sabine didn't believe a word he was saying. Either he was totally ignorant or lying. She imagined it was the latter. But she left it at that. She'd already planted the seed inside his head. "Go back inside and be with your fans, Scott."

Scott's eyes brightened, and he breathed an obvious sigh of relief. "So, we're good?"

Watching Scott reminded Sabine of a fat raccoon trapped inside a dumpster. "We're good."

"The past is dead and buried?" Scott said slowly.

"Yes, Scott," Sabine replied. "You have nothing to worry about. Dead and buried."

🐦 Chapter 6 - Love Letters

It would be a simple task, to be done under the cover of darkness when most clandestine things happened.

She waited until it was almost midnight, then poured the rest of the bottle of red wine into her glass, carried it, together with the red shoebox, which was wrapped with a single red ribbon, out to the backyard and down the slope to where the stone firepit sat, the fire still burning from when she had lit it an hour ago.

The moon was a dirty-yellow ball hanging in a cold expanse of nothingness surrounded by glistening pinpricks. After placing her glass down on the arm of an Adirondack chair, Becca threw another log on the fire and waited for the flames to grow again. She had left the book signing early, shared a drink with Josh before telling him she had an early start the next day, which wasn't exactly a lie.

Satisfied that the fire was sufficiently hungry, she opened the lid of the shoebox and, without looking at the contents, tossed, into the leaping flames, each of the bundles of letters that were tightly wrapped in colorful ribbon, followed by the shoebox itself.

Then she sat down on the chair and slowly savored the wine while the small bundles of paper caught and began to break apart, sending tiny cinders swirling upward into the darkness.

And when there was nothing but powdery, glowing ash, she sat back in the chair, wondering if the newfound warmth she felt inside her was from the heat of the fire or from the earthy, rich red she had been drinking—or from the deep sense of contentment she felt in watching the final link to her past vanish before her eyes. She had finally purged herself of Michael, her dead husband. The burning of the letters was the last act of removing Michael's stain on her life.

And as she sat there in the cold, Becca felt renewed, reborn, with a whole new life ahead of her. Over time, all thoughts of Michael would fade but not her memory of him. That would be impossible. There would always be some residual, granular muck lurking somewhere in her mind, like house dust, stubbornly lodging itself into some hard-to-reach corner.

Leaving the fire to burn itself out, Becca turned and began to climb the slope again—then stopped.

She looked down, the dirt washed with watery moonlight.

Footprints.

She aligned her right foot next to one of the footprints and pressed down with her hip, leaving her own impression next to it. She crouched down and compared size and tread patterns. Becca was a size seven, and the foreign footprint was at least a size eight, maybe nine. The tread pattern was different, too, more distinctive, chunkier, leaving a deeper impression. The person—the intruder, whoever it was—was heavier than herself. And Josh's crew had no reason to be walking around on this section of her land.

Becca stood, and for whatever reason, driven by gut instinct or by a prickly suspicion, looked across her backyard toward the house on her right, Zoe and Jason's old home. At Number Ten, the new neighbor's house, a light glowed from a second-story window that Becca was certain wasn't on before she had walked down to the firepit. The rest of the house was in darkness. Farther up the slope, just inside the boundary between her house and Number Ten, sat a mini excavator Josh had been using to shift dirt and dig trenches on the opposite side to where she was standing.

Cautiously, Becca edged forward toward the excavator, using its hunkered shape to shield her as she approached her neighbor's backyard, her eyes never leaving the glowing window.

Reaching the excavator, Becca peered around the edge of the cab to get a better look at the house and backyard next door. Up until now, Becca had shown no real interest in her new neighbor. She knew nothing about them, other than they had supposedly moved in a few weeks ago. At their coffee meetups , neither Maggie nor Paige could shed any more light on Mill Point Road's newest resident either. Becca had seen delivery drivers come and go, leaving parcels in a secure lockbox that had been installed on the wall near the front door. But no one had actually seen who was living there.

Perhaps they worked the night shift or were away, and the lights were set on timers to turn on after dark? Someone had definitely moved in because Becca had seen a moving van and men unloading boxes. But since then, only minimal signs of life. Late one night, a few days back, Becca had heard a car drive past her own house and pull into the driveway next door. By the time she'd gotten to the window, hoping to catch a glimpse of her new neighbor, the car had already driven into the garage, and the automatic door was closing.

Still, Becca could see no movement from the second-story window. Slowly, she backed herself out from behind the excavator, withdrawing toward her own home. When she was a sufficiently clear, she turned, and her heart jumped up her throat.

Someone was moving around the ground floor of her house, inside the unfinished, open section near the laundry room.

🐦 Chapter 7 - Fly Fishing

On cold winter mornings like these, the wild brown trout that lurk in the spring-fed waters of Beaver Creek can be a little lethargic.

Some say they are the most aggressive of all the species, and while they can be caught with brightly patterned lures, any seasoned angler would tell you simple primary colors are best. They would also tell you that catching such a stealthy fish is a game of infinite patience and ultimate mimicry—the subtle art of imitating something. If the fish must be enticed out of its hiding place to be caught, then you must mimic something that it wants, something that it can't resist.

Haley Perez buried her chin into the collar of her all-weather jacket as she trudged down the path of frozen mud, snow, and ice toward the creek. Driving there along Black Rock Road, Perez couldn't help but think about Adam Teal and where his body had been dumped. She made a mental note to call on Adam's mother, Valerie, on the drive back, to see how she was doing.

Dense foliage dusted white pushed in on both sides as Perez walked, and the sound of running water grew louder with each step. The foliage fell away, and she saw him immediately, a solitary figure, knee deep in the middle of the creek, the dark waters cutting a swathe around him. The edge of the creek on both sides was crusted white and glistening in the late morning sun.

If he'd seen or sensed her standing there watching him, he didn't show it. He seemed totally absorbed in casting the line back and forth with a whip of the thin rod in his hand. The fly finally settled on the surface of the water before Marvin Richards turned his head toward Perez standing on the creek bank. He smiled, but in his face she saw apprehension.

Her impromptu appearances usually started with typical social banter but soon descended into a more serious, darker tone as to why Perez was visiting her now-retired boss, although never retiring mentor. Outside of their careers, they had little in common, were born in completely different eras, and often had competing views of the world. Yet they somehow managed to work together, each acting as the counterweight of the other, moving in differing trajectories, united in a common, shared bond: murder.

Richards reeled in his line and waded over to where Perez was standing.

"Hungry?" he asked.

Perez shrugged. "Maybe."

They sat by the edge of the creek, on folding camp stools, drinking hot coffee from a thermos and eating thick sandwiches.

"Do you always bring enough food for two people?" Perez asked.

Richards finished chewing before answering. "I never know when you're going to drop by." Richards nodded to the sandwich partially wrapped in cling film that Perez was halfway through. "Just to let you know, that's my afternoon snack you're eating."

Perez took another bite. Two-inch-thick homemade bread, triple-meat cold cuts, slices of dill pickle cut just right, lengthways, not sliced, and lashings of a special green tomato and red-pepper relish Richards cooked and preserved himself. It was the same food he prepared each time he went fly-fishing.

They ate in silence for a moment, contemplating the

hypnotic ripples of the creek, lost in their own separate thoughts, each knowing the inevitable reason for Perez's visit would soon be brought up.

After wiping his mouth, Richards balled up the cling film and placed it inside a wicker fly fishing basket by his feet. He topped off Perez's enamel mug with more coffee before filling his own, then stretched his legs out, his somber eyes scanning the surface of the water as he drank in silence. Two colleagues sharing comfort food, good coffee, and the white solitude of winter all around them.

Finally, Perez spoke. "You know if anyone wanted to kill you, you wouldn't be hard to find." She took a sip from her mug.

Richards flexed his neck, then slipped off the straps of his waterproof waders. "We're all creatures of habit. It was one of the first things—"

"I know," Perez interjected, nodding, "that you said to me, our habits define us. It's the same for killers. And once you can accurately define them, you can find them, like—"

"A word in a dictionary." It was Richards turn to finish one of the many words of sage advice he had given Perez in the short time he had taken her under his wing when she was just a rookie patrol officer.

Richards stood and looked down at Perez. "Who'd want to kill me anyway?"

Perez set down her coffee mug, unzipped a jacket pocket, and pulled out a folded piece of paper. She held it out to Richards and said nothing.

Richards looked down at the piece of paper in her outstretched hand.

To Perez it looked as though he was unsure if he should take it or not, as though the act of unfolding the paper and reading its contents would spell the end to his peaceful, relaxing day of fly fishing.

Richards took the paper, unfolded it, and began to read.

As his eyes went back and forth across the page, Perez could see a gradual creasing at the corners of his eyes, the slow tightening of his jaw, and the relaxed expression she had seen before in his eyes, slowly fade to a cold, calculating look she had witnessed many times before.

Richards finished reading, handed the page back to Perez, and without meeting her gaze, or saying a word, turned and walked out to the edge of the creek bank.

Perez gave him a few minutes to himself before downing the rest of her coffee and then moved next to him. Together they looked straight ahead at the wall of frosted woodland on the opposite bank.

"What did you do with the black roses?" Richards asked.

"In the trash."

The answer seemed to agree with what Richards was thinking. Perez knew whoever had sent the flowers and accompanying note was too clever to leave any hint of trace evidence on the bouquet, black cellophane wrapping, black ribbon, or the note.

"Delivery company?"

"None," Perez replied. "I checked. Just the roses and the note."

"So how did they arrive?"

"No idea. Someone had placed them outside my apartment door."

"So, he knows where you live?"

Perez lived on a vibrant, little neighborhood block, the street lined with small grocery stores, a deli, various café's, and convenience stores. Her apartment was above a grocery store that was owned by a family who also owned the liquor store across the street and a laundromat two doors down. She became known on the block as the lady cop who lived above the grocery store. Locals seemed pleased to have her around.

Richards glanced at the sky. It was dimpled and gray like hammered pewter. "Black roses," he said. "They symbolize death."

"Or a new beginning," Perez countered. She had done her research. "The start of something new."

Richards tilted his head side to side, as though trying to alleviate some niggling irritation. "That's what I'm afraid of." He turned to Perez, his eyes guarded. "If what's in that note is true, then The Eden Killer was just a small fish." He looked out across the dark, rippling water. "A student doing his master's bidding."

Perez followed his gaze. "Caught anything today?"

Richards took a deep inhale and shook his head.

"So how do I catch him?" Perez said, cutting to the chase, literally. "This so-called person who taught The Eden Killer everything that he knew?"

Richards rocked back on his thick rubber boots. When he spoke, his gaze was still across to the other bank, like he was searching for someone hidden among the snow-caked trees and tangled white undergrowth. "Do you fish, Haley?"

"Never."

"Not even once?"

"Nope."

Richards frowned. "The fish have been elusive today. Sometimes, the dumb ones are an easy catch. They make mistakes, get too confident, flirt with being caught by taunting the fisherman."

As Perez listened, she got the feeling it wasn't fishing he was talking about.

"The reckless ones come to the surface, will chase anything that moves," Richards continued. "They're easily fooled by the bait, by the lure, thinking that it's a real insect, like a mayfly or midge, or caddis fly. The lure is designed to mimic a natural adult flying insect."

Perez nodded. "Like cheese in a mousetrap."

Richards gave an amused smile, then laughed, breaking the philosophical weight of the conversation. "Almost."

His laughter died down, and he continued. "Fly fishing has taught me a lot over the years, about how to catch killers. Where they hide, their natural habitat, idiosyncrasies and habits, where and when they feed." Richards nodded toward the water. "Brown trout can be lazy, preferring the food to come to them rather than swimming out and finding it. They like to hide behind things."

"Like wearing a mask?" Perez offered.

Richards glanced at her. "No…I mean, not in this case." He pointed at her jacket. "That note you have, from your 'admirer' as he likes to call himself. He knows who he is, is comfortable with *what* he is. He has no need to hide behind a mask." Richards turned back and gazed at a fallen log that was jutting halfway out of the water. He pointed. "You see that log?" He swept his hand to the opposite bank. "And those rocks over there?"

Perez saw both. "Yes."

"That's where you'll find the big fish. Hiding behind objects, behind other people. But just dropping a line in and hoping they'll bite is not enough. You have to coax them out, fool them, lure them to the surface, out into the daylight."

Richards turned back to Perez; his eyes had a hint of sparkle to them. "He is special. He won't be found easily, and certainly won't be fooled easily either. He thinks he's cleverer than most, superior, a master, or teacher. And he is."

"So how do I find him?"

Richards plucked a fly lure off his vest and held it up, admiring it.

With a greenish abdomen, tiny bristle-like wings, a coppery head, and swallowtail, to Perez it looked like someone had skewed a fishing hook through a tiny, colorful dragonfly.

He looked at Perez. "By giving him something he wants. Something he can't resist."

"Like what?"

Richards hooked the fly back onto his vest. "The answer is obvious," he said. Perez watched as he turned, walked past her, and back toward the folded camp stools.

Then a single chilling word floated back to her on the equally chilly air.

"You."

🐦 Chapter 8 - The Three

Leaving the sound of power tools, hammering, and swearing fading in her wake, Becca crossed Maggie's front lawn for an impromptu, morning-coffee catch-up.

Now it was just the three of them: Becca, Paige, and Maggie, and they had agreed to meet just once a week instead of every two to three days as they had done before. However, in the fallout after Sabine Miller's sudden appearance at the book signing last night, Maggie had texted Becca, insisting she and Paige meet at 10:00 a.m. at her home.

Before dawn, Becca, unable to sleep, had risen, showered, and dressed in casual, comfortable clothes. She'd taken her morning cup of coffee and sat out on the half-built porch and watched as the black sky slowly cracked open, bathing the town of Ravenwood in a sulfur-yellow dawn. She was in two minds about telling Josh about her uninvited "visitor" last night.

Maggie—as she always did—greeted Becca at the front door with a warm, genuine hug, then ushered her inside and through to the open kitchen where Paige was already seated at the huge slab of watershed-finished walnut that formed the breakfast bar counter. Without asking, Maggie poured Becca a tall cup of coffee and placed a piece of Paige's homemade, triple-layer hummingbird cake in front of her. "Eat something, honey; you're wasting away."

Becca looked down at the piece of cake. After consuming an entire bottle of red wine last night, the banana, pineapple, and cream-cheese frosting creation was making her stomach turn.

"Where's Mallory? I was looking forward to seeing her."

"She's with the nanny," Paige replied. "She's been a bit cranky this morning. Kept me up all night."

"The baby or your nanny?" Maggie said with a suggestive smile.

Maggie shuffled around the counter and took a seat next to Becca. "I still can't believe where you managed to find a male nanny from," she said, digging in to her second helping of Paige's cake. "He looks like a Brazilian Calvin Klein model. I can picture him standing on a beach, wearing nothing but a drenched pair of white boxers."

Paige gave a shrug. "He came recommended from one of the best agencies on the East Coast."

"I bet he did," Maggie whispered out of the side of her mouth, nudging Becca in the ribs.

"And Mallory took to him instantly," Paige continued, seeming to ignore Maggie's comments.

"Why did you get a male nanny, in particular, Paige?" Becca asked.

Paige gave an aloof flick of her head. "I have my reasons."

Maggie took another mouthful of cake, then closed her eyes in blissful ecstasy, making a moaning sound. "Geez, Paige," she said dreamily between bites. "This cake is like a Labor Day weekend of tag-team sex with five barely legal young men all in the same bed."

"And how does that compare to sex with Hank, then?" Paige cocked her head.

Maggie's eyes flew open. The pleasure drained from her face. "Like eating a Twinkie that's three years past its shelf life," she said drearily. "And the dimensions are about the same too."

"So, what about this new man in your life?" Paige asked

Maggie. "You've hardly mentioned anything about him, except that he's a businessman from Baltimore. Why all the secrecy?"

"It's just the early stages," Maggie said. "We're taking it slow, and James is a very private man."

"James?" Paige said. "Well, that's a start. You never told us his name before." Paige gestured at Maggie. "You've got cream on your chin."

Maggie expertly slithered her tongue down past her bottom lip and lapped up the cream. "Tastes almost as good as Ricardo's crea—"

"I wanted to ask you both something," Becca hastily cut in over Maggie.

Paige raised one perfectly sculptured eyebrow. "Ask away, Becca," she said, raising her coffee cup, her eyes darting to Maggie before she gave Becca a subtle wink, like she had done before on many occasions. Anything to stop Maggie droning on about her personal trainer and the fabulous sex they'd had.

"I had an unwelcome visitor last night," Becca said.

Maggie stopped chewing.

Paige's coffee cup paused along its path to her mouth, an inch from her lips.

"Was he naked and good looking?" Maggie asked, managing to speak and resume chewing at the same time.

Becca shook her head.

"Didn't happen to be your very well-built, young, and devilishly handsome builder, Josh?" Paige suggested.

"Butt naked except for his tool belt?" Maggie offered, a look of desperate hope in her eyes, as though she could visualize what that would entail.

"No," Becca said emphatically. "It was a woman. I'm certain of it."

Paige carefully placed down her coffee cup. "Sounds mysterious. Do tell."

"How do you know it was a woman?" Maggie asked.

"I could tell from their shape, how the person moved. They were snooping around the unfinished areas of the ground story of my house." Becca went on to explain about the muddy footprints Josh had pointed out to her and those she had found on the slope up from the firepit last night, leaving out the part about her burning the letters.

"That bitch Sabine!" Maggie growled. "Fancy her turning up to the book signing, then spouting some bullshit story that she's a changed person, a self-help guru." Maggie shot a scowl at Paige. "Surely you didn't invite her, Paige?"

Paige shook her head. "It was open to the public. I had no idea she was back in town."

"She's not broke; let me tell you," Maggie said, pushing the cake away, a look on her face, as though she'd taken a bite of something nasty. "That cunning little whore squirreled away money—my money—that the feds will never find. Fraudsters like that always have an escape hatch."

"It wasn't her," Becca said, not wanting the topic to stray to Sabine Miller.

"How do you know?" Paige asked. "Did you confront them?"

"Look, I can't be certain it wasn't Sabine," Becca said. "And no, I didn't confront them. The person saw me and took off around the front of the house. They were too fast, and I lost them."

"You chased them?" Maggie said in disbelief.

"Good for you, girl," Paige interjected. "Who do you think it was?"

"What about our mysterious and invisible new neighbor in

Number Ten, in Zoe and Jason's old house?" Maggie added. She gave a slight shiver. "Even after all this time, just thinking about those two and what you saw, Becca, still makes my skin crawl."

"I have no idea who it was," Becca replied, "except it was a woman, size eight feet, maybe. It wasn't totally dark. I could just make out her shape before she took off like a jackrabbit."

Maggie threw her hands in the air. "What the hell is happening around here! I thought the security had increased, given all the reporters that were snooping around."

"That was almost twelve months ago, Maggie," Paige said. "They've lost interest now, in the place." Paige scrutinized Becca. "Did you tell Dwayne at the gatehouse? I thought they beefed up security, especially at the bottom of the ridge, along the fence near the road."

Mac, the previous security guard, had retired. He was replaced with a younger guy, named Dwayne. As far as Becca was concerned, Dwayne seemed more than capable.

"Fuck knows we pay enough in service charges to that new security company," Maggie continued, grumbling.

"Maggie!" Paige glared at her. "Profanity, please."

"Sorry," Maggie said sullenly. "You know how easily I get worked up."

"The new security company has fixed all the holes in the fence that surrounds the entire property," Paige explained. "And updated all security cameras, and installed a few more in new locations. Didn't you get the email?"

"I don't read emails," Maggie said. "And people think they can just come and gawk at us like we're some kind of tourist attraction." Maggie got up and went to the coffee machine. "It's that damn book Scott has written, Paige," she said over her shoulder as she busied herself refilling the water reservoir and making a fresh batch of coffee. She turned back toward Paige. "Dragging up all that senseless pain and suffering again. He has no right in doing that."

"I cannot stop him from writing it," Paige replied. "God knows where he got his information from. Certainly not from me."

"It's not some eager reporter jumping the gun," Becca said, trying to ease Maggie's concern. "This is something…different."

Maggie did a double take. "Different? How?"

Paige leaned forward. "Yes, Becca. What do you mean?"

Becca glanced at both women, then slipped her hand into a pocket. She pulled out something in a small, plastic bag and placed it on the bench top. "The person, the intruder I chased, dropped this."

Maggie shuffled forward and stared down at the small object on the counter. Her jaw tightened and her nostrils flared.

Paige craned her neck at the object, her eyes blinking wider. Her lips parted slightly. "You're…fucking…kidding…me," she whispered.

All three women looked at each other.

🐦 Chapter 9 - Big Boy

Ensconced in his writing den, Scott Hamill stared at the blank computer screen.

Why was it so damn hard today to get into the flow?

He was on a deadline, had to turn in the first draft of his manuscript for his sequel to *Mill Point Road* in less than six weeks.

Scott looked wearily at the computer screen, feeling as though the white pixelated landscape was like a snow blizzard, threatening to swallow him up. What else could he write about that wasn't covered in the first book? He tilted back in his chair and swiveled around in place, his hands behind his head. He needed inspiration, new facts, fresh ideas—anything. The sequel was supposed to be an exploration of the town, its people, and the residents of Mill Point Road in the aftermath of catching The Eden Killer. The problem was nothing had happened during the damn aftermath! Ravenwood went back to its typical mundane self, and everything there was to know about The Eden Killer had been publicized, scrutinized, analyzed, and hypothesized in both the mainstream media and in local newspapers. There was nothing new to tell without sounding like you were just parroting what had already been said.

While the first twenty thousand words had flowed so easily—clever little regurgitation of the first book—Scott's imagination had now come to a grinding halt.

Maybe he should start lying again, invent stuff, make up shit, like he'd done in the first book? His editor didn't fact-check it anyway. How could she? She wasn't there, living on Mill Point

Road where it all had happened. Sure, there had been some facts Scott had been able to glean from sources, especially Paige, his wife, then cobbled them together with some speculation, and repackaged with some local news articles, with a dash of rumor and suggestion. But now he'd exhausted everything, needed some fresh meat to add to the sequel; otherwise, it would just be a rehash of the first book. Readers wouldn't take too kindly to that. Especially after he had cleverly reinvented himself in the public's eye and in the media as an authority on what happened on that fateful night when Sabine Miller and Rebecca Cartwright had faced off with The Eden Killer in Rebecca's home. After all, he lived two houses away.

Truth was, he didn't have firsthand knowledge of what had happened. Rebecca Cartwright, that smug-faced little bitch, certainly did. Yet she had refused to talk to him, tell him all the gory, juicy details, no matter how many times he'd asked her—almost begged her.

And Paige had refused to be Scott's covert emissary, to go on a secret fact-finding mission to Becca. Paige said she "wouldn't betray my friendship with Becca!" Maggie was tight lipped too. Mind you, Scott imagined she didn't know much either—too busy banging young men. *Christ! The old hag didn't even know her own son was dead. What kind of dumb cow was she?*

Sabine was totally useless, too, telling everyone at last night's book signing that she had amnesia, couldn't remember a thing.

Scott took another spin around the room on his chair, thinking of Becca Cartwright. Smug-face had probably already spilled the beans to Paige, told her all the delicious details. Maybe it was Paige who was the tight-lipped one.

Scott's chair came to a gradual halt in front of a framed copy of *Mill Point Road* on the wall, a gift from his publisher when it had hit *The New York Times* Best-Sellers list. Looking at the framed book, Scott was suddenly filled with a sense of awe—and bitter disdain.

Could he do it again? Write another best seller that everyone would again clamber over each other to buy in all the bookstores? Had he seen his last Manhattan cocktail party? Ridden in his last limo? Done his last *Good Morning America* interview? Flown in his last private jet to Hollywood to chat with Jimmy Kimmel?

Maybe the world had moved on? The book was slowly slipping out of the charts, yesterday's headline. He was in a good spot at the moment, didn't want to give that up, a man standing on his own two feet for a change, thanks to the upfront royalty his publishers had paid him for the first book. Admittedly, he had to spice the book up a bit, took some creative license with the content, but hadn't everyone done that recently in the media? Fake news, wasn't it?

The problem was, though, it would be another twelve months until the next installment of his royalties. It was the deal he had to take from his prick of an agent in New York. Scott was a newbie, unpublished, a first-time author, which meant he had no bargaining power. Take it or leave it, he'd been told. To say it left him a little jaded was an understatement. While everyone else got paid first, and in full—the agent, the publisher—it was the poor, hardworking author who had to wait years.

Things would be different now. Given the unexpected success of his first book, with the next book, the sequel, Scott had managed to negotiate a better deal on the advance royalty and subsequent installments. Still, it meant he wouldn't get the first installment on the advance until he turned in the first draft for review.

He stared at the computer screen some more. Twenty thousand

words down, another eighty thousand to go. *Christ, how am I going to manage that?* His well of inspiration—together with nearly all of the advance from the first book—had all but dried up. He had lied to everyone about it, too, especially Paige. He told her he had received a hundred thousand dollars, when, in fact, it was two hundred thousand. He'd squirreled away way half of it into a secret, offshore bank account that he could draw on at any time and had, heavily, in the last few months, trying to inspire himself to replicate that initial success.

And why shouldn't he? It was his money. He left the other hundred thousand in their joint checking account, untouched. That earned him some brownie points with Paige. The delusional bitch thought he was being frugal, careful. He was being careful all right, careful that the gravy train—the fat monthly allowance Paige got from her rich parents—kept running on track and on time.

If he'd put the full two hundred grand in their account, told Paige that was what the real advance was, then "Daddy Big Bucks"—a term coined by Scott himself to describe Paige's father, a senator in Washington—might reduce their allowance, even though the advance was a pittance compared to what Paige stood to inherit as an only child. The mansion in Georgetown. The sprawling, beachfront estate on Long Island, complete with a sixty-foot cruising yacht. Scott had often pictured himself sailing around Martha's Vineyard, bare-chested at the helm, with a boatload of bikini-clad babes, and accidentally kicking overboard the urn containing Paige's father's ashes. *Oops! Sorry! More like good riddance,* he thought. The gravy train would come to a stop because, by then, he would be running the entire damn railroad, riding trains to all destinations!

But until then, Scott needed a new scandal or an exclusive

that he could hang the new book on. His mind drifted back to Sabine. Maybe he shouldn't have blown her off that quickly. Maybe he still could squeeze a few new tantalizing details out of her. And her bout of selective amnesia? Maybe she was planning to write her own tell-all book? The woman was financially ruined anyway, or so she'd told everyone. Perhaps that was why she had returned, saw all the publicity Scott's book was getting, and wanted to cash in on it too: steal the glory and attention from him.

"Yes! Yes! That's it!"

Scott sprang to his feet, knocking back his chair, his paranoia racing. He began to pace back and forth, rubbing his chin, his eyes wide. If he approached Sabine, he'd have to do it in private. Paige could never know. Had Sabine changed? Was she the born again, self-help guru that she claimed to be the other night? He doubted it. Everyone doubted it, particularly Paige.

He decided to reach out to Sabine, find out if she had any new information or was plotting against him with her own book. Scott took a deep breath, the wave of paranoia and fear slowly abating. He went back to his desk, picked up the chair, and slumped down into it.

Instinctively, he glanced over his shoulder at the locked door. No, Paige was not on the other side listening. She had gone next door to Maggie Vickerman's house.

He turned back to the blank computer screen, safe in his thoughts that Paige was oblivious to his plans with Daddy's cash. Until then, he needed to play it cool, safe, secretive.

Then there was the issue of Mallory. To Scott, she was a blessing and a curse all wrapped up in a swaddling cloth filled with piss and shit and smelling of vomit.

She was a blessing in the sense that it tied Paige's parents—

Mallory's grandparents—to Scott and Paige. With a new grandchild in the mix, the chances of Paige's father turning off the tap was practically nonexistent. The stupid old bastard doted on Mallory, and he had already mapped out her entire life. The best Ivy League schools. The best colleges. Want for nothing. Scott didn't care, just as long as he didn't have to fund it out of Paige's allowance.

Thinking about Mallory brought Scott back to another, more pressing issue, a mystery, a biological puzzle that had been eating away at him for the better part of twelve months: who the hell was the father?

Scott had tried finding out who the elusive sperm spreader was, the sly, swinging dick who had sneakily slipped between the sheets—and Paige's spread legs—and fed her his dirty seed, ultimately giving her the one thing she wanted, and the one thing Scott didn't want, a child! When Scott had run out of ideas, he had then engaged a private investigator, and twenty grand later, nothing. Not one credible lead as to who had impregnated her. And Scott knew Paige wasn't the kind of gal to do it herself. No frozen bag of jizz, a microwave, and a turkey baster for her.

The only problem was, in finding out who "Daddy Burger Banger with the special sauce" was—another term coined by Scott—what would he do with the information? Confront Paige and risk derailing the gravy train? Such marital honesty could be grounds for divorce.

No. It was best to continue with the charade, not tell anyone about Dr. Snip Snip—a phrase Sabine Miller had come up with when Scott had told her. But information was information, and it had a value. Sabine had taught him that. Once he found out who the real father was, he would take that bit of information and store it for a rainy day, use it as leverage, as collateral.

Until then, Scott just had to smile, be the doting father he wasn't, the caring and considerate husband he hated being, and be the perfect son-in-law, which made him want to puke.

The new nanny Paige had employed had also given him cause for concern. It gave Scott the shivers just thinking about the nanny. At every twist and turn, he seemed to be watching Scott out of the corner of his distrusting eye. Strangely enough, Paige's micromanaging of Scott, wanting to know what he was doing every waking moment of the day, had evaporated.

It could only mean one thing. The nanny was a spy! Scott glanced at the locked door again, thinking maybe it was the nanny, not Paige, crouching down on the other side, peeking through the keyhole? As well as wiping the baby's ass, the nanny was keeping a watchful eye on Scott's ass. However, Scott had taken precautions, used some of his secret royalty advance, to set up his computer in his den just as he wanted it. He had a separate encrypted email account and a VPN so his questionable web browsing would not be detected. There was no way Paige or the nanny would know what he was really up to at times in his writing den.

Scott closed his eyes and took a deep breath, trying to clear his head. Opening his eyes, he glanced at the computer screen and was tempted to punch his fist through it.

It was no good. He needed a break, had been hard at it for an hour now. Scott turned on the computer's VPN, navigated to a familiar web page, logged in, and then waited.

Moments later, the screen blinked to life.

Scott craned his neck, licked his lips. There she was. Mistress Molly. The young girl leaned forward toward the screen, pushing out her perfect little titties, which were poking out of a quarter cup bra, complete with little red tassels on her nipples.

"Hey, babe!" Mistress Molly said, her voice soft and sticky, like thick molasses. "How's my big boy doing today?"

She always called him big boy, and he liked it. "Help me, Molly. I need some inspiration. What's on the menu?"

Molly bit her lip guiltily. "I've got something very special on the menu for you today, Big Boy." She did a boob shimmy, making the tassels twirl like little fans. "But first, you know the drill."

A pop-up appeared on Scott's screen. That was Molly. All business before pleasure. He entered in his credit card details—his secret credit card, the one linked to his offshore account—then hit the *pay* button. Scott had already spent thirty grand in the last six months on Molly. She was his vice, his guilty pleasure. And she was worth every cent.

Molly's eyes darted away, no doubt checking her bank account online. She gave a sweet smile. "Thank you, Big Boy." She wiggled her buttocks on her seat, like a hen settling on a clutch of eggs. "So, today on the menu, we are offering either meat or vegetarian?"

Scott frowned. This was certainly new, but he still got excited. "Meat or vegetarian? I hate fucking vegetarian!"

Molly gave a slow, sultry nod. She reached for something off camera, brought her hand back holding something.

Scott angled his head forward, toward the screen.

In her hand, Molly was holding a dog beef roll wrapped in a plastic sleeve, the kind you find in the fresh pet food section of the grocery store. Not the two-pound version either, but the big, thick six-pound roll. She held it up for Scott to see better.

Scott read the details on the label. Six pounds of chunky beef and vegetables, with a picture of "Buster" the dog, one paw raised, tongue dangling from its mouth, begging for his meat.

Scott felt his own "Buster" beginning to rise in his lap.

Then with a suggestive tilt of her head, and without taking her eyes from her Webcam, Molly reached down out of frame with her other hand, and pulled into view something else.

Scott gasped.

"Or you may prefer the vegetarian option." Molly gave a cheeky smile.

Scott stared in disbelief. There, in Molly's other hand was the biggest zucchini he had ever seen. His eyes darted between the dog roll and the zucchini, trying to work out which one was mathematically bigger. While the dog roll was thicker, the zucchini was longer, easily as long as his own forearm, from elbow to fingertips.

"Vegetarian," Scott breathed out, nodding his head like one of those wind-up toy puppies that barked and did back flips.

Molly nodded. "Good choice." She made a pout. "Too much meat in your diet isn't healthy." And with that, Mistress Molly placed the dog roll down, grabbed a large bottle of baby oil, and poured a healthy dollop on the top of the zucchini and began rubbing it, spreading the baby oil all over its dark green surface with long, practiced strokes of her hand.

She raised one eyebrow at Scott. "Who's the big boy now?"

🐦 Chapter 10 - Crushed Butterflies

The cabin was small but functional with some homey touches.

A racked ceiling looked down over two battered yet comfortable-looking sofas that sat facing each other in front of a wood burning stove, the crackling fire flickering and throwing warmth into the cozy space. Bookcases lined one wall, crammed with a collection of paperbacks and hardcovers. Fishing rods and nets hung from exposed beams, while framed pictures of fish and colorful fishing flies adorned the raw timber walls.

While Richards set about making coffee in the open kitchen, Perez browsed the bookcases: Marcus Aurelius, Epictetus, and Seneca were gathered together, as though comparing their stoic philosophies. On another shelf, true crime books converged, milling together like at a crime scene, comparing notes and sharing ideas. There was a small, concentrated smattering of thriller fiction, mainly the big hitters. The spines of these books looked pristine, untouched, not creased and worn like their nonfiction neighbors.

Richards returned with mugs of steaming coffee, and they sat opposite each other. For Perez, the warmth of the fire was most welcome. She had never been inside the cabin before. Most meetings between them were either done down by the creek as before, or at a small diner along Mapleville Road that Richards frequented.

"Do you know who the most dangerous villain is?" he said.

Perez looked away from the fire and at Richards. His obscure statement had taken her by surprise. Everything Richards said or did had a practical reason behind it. Always economical with his words, he was not prone to sudden bursts of lecturing or giving condescending speeches on how much he knew and how little she did—unlike some of the other detectives in the division. However, he didn't make it easy for her, either, by spoon-feeding her the answers or readily providing his own opinion. He much preferred Perez to arrive at her own conclusions. The best answer—he had once said—was the one you deduced on your own after careful consideration of all the factual evidence presented to you. He was her guide along the bloody path of murder, not some egotistical leader on some self-serving crusade, trampling over the dead as they sought fame and glory. He stood next to her, shoulder to shoulder, not one step in front of her, allowing her to fall behind. And when she did fall back, he would stop and step back to where she was, and say, "Tell me what you see, not what you feel."

"Not the obvious villain," Perez answered.

Richards nodded. "I'm glad you remembered."

"You've always said that the most dangerous villain is the one who is not the psychopath," Perez continued, "or the sociopath, or the insane, or the person who is just pure evil."

Richards cradled his coffee mug and nodded slowly in approval. "The most dangerous villain is the one who is totally sane."

"Extremely intelligent," Perez added, enjoying their verbal ping-pong.

"They have no abusive childhood."

"No string of tortured family pets they killed when they were young."

"No history of mental illness."

"No high school girlfriend or classmate who said they were weird, creepy, or odd."

"Far from it," Richards countered. "They could very well have been Mr. Popularity back in high school."

"The star quarterback."

"Or captain of the lacrosse team."

"'Most likely to succeed' according to their senior yearbook."

"No history of family trauma or criminal record or previous violent behavior." Perez paused. "What else?"

Richards set down his mug. "They have no *need* to satisfy, no voices in their head telling them to kill. Their only compulsion is that they can: kill, that is. They see the taking of another life as a challenge."

"It feeds no fetish or desire?" Perez asked.

"No. But that doesn't mean they don't enjoy it."

"There is no urge at all they're trying to satisfy?" Perez asked.

Richards pointed back and forth between them. "Nothing you or I could ever understand." Richards sat back and stared at the flames of the fire. "They see killing as a skill, an art form, which they want to master. Like hunting deer or fly fishing, something they are constantly refining, improving on." He turned back to Perez. "To them, the joy of life is in taking another human life."

It sounded to Perez that Richards wasn't talking abstractly. He was talking as though the discussion was about a particular person he knew. "Do you know who sent me the black roses?" There was no harm in asking. "Who the person was who wrote the note?"

Richards said nothing. He simply got up and disappeared into another part of the cabin, only to return a few minutes later, carrying a battered banker's box. The cardboard on one side was ruffled, crinkled, like it had been water damaged. He placed the box on the table in front of her, and Perez immediately recognized the Hagerstown PD evidence label stuck on one side, showing the chain of custody of evidence, a chronology of who had accessed the evidence contained in the box and when. The last entry was Marvin Richards. The date, more than four years ago.

At first, Perez didn't touch the box, feeling as though it contained some dangerous specimen inside, and if she opened the lid, it would jump out and bite her. Resisting the urge, she kept both her hands firmly planted on her lap while more questions swirled madly around inside her head. How did Marvin Richards come to have this in his possession? Did he steal the evidence box or simply forget to return it when he retired? Was it recorded as lost or stolen? What would happen if it were found in her possession?

As though seeing the confusion and concern in her eyes, Richards leaned forward and tapped the box. "Don't worry. They won't miss this. It had been buried in the archives long before I was interested in these cases."

"These cases?" Perez asked. "What cases?"

After opening the lid of the box, Richards pulled out a sealed evidence bag and held it up.

The bottom of the bag was coated with what looked like black dust and the crushed wings of butterflies, dry and powdery. Then the true contents of the bag came into focus for Perez. A withered stem, dark and twisted, jutted with triangular barbs. Oval leaves with serrated edges, mottled and discolored. And a tightly shrunken head at the top of the stem, wreathed with the brittle unfurling of dead petals.

It was a black rose.

♦ Chapter 11 - I Spy

"What is it?" Maggie asked.

"It's a miniature security camera," Paige answered before Becca could. She looked up at both Maggie and Becca in turn. "Or a spy camera."

"To spy on who?" Maggie asked.

"On me." Becca looked questioningly at Paige.

Seeing Becca's face, Paige gave a nonchalant shrug. "I've got some installed in my house, two cameras in Mallory's nursery, specifically. I had them fitted before we brought her home from the hospital. I knew I was going to employ a nanny sooner or later, so I wanted to make sure I could keep an eye on them. After all, you can't really trust anyone these days."

Becca agreed, remembering the horrific footage she had seen on the internet of nannies, even parents, abusing children who were supposedly placed in their care and protection.

"Here, take a look." Paige thumbed her cell phone, smiled, then turned the phone toward Becca and Maggie.

Becca and Maggie huddled around the screen. It was a high-angle view of Mallory's nursery. A man was seated in a rocking chair, a cloth diaper draped over one shoulder, Mallory cradled his arm, her mouth sucking vigorously from a bottle he was holding for her. The man gently rocked back and forth as he fed her.

"I expressed some milk this morning for her," Paige added, tears welling in her motherly eyes. "Paulo just heats it up in the microwave and feeds it to her."

"Paulo?" Maggie said. Up until now, Paige had been deliberately thin on details about her new nanny.

Becca strained to listen to the audio coming from Paige's cell phone. She looked at Paige. "Is he—"

"Singing?" She nodded. "He sings to her each feed." Paige blinked the tears away. "He's been such a blessing. Honestly."

Becca and Maggie exchanged looks.

"He's from Sao Paulo," Paige went on. "Has a black belt in Brazilian jiu jitsu too. He's more than capable of protecting her."

Paige put away her cell. "Having the security cameras means I can get out of the house, come and meet you like today *and* still keep an eye on them both." Her face suddenly morphed into a stony coldness. "If anyone attempts to harm her"—she stared at both Becca and Maggie—"I'd kill them. No matter who it was."

Becca believed her.

Paige picked up the spy camera in the plastic bag, and her expression softened. "The usual nanny cams you can buy are too bulky. So, I called in a specialist contractor." She turned the bag over in her fingers, studying the design. It was a small square, the size of a Scrabble tile with a tiny wire dangling from it. "How the hell did you find this in the dark?" Paige asked.

"I came back with a flashlight," Becca replied, "after they had gone."

"They're not cheap. Military spec, I was told," Paige said, handing the bag with the camera inside back to Becca. "The one you found is similar to the ones I had installed. Full HD, real-time transmitting, all footage recorded and backed up. Best on the market."

"Backed up where?" Becca asked, wondering if it was, in fact, Sabine whom she had seen last night.

Paige gave a sly smile. "I could tell you, but then I'd have to kill you." She sighed. "Someplace safe." She leaned forward toward Becca. "The more important question you should be asking is, who is this woman snooping around your place in the dark, and why was she trying to install a state-of-the-art spy camera in your home?"

🐦 Chapter 12 - Olsen's

Perez's meeting with Marvin Richards at his cabin was cut short by a telephone call from Annabel Chandler, and twenty minutes later, Perez was pulling into the parking lot of Olsen's Coffee and Bakery.

It was one of her favorite places in Ravenwood to drink coffee and just watch the world pass by from behind one of the huge bay windows at the front of the store.

Olsen's had a rendered brick façade, brown and beige, with contemporary stone edging and dark green awnings. Inside, it was warm and cozy, filled with the comforting smells of freshly baked bread, gooey cookies, buttery bagels, and the earthy aroma of ground coffee. Walking in there always evoked a safe, grounded, and homey feeling within Perez. Another reason why she liked the place was that no other cops went there.

The interior was a soothing blend of rich, dark browns; warm wood veneers; rustic, exposed brickwork; and wooden plank floors. Chalkboard menus filled with neat, colorful handwriting hung from the ceiling above the counter, and a long glass display cabinet ran its entire length and was filled with a sugar-dizzying array of cookies, brownies, muffins, bagels, and pastries, all sitting on white plastic trays with cardboard labels.

"Hi, Haley," the owner Sally Monk said, peeking out from behind a huge stainless steel espresso machine, steam swirling around her face. Sally had worked as a waitress doing double shifts at a local gas station diner just to make ends meet before jumping at the opportunity to buy Olsen's, when the original owners retired.

She used what little savings she had scrimped together over the years, together with a bank loan, to buy the bakery business.

"Hey, Sally. What news do you have for me?"

Sally, while never a town gossip, was always a good source of local information for Perez, collecting and curating little snippets she gleaned from her customers.

"Slow news cycle today," Sally admitted, wiping her hands on her green apron. "Your usual?"

Perez ordered a large coffee, resisting the urge to also get the massive cheesecake brownie displayed right under her nose, thinking it would probably deliver her total daily allowance of sugar in one indulgent hit.

"Oh, there was one thing," Sally said, pouring hot coffee into a large ceramic cup.

"What's that?"

Sally placed the cup down on the counter in front of Perez, then rested her hand on one hip and rubbed her chin. It was Sally's trademark stance she adopted whenever she was about to share something that had piqued her curiosity. "Freddy said he thinks someone was following him the other day when he was walking through Kenley Lane."

Freddy, Sally's teenage son, worked—when he wasn't attending community college—at the Sheetz gas station just off the Dwight D. Eisenhower Highway. Sally was a single mom. Her husband, Freddy's father, was a drunk who walked out on them when Freddy was just five years old. It had a profound effect on Freddy who'd been bullied at school ever since. And Kenley Lane, a favored shortcut, was a narrow laneway that cut between Kenley Road and Main Street.

"Did he know who it was?" Perez asked before taking a sip of her coffee.

"No, he couldn't tell," Sally replied, staring off into space. "The person was wearing a hoodie. Their face was covered, Freddy said."

"Tell your son, next time, to stay out of that laneway," Perez cautioned. The laneway ran behind an abandoned row of small warehouse units on one side and a disused lot on the other. Two years ago, a young girl named Arual Remlap was last seen by her boyfriend entering the laneway at the northern end but never emerged from the other side. She had simply vanished. Perez had walked the two-hundred-yard laneway numerous times, checking. Even during the day, the lane had an ominous feel to it, as though you were entering a portal to another place. Stepping into the lane, everything suddenly went eerily quiet. No sound of traffic, no birds, nothing. There had been a few complaints lately of local pets, cats, and dogs going missing, only to be found months later, dismembered and strewn in Kenley Lane.

Sally shrugged. "Teenagers, you can't tell them to do anything these days."

Perez smiled and, taking her coffee, moved to one of the long wooden benches with metal high stools, and sat down. A flat-screen TV on the wall was tuned to the local news channel. An unnatural-looking, middle-aged woman stood in front of the weather map promising a clear wintry day with the possibility of snowfall at night. There was an older couple at a far corner table and two teenagers nearby, glued to their cell phones, thumbs scrolling furiously, blank expressions on their faces.

Five minutes passed, then the front door opened, and Haley turned to see a woman wearing sunglasses enter. The woman glanced briefly at Haley before making her way over to the counter to order.

Haley took a mental snapshot of the woman. It was something

Marvin Richards had drilled into her. No matter where she was, always try to commit to memory people you see. That, and the makes of cars on the street, including license plates. You never knew when you would have to recall such details, no matter how trivial. Unfortunately, Haley wasn't blessed with a photographic memory, but her recall was getting better.

She turned away and stared at the TV screen again, processing the details of the woman in her head, testing herself. Maybe close to six feet tall, honey-blonde, shoulder-length hair, pale-skinned, minimal makeup, maybe mid-forties, slim in all the right places, obviously a woman who took care of herself without being obsessive or vain. She wore functional but stylish clothing, pale, muted colors, quality without being excessive, base layers, well chosen and matching, with soft-soled boots, more suited for hiking than clothes shopping at an upscale ski village. Under the layers of clothing, she appeared lean, strong-looking, with good posture. Perez checked her watch. Chandler was late, only just, though. She slipped out her cell phone and dialed the number. A phone started ringing in Perez's ear as well as behind her.

Haley looked around and saw the woman with the honey-blonde hair standing at her back, coffee cup in one hand and her ringing cell phone in the other.

"Detective Perez?" the woman said, a warm smile on her face.

Perez ended the call.

The woman glanced down at herself. "I seem to have you at a distinct disadvantage."

"Excuse me?" Perez said. The woman's voice sounded familiar.

The woman pocketed the cell phone and slid her sunglasses to the top of her head, revealing a pair of intense blue eyes. "The last time I saw you, I was covered head to toe." The woman stepped forward and extended her hand. "I'm Annabel Chandler. She smiled again, unwound her scarf, and placed it on the bench where Perez sat. "Sorry I'm a tad late," Chandler said. "But I wanted to get the report on the dead woman from yesterday."

Chandler sat down, then looked at Perez with a singular intensity. "And I know how she died."

🐦 Chapter 13 - Beer and Pizza

After leaving Maggie's house, Becca was at her front door when her cell rang.

It was Dwayne, the security guard at the gatehouse. "Ms. Cartwright, sorry to disturb you, but I have a gentleman here to see you. He's not on the appointment list."

Becca turned and glanced back down the ridge toward the gatehouse to where a small tan-colored sedan sat parked on the other side of the gates.

Dwayne continued in Becca's ear. "His name is Phil Benton, says he's from Connecticut."

Becca tensed and stepped back under some scaffolding. "I have no idea who he is, but he's been harassing me. Don't let him in, and please advise him that if he contacts me again, I'll call the police."

"Will do."

Becca ended the call and retreated into the chaos that was her partially built house.

Inside, Becca checked on the progress of the workmen and was told Josh had gone into town to pick up more supplies. There were friendly nods and tilts of hardhats as she made her way through the framework, stepping over power cables, giving the men a wide birth, not being intrusive but watching them work, hanging drywall, cutting lumber, reframing the last sections of the walls to the downstairs area of the house. It was

Friday, which meant tools down at 4:00 p.m. and pizza and beer, put on by Becca. It was a small gesture by her, to thank them for the week's work—even though they were paid well, well above the going rate around town. However, *Beer and Pizza Friday* was frowned upon by Josh. "Don't encourage them. They'll get used to it," he'd scolded Becca when she first returned one Friday afternoon with a trunk load of hot pizza boxes and a case of cold craft beer from Antietam Brewery in Hagerstown.

"I don't care," Becca replied. Putting on Friday food and drinks gave Becca the chance to casually talk to the crew, gauge their thoughts and ideas about the house, and put forward possible suggestions. She valued their input, not just Josh's. Maybe talking to the guys over a slice of pizza and a cold beer made Josh jealous, after she had repeatedly rebuffed his invitations for a date.

Pausing at an open section of external wall near the laundry room, Becca made a note to tell Josh she wanted the entire downstairs area buttoned up tight as soon as possible. She didn't want anyone else—friend or stranger—wandering into her house, day or night. Not that she didn't feel safe. She still had her gun after all. The police had given it back to her after they had forensically examined it and checked her permit. She decided not to tell Josh what she had found, the tiny spy camera. And she didn't believe it was one of his crew who had dropped it. Any one of them had plenty of opportunity while working on the site during the day to properly hide a spy camera.

Whoever it was, Becca was going to find out herself.

🐦 Chapter 14 - Thaw

"Hypothermia?" Perez said.

Annabel Chandler nodded. "It's early stages, and the autopsy is yet to be done, but that is my personal opinion based on the preliminary physical characteristics of the body I examined at the scene. Please don't quote me on this yet. I just wanted to give you some initial feedback."

Perez appreciated Chandler's help yet couldn't help but feel a little disappointed. The dead woman's lifelike pose, sitting against the stone monument, two dark hollow pits for eyes, her face a ghoulish Halloween mask. It all made the macabre scene seem so much more than just death by misadventure. Maybe the autopsy would reveal more. "So, she died of exposure?" Perez asked. "She was hiking, got lost, and somehow staggered up to the Washington Monument and died there?"

"Most likely," Chandler said. "And the ravens had a feast on her eyes, and face."

Something was bothering Chandler. Perez could tell. "What else can you tell me about the body, and how she would have actually died?"

Chandler took a sip of her coffee. "She displayed all the typical signs of hypothermia and frostbite damage to her extremities. Her fingers, ears, lips, and nose. Your core temperature usually sits around ninety-eight degrees. When that drops to around about ninety-five degrees, the onset of hypothermia is most likely. There's a lot of other variables that can bring it on quicker, such as immersion in cold water, your age, health, and clothing worn. The critical organs begin to shut down, like the brain and the heart as a result of the reduced blood flow. The victim will experience liver failure, kidney failure, and then cardiac arrest—heart failure."

Perez took a few moments to digest what Chandler was saying. It seemed strange. There had never been a case—as far she knew—in Ravenwood of death from hypothermia. Perhaps the victim didn't recognize the early signs, such as sleepiness, drowsiness, confusion, and disorientation.

"She probably thought she had overexerted herself." Chandler cut into Perez's thinking, as though reading a thought bubble floating above the detective's head. "So, she decided to sit down, take a rest for a moment, closed her eyes, then slipped into unconsciousness."

"She had no cell phone, no ID on her," Perez said, more to herself. "Who goes hiking anytime, let alone in winter, carrying nothing?"

"I agree," Chandler said. "It is strange."

"And she was sufficiently clothed," Perez said.

"Hypothermia can affect people in different ways. There's been cases, albeit extreme, of people surviving for hours in subzero temperatures practically wearing beachwear. The human body is both a strong and fragile thing. It can be unpredictable."

"But you think there's more to it?" Perez said. "That she didn't just die from the cold?"

Chandler played with the lid of her take-out cup. When she spoke again, her face was grim, her voice lower. "I think there's something more sinister at play here."

"Like what?" Perez asked.

"Like I said, I cannot be certain until the autopsy is done, including a full toxicology, but…"

"What?"

Chandler gave a thin smile. "I think she was deliberately frozen, then dumped there to thaw out."

🐦 Chapter 15 - Peggy Scott Tuttle

Outside in the parking lot of Olsen's, Perez and Chandler parted ways.

Chandler headed into Baltimore to follow up on the body, while Perez headed back to Hagerstown, the image of a pale-skinned woman, blue lips, eyelids frosted white, sitting peacefully in a freezer, firmly on her mind as she drove.

After two hours at her desk, clearing paperwork, Perez got a call on her cell. It was Annabel Chandler.

"Haley," she said. "We might have an ID on her."

Perez was thrown by being called her first name, so she didn't immediately respond. She'd grown so accustomed to others in the department calling her Perez. Even Marvin Richards still called her Perez.

"Yes," Perez said. "Might have an ID?"

"A Maryland driver's license was found wedged deep inside a pocket. I didn't know about it until they removed all her clothing. She's been placed in the fridge awaiting the autopsy."

Chandler's theory, that the victim had been frozen, then left out in the cold to thaw, only to be placed in a refrigerator for safekeeping, reminded Perez of store-bought frozen meat. "Nothing else was found on her body?"

"No. The name on the driver's license is Peggy Scott Tuttle. I was told her prints were taken and escalated for testing, that's if she's in the database. Judging from the photo on the license, there is a facial resemblance. A DNA match would confirm for certain, if you can get a sample." Chandler read off the address from the driver's license. "The vitals on the license seem to match her," Chandler added. "All except the eyes."

All except the eyes, Perez thought, jotting down the name and address.

"Do you know where Erinsville is?" Chandler asked.

Perez knew what Chandler was hinting at. Go to the address on the driver's license, and see if she could obtain a sample of hair or any other biological material for forensics to cross match to the body's DNA. With hair, you required multiple strands, eight to ten, not just a single hair, as is often wrongly depicted in glamorous television crime shows, where an impossibly beautiful lab technician with perfect skin, teeth, and makeup jumps up and down with excitement because they found a single hair in a suspect's trunk or bed. The sample strands also must have roots. Cut hair is useless because the hair root is where the DNA is stored.

"My gut feeling is telling me it's her," Chandler continued. "Why else would she have that driver's license on her?"

For Perez, it wasn't a perfect situation, to turn up at someone's home or last known address and start making inquiries of family and friends on the basis that the victim *might* be known to them. She would need to tread cautiously. She needed the DNA, though, to also eliminate the possibility of the owner of the driver's license not being the victim as much as to confirm the true identity of the victim. Why did she only have a driver's license on her? Perez thought of a morbid gift with a name tag, then dismissed the idea.

Chandler continued, saying the autopsy might be done later or first thing the following morning.

Perez thanked her for the heads-up and told her coffee and cake at Olsen's was on her next time they met, before ending the call. She swung around to see Nate Garland stroll in and slump down in his chair.

He glanced over at Perez. "Hey, Perez, heard you're down for the stiff in the park."

"Looks like it."

Garland gave a dismissive wave. "You take it. I've got enough on my plate. It won't amount to anything. You'll see."

Looking over, Perez noticed just two case folders on his desk. The rest of the desk was littered with a mix of old take-out cups, fast-food boxes, balled-up paper, and yellowed copies of the *Ravenwood Daily* stacked in a pile. Perez went back to her work, and no more than two minutes had passed before Garland sprang out of his seat and headed for the door, his cell phone pressed to his ear. "Hey, Ronny, it's me. Got a tip on the fourth at Pimlico today. Lucky Eight. What odds can you get me? And don't gyp me either!"

Shaking her head, Perez sat back in her desk chair for a moment, contemplating the Peggy Scott Tuttle case. There were too many unknowns for her liking. She stared at the name and address she had jotted down. It was a thin slither of information, not as much as she had hoped, but Perez wasn't one to wait. She swung into gear and kicked her workstation to life.

First, she pulled the DMV details for Peggy Scott Tuttle and confirmed the address Chandler had given her. The face of Peggy Scott Tuttle smiled back at Perez. Twenty-one years old, five foot eight, hundred and thirty-two pounds, and an organ donor. Studying the DMV photo, Perez tried to superimpose the big, bright brown eyes, smiling, youthful face, glowing with life and vitality, and a lustrous fall of hair, to the ghoulish death mask she had seen, with two large, ragged holes for eyes; waxen, translucent skin; and unruly, frozen hair.

Was it her? Were they the same person? Perez didn't know, but Chandler seemed to think it was. Then again, Perez figured Chandler, in her profession, had seen many more dead bodies than she had or ever would, such that the forensic investigator was able to breathe life into any dead face and imagine what it had once looked like before all life was drained from it.

There were no other records for a Peggy Scott Tuttle in the databases. No missing person's report, not even a parking infringement. The young woman was a law-abiding citizen, a good girl, or so it seemed. Yet, behind the young woman's smile, Perez sensed something else lurking. The slight lopsidedness of her mouth. The minuscule curl of her upper lip. One eyebrow raised questioningly, and that slight rebellious gaze in her eyes.

Perez may have been mistaken, but Peggy Scott Tuttle's DMV photo had a flirty, bewitching, yet guilty quality to it.

Perez's phone rang. It was the desk sergeant. "Perez, I've got some guy here at the front desk who wants to see you, and claims he knows you."

"What's his name?"

"Philip Benton."

Why did the name sound familiar to Perez? Then it struck her. She'd only met the man briefly, twelve months ago, in the station lobby where he now apparently was again. It was Marvin Richards, not her, on that occasion who had spoken to Benton at length. Perez let out a loud breath of frustration. She didn't have the time or the inclination to speak to the man. But before she could convert her thoughts to words, the desk sergeant spoke again.

"He says it's urgent. That it's about a murder."

🐦 Chapter 16 - Phil Benton

After almost five minutes of Phil Benton practically begging, pleading with Perez for a few moments of her time, she finally relented, choosing the diner across the street for privacy.

Perez watched on as Benton hungrily devoured a plate of eggs, bacon, and grits, as though he hadn't eaten in weeks.

At first, she didn't recognize him, thought it was someone else using his name. The memory she had of the insurance investigator was of a well-dressed, clean-shaven, articulate man with a ramrod posture, perhaps mid-forties, with styled dark hair, who was slightly overweight—well nourished, using the forensic term—wearing a tailored suit and Windsor knot silk tie, and carrying a calfskin briefcase.

Now watching him eat like a vulture, reminded her of a homeless person, aged in their sixties. Benton was gaunt, his skin ashen, matching his unkempt hair. He was dressed in a chaotic rumple of clothing that looked like he had slept in them, and not just for one night either. His eyes were red raw, shoulders slouched, his face slack with hopelessness. He had the dejected look of someone whom the world had beaten down, ground into the dirt. His emaciated appearance wasn't from some trendy Beverly Hills diet he had adopted either. It was from a lifestyle not by choice. She didn't feel sorry for him. She felt confused, and a little concerned for his well-being and state of mind. There was no scent of alcohol on his breath, a saving grace. However, she got the distinct feeling that some other addiction, not alcohol or drugs, had gotten hold of him and was slowly poisoning him, both physically and mentally.

Sitting on the tabletop was a thick, dog-eared manila folder Benton had retrieved from a sun-bleached, tan-colored sedan that was parked in the department parking lot. The folder was torn at the edges and stained with coffee ring marks, smudges of ketchup, and streaks of orange that Perez could not determine. Stamped across the file in big, red lettering were the words, *File Closed*.

For a full ten minutes, pausing only to slurp black coffee and shovel eggs into his mouth, with yolk dribbling down his chin, Benton never took a breath, talking nonstop. It wasn't long before Perez realized she had unwittingly become the sympathetic ear for his outpouring, someone to listen when it seemed no one, neither friend nor work colleague, had wanted to listen to him during the last twelve months.

Wrapped in a manic bitterness, Benton explained how he'd lost his job at the insurance company where he had worked for the last sixteen years, without so much as taking a single sick day or arriving late for work. The bank then foreclosed on his house, and his meager share of the fire-sale proceeds, together with what little savings he had, was now almost gone.

Benton poked his fork at Perez. "Your boss, Richards, sent me packing after our meeting, said I had no solid evidence to support my theory that Rebecca Cartwright may have murdered her husband, Michael Cartwright, in order to claim his life insurance. He wasn't willing to listen, like my old boss wasn't." Benton took another slurp of coffee. "I'm glad you told me he's retired." He forked more egg into his mouth, and a fragment of yolk fell, just missing the file. "Maybe you'll be more understanding."

Perez's cell rang and she answered it.

"Hey, Detective Perez!"

"Who's this?"

"It's Katie Kundy from R-A-V TV. I was wondering if you have a moment to talk about the Eden Kil—"

Perez hung up. "Sorry," she said to Benton, turning her cell to silent. "So, you were saying?"

Benton went on to explain how he'd refused to give up on the Cartwright file even when his employer had closed the file because of a lack of evidence, directing him to move on to other, more viable fraud cases he had been assigned. And when he didn't, and after repeated warnings, they fired him. But that didn't stop Benton from stealing the file when he left. He continued working on it ever since, explaining to Perez that he was on a crusade for truth and justice. Deep down, he believed Michael Cartwright didn't commit suicide, that he'd come to his untimely demise at the hands of his wife, Rebecca.

After finishing his food, Benton looked like he was going to lick the plate. Instead, he wiped his face with a napkin and pushed the plate aside. He looked up at Perez, his eyes a little less bloodshot. "Like I was saying before, it was Rachel Gideon, Michael's lover, who approached me after his death. She told me Michael would never even contemplate suicide, let alone go and do it. He was killing it at work—pardon the pun—had just gotten a huge pay raise, promoted to a corner office, and was on the up and up." Benton picked a piece of food lodged between his teeth. "She told me she was pregnant, that Michael was thrilled, over the moon at the fact of being a father for the first time. They were making plans, setting up a new life together as a family."

"So, had Michael and Rebecca Cartwright divorced during that time?" Perez asked. "Before this Rachel Gideon fell pregnant and before they started picking out baby clothes together?"

Benton looked sheepish. "Not exactly."

"Were separated?"

"No."

"So how long had Michael been having an affair behind his wife's back?" Perez asked, before adding, "Not that I'm being judgmental. I just want to put everything into perspective, for both parties."

Benton gave a shrug. "Three years."

Perez's judgmental radar suddenly kicked in. It wasn't illegal, and it happens. Yet three years was certainly a deep marital betrayal, not to mention Michael getting his lover pregnant and them making family plans, all the time keeping it a secret from his wife. People had killed for less. However, it had nothing to do with Perez. "Look, I can't see how I can help you. This is Maryland. If you are concerned that a crime has been committed, then surely you should contact the police in Connecticut, where Michael Cartwright died."

Benton's ensuing silence gave Perez her answer. Benton had contacted the police in Connecticut and got the same response that Marvin Richards had given him, and that Perez was about to give. Richards had told Perez of his meeting, that Benton had made wild, unfounded accusations about Rebecca Cartwright's involvement with Michael's apparent suicide. It was all circumstantial, certainly not enough to arrest someone, let alone build a solid case for a murder conviction to stick.

Benton leaned forward, desperation in his eyes, and pushed the file toward Perez. "Here, take the file, read it, at least. I've got more proof this time. I've spent the last twelve months going back over every detail, and added more proof."

Perez shook her head. This wasn't for her. It wasn't her jurisdiction. "I can't help you. If the police in Connecticut couldn't, then I can't either. I can only act upon an arrest warrant from another state if one is issued by that state. As far as I know, Connecticut hasn't made such a request."

Benton looked forlorn, at the end of his tether, on the brink of a mental breakdown.

"What substantial motive would Rebecca Cartwright have in murdering her husband?" Perez asked, now feeling slightly sad for him. "What possible reason would she have in killing him, then making it look like it was suicide, as you're claiming?"

Benton's eyes suddenly sparked. He sat a little straighter. "How about five million reasons?"

Chapter 17 - Vengeance

It took supreme effort for Haley Perez not to balk at what Benton had just said.

Five million dollars? She had no idea the insurance payout was that much. Richards hadn't gone into actual specifics about his meeting with Benton, just that the man was on a fool's errand.

"She got paid five million dollars?"

Benton slowly nodded, a cunning little smile spreading across his egg-stained face. "That's right. In cold hard cash."

"You told me that the coroner's report concluded that it was suicide. No one pays out on suicide." Perez had a life insurance policy through the police union and remembered it listed a specific suicide exclusion.

Benton drained his coffee cup. "Michael Cartwright had a suicide clause in his policy. It's rare, but he had one."

It still didn't change anything for Perez, other than filling in some backstory on one of Ravenwood's more prominent residents. She took out her notebook. From what little interaction Perez had with Rebecca Cartwright, the woman didn't seem like a black widow, someone who would kill her husband purely for the sake of money. The affair was an added reason though. Then a thought occurred to her. "And how much of the five million do you stand to get?"

Benton's mouth twitched.

"Let me rephrase," Perez said, her pen poised. "What would your cut have been for proving that a fraud was committed? How much did you stand to make?"

"Twenty percent."

Boom! There it was. Now it was starting to make sense to Perez. No wonder Benton looked so slickly dressed the last time Perez had seen him. The guy was obviously good at his job, had done very well from it. Now it was all gone, replaced with more than a little resentment as far as Perez could see. "So, you stood to gain one million dollars by proving Michael Cartwright did not commit suicide, and was instead murdered by his wife for financial gain?"

Benton spread his hands on the tabletop. "I deserve that money if I'm right. It's my money."

Perez glanced down at his hands, the nails chewed to nothing. "And this Rachel Gideon?" Perez made a shorthand note. *Benton's motive: greed. Feels cheated by Cartwright.* Perez glanced up. "Michael Cartwright's lover? What does she stand to gain if you can prove it wasn't suicide?"

Benton gave a shrug. "The truth. Justice. Closure on Michael's death. Clearing his name. And if he was murdered, to see his murderer, Rebecca Cartwright, behind bars."

Perez sat back, contemplating all the information Benton had told her so far. It still wasn't enough to convince her. "What about the child?"

"What child?" Benton said, looking as though his mind was dwelling on the prospect of not getting his million-dollar payday.

"You said Rachel, Michael's lover, was pregnant. What happened to the baby?"

A flash of sadness crossed Benton's eyes. "At Michael's funeral, there was some kind of confrontation between Rebecca Cartwright and Rachel. Accusations were apparently made by Rebecca. She made threats that she would go to Rachel's employer, as well as spread word around the town that Rachel was a home-wrecker, a marriage destroyer. Cartwright called Rachel a whore, a slut who sleeps with other people's husbands." For some inexplicable reason, Benton started playing with the packets of artificial sweetener in the condiment caddy while he continued. "Coupled with Michael's sudden death, it was all too much for Rachel. She suffered a miscarriage. Apparently, it was a girl."

No one said anything for a moment. Finally, Perez spoke. "So, Rachel blames Rebecca Cartwright for the loss of her child?" It certainly was a valid question to ask.

Benton threw a glare at Perez, as though her question deeply offended him."Any woman would take that view, given the circumstances," Benton said, bitterness in his voice. "She believes, as well as killing Michael, Rebecca Cartwright also killed her unborn child."

"That's certainly a stretch," Perez said. There were no direct grounds for blaming Rebecca Cartwright for the miscarriage, and Perez knew no court or judge in the land would give that accusation any serious consideration. Perez made another note. *Benton has made this personal.* These details certainly made Perez think about Rachel Gideon's ulterior motives. Was she pursuing Rebecca Cartwright through some kind of personal vendetta? A woman's scorn for losing her lover—and future husband—coupled with a mother's grief in losing her unborn child?

"Is Rachel Gideon paying you?"

Benton's eyes flared wide, the blood vessels around each iris seeming to pulse and throb. "No! Definitely not."

Maybe she should be, Perez felt like saying. "Have you told her where Rebecca Cartwright lives?"

"No."

"You're positive?" As far as Perez was concerned, Rebecca

Cartwright was an innocent citizen. As such, Perez, as an officer of the law, owed a duty of care to her, to protect her, especially if Rachael Gideon decided to take matters into her own hands and come to Ravenwood seeking vengeance.

"I'm not stupid," Benton retorted. "She thinks I'm still making inquiries in Connecticut. I'm—*was*—an insurance investigator, not a private eye." Benton pushed the file farther across the table, almost tipping it in Perez's lap. "Please." His expression softened."It's all in the file. Just take a look, and tell me what you think."

Perez looked at the file, knowing if she so much as laid a finger on it, the dynamic of the meeting would instantly change. She would be giving Benton false hope. The only reason why she was still sitting there talking to him was to glean what information she could about Rachel Gideon in case the woman decided to enter Ravenwood and cause trouble. Michael Cartwright's death was a matter for the Connecticut police, and they had already given their verdict to Benton. She pushed the file back. "You keep the file. It's your property." She was more concerned about his health and well-being. She didn't want him to do anything stupid.

She flipped her notebook to a fresh page. "Tell me where you are staying in Ravenwood, and how I can reach you." It was a subtle way of getting a fixed address for him, in case he did do something rash.

Benton gave Perez his cell phone number.

She looked up expectantly. "And where can I find you? Where are you staying? At a motel?"

Benton looked down at his hands and shook his head slowly, not offering an answer.

Then it dawned on her. She cast her mind back to his tan-colored sedan she had seen. While she didn't get a good look inside the vehicle, Benton's sudden embarrassed look said it all: he'd been sleeping in his car. For how long, she had no idea. It was no way for anyone to live. He was probably showering in public rest stops, and using cafés and diners as his office to conduct his work.

The server came, topped off their coffee, and placed the check on the table before leaving. Perez quickly snatched up the bill, noticing a grateful smile on Benton's face. "I should probably buy you breakfast," he said. "For agreeing to meet and for listening to me."

Perez dealt out a few bills, placing them on the check, then used her cup as a paperweight. "You owe me nothing," she said. "And I owe you nothing." She felt guilty, felt bad saying the words. And yet she found herself wanting to know more about the case despite not being in a position to do anything about it. Maybe it was just her detective's curiosity coming to the forefront.

"You mentioned that Michael Cartwright hung himself?" Perez asked.

"The coroner's report is in the file. They also found alcohol in this bloodstream. He was fairly intoxicated at the time of death."

"Were there any reports of domestic violence? Was Rebecca Cartwright physically abused by him?"

After reaching into his pocket, Benton withdrew a pair of spectacles and slipped them on. One of the arms of the spectacles was held together with white tape, causing them to sit crookedly on his nose. Benton seemed to open the thick file at the exact location he was looking for, as though he possessed a mental index for every page in the file. His eyes ran down the page, then stopped. "There were three incidents in the six months prior to Michael's apparent suicide, where Rebecca Cartwright had been admitted to the ER. Broken forearm, fractured cheekbone, and a grade-two concussion." He looked up from the file, the thick lenses of his spectacles magnifying his eyes into two red, angry orbs. "In each case, the attending physician noted possible domestic violence down on their report. However, there was no record that I could find of Rebecca Cartwright ever lodging a complaint or bringing charges against her husband for domestic assault."

Perez cycled through the list of injuries, imagining what each entailed. Broken forearm—a defensive wound. Shattered cheekbone—when Michael's fist got past her guard the next time and smashed into her face. Grade-two concussion—another blow rendering her unconscious for as much as a few minutes. The fact that Rebecca Cartwright hadn't lodged a complaint with police didn't surprise her at all. Most victims of domestic violence suffered in silence under the fear that making a complaint against their spouse would only escalate the abuse. And when they finally did have the courage to contact police, it was usually too late.

When looked at individually, the insurance payout, adulterous husband, and domestic abuse, there may not be enough of a motive to warrant a wife murdering her husband, then staging it to look like suicide in order to claim insurance money. However, when taken together, greed, retribution, and fear did form a powerful accumulation of several motives for someone to act upon.

Rebecca Cartwright seemed to possess two of the three elements of the criminal trinity required for murder: means and opportunity. She lived with her husband, so she had the opportunity to get him drunk to the point of where he passed out, for her to then easily slip a noose over his head. And she had the means. Rope could be purchased from any hardware store or supermarket.

But where was the third element? What was her solid motive? Self-defense? Greed? Revenge for Michael having an affair? There had to be more, Perez felt. She didn't know Rebecca Cartwright's side of the story, and there seemed to be something substantial missing to have triggered her to take such a leap from victim to attacker.

Rebecca Cartwright didn't seem like a cold, calculating killer.

🐦 Chapter 18 - Rooms Within Rooms

Becca spent the rest of the afternoon in her makeshift study, going through samples of paint colors, wooden flooring, and a myriad of window styles Josh had given her to choose from.

All of this, on top of the thick file crammed full of brochures from plumbing supply companies and kitchen studios that she combed through, didn't make Becca feel overwhelmed. Truly the opposite. She wanted to be involved in every aspect. This was her house, *her* new home, designed by her, with every faucet, tile, light fixture, shade of paint, chosen by her and not by a previous homeowner. She wanted to put her mark on it, from the lowest foundation to the highest roof tile on the tallest gable. Plus, there were a few features of the house, for safety and security reasons, Becca had insisted on. Features, by their very design, hid their true purpose from the crew, including Josh. Making him privy to everything on the build was a risk, and after he and his crew finished the project and had packed up, another smaller team of contractors were due to arrive to install what Becca had in mind.

While leafing through a bathroom-fixtures brochure, nothing caught Becca's eye. There were too many choices, turning the task of selecting the right faucets, door and drawer handles, bathroom fittings, light fittings, and everything else in the house, into a long, drawn-out process. She much preferred just a handful of options to choose from.

The afternoon dragged on until she'd had enough. Grabbing

her jacket, she went outside for a walk. The temperature had begun to drop, and the low sun threw long shadows from the woods across the backyard. Playing on her mind the whole afternoon was the fact that Phil Benton had turned up to the gatehouse, asking for her. She had last seen him, what, twelve months ago? He had tried to strike up a conversation with her outside the police department. She briskly ignored him and kept walking to her car. Surely he hadn't stayed around Ravenwood since then? Becca wondered who else Benton may have tried to contact to talk about her. She wasn't overly concerned; the past was the past, and she had taken precautions, taken great care. If she hadn't, then the insurance company wouldn't have paid the money they had. And if it was a problem, why hadn't she heard from them in a letter or email?

The back of the house was covered with a network of scaffolding, and Becca took a moment to watch workmen scurry up and down like spiders, attaching external cladding. Then something moved higher up, a dark outline against the backdrop of pale blue. Perched on the peak of the top gable, at the highest point of the entire house, a raven sat looking down at her. Was it the same raven she had seen before, sitting on the porch? The bird gave a shake of its head, ruffling its thick throat hackles. Becca turned away and looked toward the woods behind her house, where a path led through the woods, down the ridge, to the fence at the bottom. She hadn't ventured into the woods since she had a prowler on the property last year. While she couldn't erect a separate fence along the rear of her property, Becca was determined to make sure she was safe in her new house. Her mind went back to the person she'd seen the previous night. Had they used the same path through the woods? A gurgling, mocking croak startled Becca out of her thoughts.

Another raven was perched calmly on a branch in the tree line, its cold, black eyes watching her.

Ignoring her feathered spies, Becca walked to the western side of her house, to where Zoe and Jason had lived. She had no idea where they had gone to. They just disappeared, up and left in the middle of the night. Leaving no forwarding address. Two days after they vanished, a tight-lipped moving crew arrived with a truck, and packed up all their furniture, clearing the house out.

Maybe they had moved to another town, another state, and continued their charade as a happily married couple.

🐦 Chapter 19 - Eighteen

It was late by the time Perez had finished reviewing what little material she could find on Peggy Scott Tuttle.

Tomorrow she would visit where Peggy lived with her mother, Vera Tuttle, in Erinsville, a small, unincorporated community just outside Ravenwood.

For now, Perez was content to sit in her apartment, with an evening breeze coming in off the small balcony, eating her takeout she'd picked up on the way home from one of her favorite eating places in Hagerstown's downtown district, The Broad Axe.

While eating her firehouse burger with a side of slaw, she thought about what Annabel Chandler had said, how Peggy Scott Tuttle had been frozen, then dumped in the state park to thaw out. This meant she could've been kept on ice for any amount of time. But frozen where? Frozen how? Perez had read grisly cases where bodies had been dismembered, then frozen to make it easier to dispose of later, piece by piece.

But to freeze an entire body, without anyone knowing, to then transport it to a state park? That required some serious planning and a degree of privacy. The person who did this to Peggy Scott Tuttle most likely lived alone, had the space for a large freezer or access to one. Perez took another bite of her burger, resigned to the fact that there was nothing more she could do on the case until the autopsy results came back, and until she spoke to Vera Tuttle.

Then there was the meeting with Phil Benton and his accusations about Rebecca Cartwright. While it had aroused her curiosity, given the size of the insurance payout, suggestions of domestic abuse, and a resentful ex-lover, after thinking about it some more, Perez decided to park it to one side and concentrate on the Peggy Scott Tuttle case. She didn't need the distraction. Without solid evidence of premeditated murder, it was still only an insurance fraud issue, if there was an issue at all, and like she had told Benton, it was up to the authorities in Connecticut to deal with it. As far as Perez was concerned, Rebecca Cartwright hadn't broken the law in Ravenwood, and had been cleared of any wrongdoing with The Eden Killer case last year. That didn't mean Perez wouldn't keep her ears and eyes open if Rebecca Cartwright came across her radar.

After wrapping up her take-out container and tossing it into the trash, Perez came back and settled on the floor with her back pressed up against the sofa. She glanced at the banker's box Marvin Richards had given her. It sat silently in the corner, untouched, an abandoned child no one wanted. It wasn't that Perez didn't want to know what was inside the box, to see how it related to The Eden Killer, and the note she was given. Moreover, what kind of horrors would fly out of it if she opened it?

It was no use. Her inquiring mind couldn't tolerate it anymore. So, with some reluctance, she dragged herself off the floor, lifted the box, and brought it back to where she sat on the floor.

And when she did lift the lid, all of the demons, monsters, and malignant spirits she never knew existed in a peaceful town, such as Ravenwood, came crawling, slithering, and shambling out.

And for the next few hours, Perez slid into a world filled with questions and no answers.

She watched from the bedroom window on the second story, craning her head enough to see across Maggie Vickerman's front yard, to the driveway of Paige and Scott Hamill's house.

She hid in the darkness, partially behind the curtain, and watched intently as Paige Hamill came down the steps at the front of her house, carrying an infant car seat that she secured onto the rear seat of the SUV.

Moments later, Scott came bounding out of the house, a big grin across his face. *Stupid, doe-eyed fuck*, she thought as she watched him lean through the open rear door where the baby was and pull an idiotic, goofy face and wiggle his fingers like a half-wit.

Scott closed the SUV door, then walked around to the driver's side window to where Paige was sitting—like the pretentious, regal bitch she was—and gave her a long, nauseating kiss.

How pathetic.

Sabine then watched as Scott climbed into the passenger side before the SUV backed out of the driveway and roared down the curve of the ridge toward the gatehouse.

Sabine stood there for a few more minutes, watching their house, until she felt a slight pain in her hand. Looking down, she saw the edge of the curtain bunched in her fist, the skin drawn tight across the whites of her knuckles. She let go of the curtain, and without a sound, slowly retreated from the window, the shadows gradually inching over her face until she finally vanished into the darkness.

Brenda O'Donnell, single mother and waitress from Ravenwood, vanished from the diner where she worked sixty hours a week to put food on the table and her only son through college. Her bag, car keys, and cell phone were discovered in a culvert under the rail track not two hundred yards from the diner parking lot where her car was left.

Mary Bickford, mother of three, disappeared at a roadside picnic spot. Mary went to use the restroom while her husband and three sons sat not more than thirty feet away on a bench, eating lunch. The family from Springfield, Illinois was passing through Ravenwood. Mary Bickford was suspected of having run off with another man when her husband, three weeks after her disappearance, received a text message from her saying that their fifteen-year marriage was over and not to try and find her.

Kevin Cross, twenty-six years old, unemployed, and from Erinsville left his live-in boyfriend, Alex Madden, one evening and never returned. A week later, his boyfriend received a voicemail message on his cell phone from Cross saying he wasn't coming back and to sell what possessions he had and keep the money for his share of the rent owed. Madden became suspicious and notified police and was told Cross wasn't considered a missing person.

Closing the last file, Perez stifled a yawn, then using her fingers, massaged the tight and knotted muscles at the back of her neck. Then she stretched her tired limbs and lifted her butt cheeks, one at a time, off the floor to relieve their numbness.

She looked at her watch, amazed at the time. So immersed was she in the files in the box, that it was already past midnight. Looking down, she saw the plastic evidence bag containing the crushed, dried remains of a black rose. It had been found on the passenger seat of Brenda O'Donnell's car. Eighteen people gone, vanished in and around Ravenwood over the years. Some had left text messages to loved ones, explaining their sudden departure. Others, like Brenda O'Donnell, never left any clue as to their whereabouts and was never heard from again.

Perez understood that people went missing every day of every year, thousands of them. Some finally turned up, living happily in another town or state, wondering what all the fuss was about. While others just vanished off the face of the earth. Marvin Richards believed there were more people missing in and around the town, that Ravenwood and its surrounding communities had an unnaturally high propensity of missing persons when compared to other places.

It was an anomaly that had caught his eye when he first arrived in Ravenwood. But over time—and given his heavy caseload as a detective—he had pushed the anomaly aside to focus on his work, only returning to his unproven theory when he could afford a little time on the weekends.

His theory, as he had explained to Perez at his cabin, was both as simple as it was frightening. That in some small towns, because of limited police resources, the chances of someone being caught for murder was less than in other towns that had larger police departments and manpower to throw at homicide cases. To Perez, this seemed logical, and it wasn't a criticism of law enforcement. It was just a fact, that every county had a different homicide clearance rate, that is the percentage of murder cases cleared by someone being charged versus never being solved, and the perpetrator remained in the community, untouched, to go on and reoffend. That was the simple part of his theory. The frightening part was, however, that these stats were easily available to anyone online and could be used by serial murderers to find the best town or county to move to where the chances of them being caught was minimal. Like a *Forbes* Best Places to Live list for murderers.

However, Richards had added another layer of evilness to his hypothesis. To further hide a murder, you simply reconstructed or staged it to make it look as though the victim was a missing person. Then their true fate—the fact that they had actually been murdered and their body disposed of—would be hidden forever. A missing person case never got the same level of effort or resources that unsolved homicide cases did, simply because with an unsolved homicide, the perpetrator was still roaming the community and likely looking for their next victim.

Perez glanced at the neat stack of files next to the banker's box. Was Ravenwood one of those places? A small town that had drawn murderers to it because, statistically, the chances of them not being caught was in their favor?

🐦 Chapter 20 - New Man

She loved his smell, his scent, a warm, earthy mix of leather and almond spice with slight floral undertones.

It was a subtle, lingering fragrance that always made the hairs on the nape of her neck stiffen, her nipples bristle, and her loins unabashedly salivate.

She may have just turned seventy, but Maggie Vickerman had needs and desires, just like any woman, regardless of age.

"God, that smells wonderful, James," Maggie said.

The man standing at the cooktop in her kitchen turned and smiled, wooden spoon in hand, a dishcloth draped over one shoulder, steam rising from a large pot gently simmering on the flame. "It's an old family recipe, handed down by my grandmother." His dark, sensual eyes smothered her.

Maggie watched him for a few moments, wishing he would stir his own spoon inside her desperately aching pot. She let out a gentle sigh, watching as he slowly dipped the spoon into the red, viscous liquid, not so much stirring it, more like coaxing it lovingly to mingle and infuse.

Maggie had grown tired of younger men; they had no substance, nothing to carry them beyond the physicality of sex. Sure, she had welcomed the unrelenting stamina and youthful enthusiasm a young, virile man brought to her bed. However, it left her wanting more, a deeper connection, more meaning, and a half-decent conversation long after the sweat had dried from her back. She didn't tell Becca and Paige this fact, however. She still had a reputation as a sex-hungry vixen to uphold. Yet, more than anything now, she craved the intimacy and intellect Hank had starved her of for so many years while he tinkered away for endless hours in his basement of depravity.

James had come into her life at just the right time, during her lowest point when she had recovered from the physical injuries Hank had inflicted on her, when she felt as though the large, lonely house would swallow her.

They had met on a dating app despite Maggie swearing herself off such a frivolous and superficial meat market. But then James Mohels, a forty-two-year-old, Tesla-driving, cryptocurrency trader from Baltimore dropped into her feed and waved. He took the initiative, reached out to her, and Maggie liked that.

James brought a certain level of intellect, maturity, and finesse to their fledgling relationship, which was barely two months old. The fact that he looked like Hugh Jackman, the Australian actor, was the cherry on top of a very delicious pie. Rarely did anyone's online picture on such dating sites match the flesh and blood of their reality. James, however, was the exception. With the tall, lean physique of an Olympic swimmer, short dark hair, intense, hypnotic, coal-black eyes, and smudge of stubble across his jaw, his online photo certainly didn't do him justice. So much so, for the first time since she could remember, Maggie actually felt inadequate when she had met him for an initial drink. And his clothes, no matter what he wore—from a classic, dark, tailored suit to a simple T-shirt and jeans—always seemed to fit him so well, hugging in all the right places.

"I meant *you* smell wonderful, not the pasta sauce," Maggie said, approaching James and then wrapping her arms around his waist. "When will it be ready?" she asked, her fingers of one hand moving seductively down past his belt buckle, probing and searching for something substantial to eat. "I'm hungry," she crooned, low and throaty.

James playfully slapped Maggie's wandering hand away. "I told you; all good things come to those who wait."

Maggie peeled off and gave him a pout. "You're no fun."

He still hadn't fucked her yet, and that fact was driving her crazy, making her hungrier to devour him.

James reduced the heat to a slow simmer and poured Maggie a glass of wine. Maggie regarded him as he leaned back against the kitchen counter, the sleeves of his crisp white shirt rolled up, his blue jeans hugging his groin and thighs, leaving little to the imagination. Only he could make such a domesticated pose look so damn sexy.

He gave her a questioning look. "Aren't you concerned at all about Hank being released from prison next week?"

Maggie rolled her eyes and took a sip of the wine. Why so many questions about Hank? She'd already told James almost everything about her ex. How he'd attacked her in their own home, how—to her horror and dismay—he had secretly placed spy cameras throughout the house to record Maggie, leaving out the part that Hank had done so to catch her having sex with her many lovers. Hank had even placed a spy camera in her car. Not to mention the hundreds of child abuse videos he had amassed on his home computer hard drive, which the police had discovered in his basement lair of sin and debauchery. And how he was indirectly responsible for the murder of their son, Adam.

"Hank is useless, a weak man, always has been. Without me, he's lucky if he can wipe his own ass. He's incapable of doing anything on his own." With glass in hand, Maggie went to the touchscreen display on the wall. "And I've had a totally new security system installed." She pressed a series of numbers on the lock screen, and the display came alive. "New hi-tech security cameras, keypad locks on all the doors, even motion sensors along my backyard where the woods are in case he decides to creep up the ridge behind the house."

"Impressive," James said.

"I'm more than capable of taking care of myself," Maggie replied breezily. While the last twelve months had been financially challenging for Maggie, she had managed to salvage what was left of her retirement savings and was managing the small portfolio of funds on her own—doing quite well, really. She had always been self-reliant, a free thinker, and the trials and tribulations of the past had only bolstered her resolve to steer her own destiny. Her life was her own ship, and as captain, she needed to spend more time in the wheelhouse. While men were essential, they were confined below deck, stoking her boiler, nothing more.

James raised his glass in a toast. "I totally agree. Here's to strong, independent women and their gadgets."

"Absolutely." Maggie raised her glass and then drained it. Placing it on the countertop, she sauntered toward James. The boiler needed stoking. "And I've got you to protect me," she said, pushing up against his chest, her fingers slipping not so innocently between the buttons of his shirt, feeling the hard folds of his chest muscle. "You're big and strong. I'm sure you'd be able to snap him in two if he so much as shows his face around town." Maggie felt a spark of heat in her loins, an empty furnace that needed stoking.

"I'm not a violent person," James replied, looking down at her. "As I've told you numerous times, Maggie. I wouldn't even hurt a fly."

Maggie raised an eyebrow, her hand now buried inside his shirt, her fingers probing, searching, finding, then twisting his nipple. "We'll see about that," she whispered, pulling him toward her.

🐦 Chapter 21 - Collusion

Jessop's Hardware was located on the outskirts of Ravenwood, and Becca turned into its dirt parking lot at just after 9:00 a.m.

The outside of the store was layered with rows of ladders, wheelbarrows, pallets of fertilizer, and an assortment of gardening tools.

As Becca pushed open the door, the familiar sound of a brass bell rang above her head, and a warm, comforting feeling settled on her. It was like stepping back in time to an era when attention to detail and traditional values meant something, and *Made in America* was the norm, not the exception. Immediately, she was hit by the pleasant smell of raw lumber, wood shavings, and beeswax. The floor had seen a million feet over the years, the original stain worn back to a dirty olive smear. There was a long counter along one side of the store, and behind it was a tall wall with built-in pigeonholes crammed full of small tools, parts, cardboard cartons, small boxes, and hardware bric-a-brac, all neatly and carefully stacked. A ladder on a slant ran along a rail halfway up the wall to gain access to the top where larger boxes were stacked, the print on the sides faded and their cardboard sagging with age. Every conceivable space was taken, brimming with bits and pieces of hardware.

"Morning." An old man with thin hair and thick glasses shuffled out from a storeroom out the back. He wore an old-fashioned woodworking apron, checked shirt, and looked like he had been born in a sawdust pile.

"Hi, Clarence," Becca said, greeting the owner. Walter

Jessop, Clarence's father, had opened the store back in the 1950s when Clarence was just a boy. "I just came in to pick up some paint samples."

"No problem, Becca. Josh dropped off the codes a few days back, and I mixed them up. They're all boxed up out back and ready to go. I'll grab them for you."

"Thanks."

Clarence disappeared back to the storeroom, and while she waited, Becca looked around the store, walking the aisles, amazed at the size and variety of stock crammed into the place. She had insisted—as well as hiring local contractors—that Josh also source the building materials from local business owners as much as possible. The lumber for the house came from a local mill. The window glass from a local fabricator, and most of the hardware needed, Clarence Jessop either sold or could get in.

Becca stopped and looked down at the floorboards, thinking she heard something, like a hollow moan coming from under the planks. She listened some more. Nothing. Maybe just rats or water pipes groaning in the cold.

Clarence emerged moments later, carrying a carton, and placed it on the counter. "Here you go."

"How's my account going? Josh is not going overboard?" Becca had set up an account so Josh could charge everything as he needed.

Clarence shook his head. "The opposite. He scrutinizes every damn nut and bolt, whining about how cheap he can get it for at one of those big-box stores along the highway."

Becca smiled, picking up the carton. "I'll have a word with him."

Clarence gave a nod. "I'll send a statement at the end of the month, like always."

Becca knew "send" meant *mail* not *email* and smiled again as she left the store.

Outside, Becca knelt in and placed the carton of paint samples on the back seat of her car. Standing again, she glanced across the street and saw a tall, thin woman with a woolen hat pulled down tight on her head, wearing a thick scarf and dark sunglasses. Even at this distance, Becca could tell it was Sabine Miller.

But that wasn't what caught Becca's attention. It was the man Sabine was apparently in a deep conversation with. He looked different compared to the last time she had seen him. Thinner, rougher around the edges, less groomed. But it was definitely him.

Phil Benton.

🐦 Chapter 22 - Vera Ann Tuttle

According to her mother, Vera Ann Tuttle, Peggy Scott had left Ravenwood six months ago and had told her mother she was heading to LA to pursue a career as an actress.

The family home was a twelve-hundred-foot, three-bedroom, ranch-style house in Erinsville, an unincorporated community just outside the township, with a population of three hundred, according to the last census.

"Did you actually talk to or see Peggy when she told you she was leaving for LA?" Perez sat in the small living room surrounded by thick, soft, padded sofas; chunky, worn, wooden furniture; and a shabby, cream-colored rug. A fish tank bubbled away in the corner, a solitary bug-eyed goldfish peering out behind the slimy, green glass. Perez had to sit forward on the sofa for fear of losing the fight and being sucked between the deep cushions and vanishing forever.

Vera Tuttle sat across from her, a mix of concern and apprehension on her face. She seemed a proud woman. The family might not have had much, but the house was clean, neat, where repairing and repurposing household items, rather than throwing them out, was the order of the day.

For the sake of not alarming the woman, Perez hadn't told her about the body they had found in the state park. She first needed official confirmation from Baltimore.

"No," Vera said, her fingers twisting the folds of her dress. "I didn't actually speak to my daughter. I just got a voice message on my cell phone."

"And it was definitely her?"

"I know my own daughter's voice."

Becca could see that the woman was holding back tears, and her lips trembled as she spoke. Her eyes had that pleading quality to them, as though she were either constantly apologizing or begging for forgiveness. Perez so wished she could offer the woman more, put her out of her misery. But she couldn't—yet.

"Just tell me! Has something happened to my daughter?"

"Mrs. Tuttle, I'm just conducting initial inquiries about your daughter. I can't confirm anything at this stage."

"But she's not missing!" Vera insisted, her voice rising a few octaves, sounding like she was trying to convince herself, which meant there was doubt there. "She contacted me just yesterday. Told me she was auditioning for a part in a sitcom. It was a small part, but she might get it, and it could lead to a bigger role."

Perez stopped writing in her notebook, seeing now where Peggy Scott Tuttle got her apparent optimism from, if in fact, she had gone to LA chasing fame. "You actually spoke to your daughter, Mrs. Tuttle? Yesterday?"

Vera looked away, shaking her head. "No. It was a text message." She wiped her nose with a tissue she pulled out from the cuff of her sleeve.

"So, you tried calling her back?" Perez asked, a familiar wave of suspicion slowly building inside her.

"I've never been able to reach her," Vera said, with another wipe to the nose, uncertainty and optimism slowly turning into doubt and dread. "There is no number to call her back. It's like it's been blocked."

Perez made a note to get Peggy Scott Tuttle's cell phone

details so she could check her phone records.

"So, you've never you actually spoken to your daughter since she left town?" Perez asked.

"Not an actual two-way conversation, if that's what you mean," Vera replied. "Apart from that text from her yesterday, I hadn't really heard from her recently. She did text me a few days after she left town, saying that she had arrived safely in LA, and not to worry. She mentioned she would be not contactable for a while. So don't bother trying to reach her."

Perez thought it strange that Peggy hadn't actually spoken to her mother, just a voice message soon after she disappeared, and a few random texts later, including one on the day the body had been discovered. If someone had taken Peggy six months ago, maybe the voice message had been coerced out of her, recorded soon after, sent to her mother, then she was killed. Hence, no more voicemails, just texts that could easily be fabricated. As Perez reviewed her notes, a disturbing and familiar picture was starting to form in her mind, making her think of Adam Vickerman.

Perez glanced to her right. "Is it all right if I take a look at that photo?" Perez asked, pointing to a worn photo frame sitting on a side table.

Vera Tuttle handed the photo frame to Perez. "That was taken last year."

Instantly, a pit of hollowness hit Perez in the gut as she stared at the photo, and she tried to keep her expression neutral. The body found in the state park was Peggy. A DNA match would confirm it. The photo in her hand was more revealing than the DMV photo. It showed a young woman, sitting perched on a low railing, smiling at the camera. She had the same hair, similar facial features and build as the body that was found.

Minus the eyes.

There was a younger sister, Stacy Tuttle, who was autistic, Vera Tuttle had mentioned. "Stacy has no middle name?" Perez asked.

Vera Tuttle again looked uncomfortable. "No," she said. "Peggy and Stacy came from two different fathers."

Apparently, Stacy's father vanished the same day he found out she was autistic. The family had never seen or heard from him again.

"And Peggy's father?" Perez asked. Vera went on to explain that he was a long-haul truck driver, crisscrossing the country. "He's basically a drifter," Vera confessed with a scowl.

Perez thought about the truck driver she had pulled over a few days back.

"He comes home now and then—if he considers this place to be a home," Vera scoffed. "Dumps a few dollars on the kitchen counter, fucks me senseless for a few days like a rutting deer, then takes off again." She threw a sneer at Perez. "I'm sure both fathers will be back once all the hard work of raising them has been done by me. They'll then want to be part of my daughters' lives again."

Perez felt a deep remorse for the woman. Men seemed to be a blight on the Tuttle women, planting their seed before taking off, only to one day return when the sapling had grown old enough and strong enough to fend for itself, emotionally and financially.

"When was the last time you saw him?" Perez asked. "Peggy's father, that is."

"Maybe two weeks ago. Said he was heading down toward the Gulf of Mexico to look for better work, maybe pick up a rigging job. Had enough of being on the road, he said."

But he still didn't want to come home, be closer to his family, Perez guessed.

Vera explained that Peggy worked at a Sheetz gas station south of the Premium Outlets, just off the Dwight D. Eisenhower Highway and across from a Walmart superstore. Perez made a note. It was also the same gas station where Freddy Monk worked.

"What about a boyfriend, Mrs. Tuttle?" Perez said, looking up.

Vera raised an eyebrow. "She's had plenty."

Great, Perez thought. The acorn definitely didn't fall far from the tree. She made a note to follow up at the Sheetz gas station and get a list of Peggy's past acquaintances from Vera.

A phone chimed. Perez glanced at the screen of her cell.

Nothing.

"Oh, it's mine, dear," Vera said, picking up her cell phone from the arm of the sofa.

Perez's heart did a quick tap dance as she watched Vera smile hopefully at the screen. Surely not?

"Oh…" Vera said. "Wishful thinking." She gave a defeated frown. "I thought it may have been another text from Peggy."

Perez went back to completing her notes. Wishful thinking indeed.

"Detective?"

Perez looked up again at Vera. The woman's frown was still there but deeper, more furrowed across her brow this time. "Yes?" Perez asked.

"The message…it's for you."

This time Perez's heart started doing backflips. Her mind folded in on itself as the living room seemed to shrink to the size of a hall closet. *What? Me? How? Who?*

Vera Tuttle read off the screen. "It says, 'My Dearest Detective Perez. I sincerely hope that you got the flowers.'"

🐦 Chapter 23 - Ten Thousand Ways

It was almost 10:00 a.m. by the time Scott Hamill got out of bed and stumbled groggily into the kitchen, where he was greeted by a sweet and savory fragrance.

Paige bustled around the kitchen, and Scott spied two trays of muffins cooling on a wire rack. Next to the muffins sat a small wicker basket, a red checked cloth layering the insides.

"Coffee is made," Paige said as she slowly eased out the muffins and placed them carefully inside the basket.

Scott took a coffee cup down from the cabinet and poured himself a cup. "Who are the muffins for?"

"For our new neighbor, of course." Paige looked up. "At Number Ten." She went back to filling the basket. "I thought I'd break the ice, so to speak. Take them my famous welcome muffins."

"Don't you think it's odd?" Scott said, eyeing the muffins.

"What is odd?"

"That no one has really seen them?"

Paige twisted her lips. "That's why I'm taking the initiative, going by there myself this morning with these."

"What happens if no one is home?"

"Then I'll leave them on the porch, with a note I've written."

Paige turned to Scott, holding up a freshly baked muffin in her outstretched hand. "Try one. I'm sure you'll find it delicious."

Eagerly, Scott grabbed the muffin and took a bite. "Wow!

This *is* delicious," he said. "It's savory, but still delicious." Looking down at the insides of the muffin, he saw slithers of green. "What's in it?" He took another bite, his stomach grumbling for more.

Paige continued filling the small basket with the muffins. "Well, I've been thinking, Scott, that we eat far too much meat."

Scott stopped chewing. "Too much meat?" A few crumbs fell from the corners of his mouth.

"Too much red meat is not good for you." She brought the corners of the red checked cloth together and tied a neat bow before stepping back and regarding her work with a critical eye. "Good." She turned to face Scott. "I think we need to eat more vegetarian food," she said, scrunching up her face into a sweet smile. "Zucchini."

Scott felt a seed of fear take root inside his stomach. "Zucchini?"

"That's right," Paige said. "That's what is in the muffin you're eating. You said it was delicious, didn't you?" Without waiting for Scott's response, Paige went to the built-in bookcase where all her prized cookery books were. "I found this wonderful new vegetarian cookbook online. I ordered it yesterday, and it just arrived this morning." She slipped out a thick book and brought it back to where Scott was standing, holding it up so he could read the cover. "Isn't it great?" Paige said, glancing at the cover, before reading the title. "*Ten Thousand Ways with Zucchini.*"

Scott felt suddenly ill. The small shoots of fear in his stomach had grown into a creeping, tightening vine.

"Oh, by the way, how's the new book coming along?"

"Fine," Scott said cautiously, placing the unfinished half of the muffin on the countertop.

"Good!" Paige said cheerfully. "I know how *hard* it gets, when you're in your writing den, and how you don't like to be disturbed when you're in there working *hard* at it."

Scott frowned, wondering why his wife kept emphasizing the word *hard* to him. Unless…

Grabbing the basket, Paige turned and pecked Scott on the cheek before staring deep into his eyes. "You must stop *beating* yourself up all the time."

"Beating…myself?" Scott said, feeling the creeping vine inching its way up his throat.

Paige gave a concerned nod. "It's not good for you." And with those choice words of advice, she whisked from the kitchen, carrying the basket, and out the front door.

🐦 Chapter 24 - Being Watched

Perez rushed down the front porch steps and got to the curb as fast as she could, her eyes scanning left and right down the street as she went.

The street was deserted. She looked across, searching the trees, bushes, fence lines, the houses on the opposite side, expecting to see someone hiding in the shadows, an outline, a person, but there was no one.

Quickly, she scanned the vehicles on both sides. Empty. No dark shape hunched behind the wheel, looking back at her.

Riding a bicycle, a child with pigtails, tied with pink ribbons, came rolling into view on the opposite sidewalk. Perez watched her for a moment, the girl's head thrown back, face upturned to the sun, singing a tune to herself as she pedaled, immersed in her own make-believe world.

Vera Tuttle appeared in the doorway behind Perez, cell phone still clasped in her hand. "What's wrong?"

Ignoring her, Perez took off to her right, jogging a hundred yards down the sidewalk, stopped, then looked around.

Nothing.

She crossed the street and jogged in the opposite direction, pausing in front of a vacant dirt lot overgrown with grass. The rear of the block was walled with a scatter of trees and low shrubs. The wind picked up, rustling the trees and kicking up a funnel of dirt and garbage. Looking up, Perez saw the smooth, glossy, black shape of a bird perched on a branch. It gave a gurgling, mocking croak as it watched her, inviting her to step forward.

Dropping her gaze, Perez saw a flicker of movement behind the shrubs. Cautiously, she stepped forward onto the lot, bringing her hand up to her right hip where her gun was holstered under her jacket.

She stopped again. Among the weeds, an old sofa lay on its side like a body, the brown, faded upholstery slashed open, its innards spilling out. A rusted car axle. An old refrigerator someone had dumped, dented and covered with graffiti.

Movement again, in the grass near the old refrigerator. A dog, with half its fur missing, its mottled skin drawn tight across visible ribs, its muzzle deep in an old tin can. The dog looked up. The can dropped from its muzzle. Two darks eyes glared at Perez. The dog's mouth twitched, revealing a row of teeth, before it took off with a sulky limp, looking sullenly over its shoulder at Perez before disappearing into the foliage at the rear of the lot.

Back on the porch, without asking, Perez grabbed Vera Tuttle's cell phone from her hand. There was no caller ID, but the message was as Vera had relayed it to her. There was no other explanation as to how the person knew where Perez was, sitting in Vera Tuttle's house, talking to her about her daughter. It was the same person who had sent text messages to Vera, pretending to be Peggy, and had sent the black roses to Perez with the note. Mason Garrett's mentor, his teacher, had abducted and killed Peggy Scott Tuttle and was now taunting Perez, goading her.

Perez pocketed Vera Tuttle's cell phone. "I'll need this for forensic testing."

Vera began protesting, but Perez couldn't hear the words coming from the woman's mouth. Looking out to the street, Perez felt the hairs on the nape of her neck itch, as though a line of ants were crawling up her spine, the pads of their tiny feet scratching her skin. Something was wrong. Something *felt* wrong. She could feel eyes on her now, even though she couldn't see anyone. The person was there, watching her, mocking her with their cleverness.

Perez turned back to Vera Tuttle, saw her distraught face, the glassiness of her eyes.

She knew. She knew her daughter was dead.

"I need a sample of Peggy's hair," Perez said. "Maybe her hairbrush."

Vera moved her head up and down mechanically, her face stretched with grief and despair, the certainty of her daughter's fate almost sealed. Tears began to well in her eyes. "In…her bedroom," Vera said, her voice hollow and empty, as though the last two minutes had drained the last fifty years of life from her body.

"Can you get it for me, please," Perez asked. She didn't want to go into Peggy's bedroom, not yet. That would come later, when an army of forensic techs and police officers descended on the place, to trample on their already trampled lives. While Peggy lay in deathly slumber in the morgue, back home her entire life would be exhumed, laid bare for the world to examine, prod, poke, question, and judge, down to the most infinite and intimate of details.

For the moment, it was better to leave some semblance of dignity with the poor mother, even if that meant giving her a false glimmer of hope. Perez would wait until there was confirmation from DNA before shattering the family forever. Even though she was only the messenger of death, she felt somehow complicit in it.

Vera Tuttle turned and drifted, trancelike, back inside the house.

Just then a cell phone rang inside Perez's pocket.

Her gut tensed before realizing it was her own phone, in her other pocket, that was ringing.

She looked at the screen, then took the call.

It was Annabel Chandler. "The autopsy has been done, and the report will be emailed to you within the hour from Baltimore. I just wanted to give you a heads-up on what was in the report. Can we meet?"

With the cell phone pressed firmly to her ear, Perez swiveled and continued watching the street, the uneasy feeling in her gut increasing, not subsiding, with every passing moment. "I could be at Olsen's in twenty minutes."

Chandler agreed, and Perez ended the call.

With a heavy heart, Perez went back down the path toward the sidewalk and then stopped. Turning, she looked back up at the house. Eyes indeed had been watching her—from above.

A pale, innocent face peered down at her from an upper-story window. A young child. Stacy Tuttle. The young girl just stared down at Perez. No smile. No wave, almost accusatory.

Perez turned and kept walking to the sidewalk toward where her ride was parked. She needed an evidence bag from the trunk to put the hairbrush in. Twenty feet away from her car, she froze, her heart turning to a block of ice in her chest.

There, on the windshield, under one of the wiper blades, was a long-stemmed, black rose.

🐦 Chapter 25 - Cause of Death

"She was deliberately frozen alive, most likely in a proper freezer, and not from being outdoors," Chandler said. "I also believe that someone tried to resuscitate her."

They sat at a quiet corner table in Olsen's, an assortment of sugary goodies in front of them. As agreed, it was Perez's treat, but her appetite was shot. She had already given Chandler the plastic evidence bag containing Peggy's hairbrush with a request to fast-track the analysis. Perez hadn't told Chandler about what else had happened at Vera Tuttle's home: the revealing text messages, running out into the street, and the black rose on her windshield. Her brain was still trying to process it all. She hadn't thought of checking her own car first when she had torn outside. She was too engrossed at looking for an actual person on the sidewalk.

"Someone tried to save her life?" Perez said. "A good Samaritan?"

"No," Chandler said. She had already consumed two chocolate brownies and was eyeing a cinnamon bun. "She had two broken ribs, the likely result of someone applying CPR to her, trying to bring her back to life."

"Hold on," Perez said, struggling to understand this new but somewhat contradictory revelation about Peggy Scott Tuttle's demise. "Someone first killed her by placing her in a freezer, before dumping her out in the state park? Then someone else found her and tried to resuscitate her?"

Chandler shook her head. "At first that's what I thought, that perhaps someone came across her in the state forest, realized she was suffering from hypothermia and that her heart stopped. So, they applied CPR. But that's not the case now that a full autopsy has been completed. The report should be in your inbox. Check your emails."

"I will, but first give it to me in layman's terms."

Chandler gave a sigh. "She had two recently chipped teeth, a central incisor of the upper jaw, and a lateral incisor of the lower jaw. There were also cuts along the inside of her mouth, and blood was found on the mid third of her left vocal cord. Such mouth and throat injuries are consistent with her being intubated." Relenting, Chandler reached for the cinnamon bun. "Whoever had tried to resuscitate her, did a lousy job of it."

"So, she was in a hospital?" Perez said, more confused than ever now.

Chandler took a bite of the bun, her appetite seemingly immune to the grisly conversation.

Perez drew a line with her finger, on the table, mapping out her thoughts. "Or a passing hiker, unbelievable as it sounds, just happened to be carrying the equipment to put a breathing tube down her throat?"

"I don't know," Chandler replied between chews. "None of it really makes sense." She wiped her mouth with a napkin. "I'm just reporting on the medical cause of death findings. How she died. You'll need to talk to the forensic pathologist in Baltimore who did the autopsy. As a courtesy, I'm just giving you a heads-up."

"Which I appreciate," Perez said. "But I would also appreciate your professional opinion."

Chandler looked down at her hands in her lap, and Perez

could see the woman was feeling uncomfortable but wanted to say more.

"You're the detective. You figure out what led up to her death." Chandler remained tight lipped, her eyes still staring intently at her hands.

Perez leaned in. "Look, you were on scene. You saw her in situ. You're not going to get into trouble by telling me more or giving me your honest, professional opinion. Some of the people in Baltimore are noncommittal at times, don't like giving me their opinion about a death." Perez sat back. "The other alternative was that someone didn't really mean to kill the woman, someone with medical training and equipment, and they panicked, tried to save her life, botched it, then decided to dump her body in the state park."

Chandler's eyes rose to meet Perez's gaze. "I think she was experimented on."

"What?" Perez asked, not in disbelief but more as though she had heard incorrectly.

"I'm going out on a limb here," Chandler cautioned. "Above my pay grade as a part-timer."

"Understood," Perez said, edging forward in her seat. "But I value your professional opinion, and I don't care about you being a part-timer."

Chandler seemed to bristle at the compliment. She paused, then spoke in a lowered voice." I believe she was deliberately frozen, then warmed, then frozen again, in a repeating cycle by someone who wanted to see how, physiologically, her body would react."

It was Perez's turn to feel as though this was all above her pay grade. However, as tempting as it was to comment on this incredible revelation, she just nodded and continued listening, her mind swirling.

"The person who performed CPR—intubated her," Chandler

continued, "did so a little too vigorously, or was inexperienced, causing teeth, mouth, and vocal cord damage. I think the person pushed the boundaries a little too far with her and accidentally brought on cardiac arrest. There were also numerous burn marks on her chest and flank consistent with an overuse of fibrillation pads."

Perez couldn't believe what she was hearing.

"In layman's terms, she was repeatedly shocked with varying degrees of intensity. Her body bore the marks of someone with a prolonged history of defibrillation."

"Why was she intubated?" Perez asked. "Why not just shock her back to life?"

"In cases of hypothermia, when you are administering basic life support, one of the strategies is to get warm oxygen into the airway as soon as possible. The cruel thing is, the killer panicked, hence the oral injuries that she sustained from the scope being shoved too hard down her throat."

"Panicked?" Perez asked. "Maybe they were just inexperienced at playing God?" Perez contemplated the information. So, it was an experiment that had gone wrong? "Peggy Scott Tuttle was the subject of someone's sick fantasy of freezing and thawing, but it went a little too far?"

"Could be," Chandler replied. "Either way, they applied CPR and definitely a defibrillation device, maybe because they didn't anticipate her dying so soon."

"So soon?" Perez said. "Do you mean she spoiled their fun? They wanted to torture her for as long as they could. What kind of person does that?"

"Whoever did this to her is one sick bastard that we need to find. They may do it again." Chandler finished off the rest of her bun.

"Perform another type of experiment on someone else?" Perez said, finishing Chandler's line of thinking.

"Yes," Chandler replied, wiping her hands. "Sorry. I missed breakfast."

"Have you ever seen anything like this before in your line of work?"

"Fortunately, no."

"Could it be a doctor or a paramedic?" Perez questioned, "This person playing Frankenstein, by carrying out sick experiments?"

"Not a very good doctor, if it is one," Chandler answered. "And paramedics are well trained."

"So, it's an ordinary person?"

"With some limited medical training," Chandler added.

Perez said nothing for a moment, trying to fathom the unfathomable, her mind in some garish place. She looked up at Chandler. "Did she suffer?"

Chandler slowly nodded. "She would have drifted in and out of varying degrees of consciousness, but pain would have been present. That isn't the bad part, though."

"What do you mean?" To Perez, it sounded all bad.

Chandler pushed her plate away. "Well, can you imagine regaining consciousness only for the nightmare to repeat itself over and over again? The victim would have been frozen alive again, placed back into some freezer knowing full well what was happening."

Perez took a deep breath and tried to imagine the horrendous nightmare the young woman must have suffered, like a lab rat for some sick and perverted human experiment. Someone had stolen Peggy from her family, from an impoverished community of welfare dependency and crushing despair and plunged her into a worse nightmare. "What kind of sick person does this?" Perez said.

"You tell me," Chandler replied. "You're the detective." Chandler drained her coffee.

"Thanks for the heads-up," Perez said, her mind adrift. What was she going to tell Peggy's mother, Vera Tuttle? How could you reveal such nightmarish details of pain and suffering to the mother of a daughter who had been taken by such a cruel and sadistic murderer? And whoever it was, was a murderer, plain and simple. This wasn't a case of manslaughter, an accidental death in the name of medical science. The only possible outcome for Peggy Scott Tuttle was eventual death. The sicko only wanted to draw it out for as long as possible to get his kicks. The grim news Perez had to deliver would utterly destroy Vera Tuttle, condemning the poor woman to a lifetime of misery from knowing exactly what had happened to her daughter. Not to mention the impact on Peggy's younger sister, Stacy.

Most of the time, Perez loved her job. But it was times like these when she truly hated it.

"There is some sick bastard out there we need to find," Chandler said, her face gaunt and tight, but offering a glimmer of a smile.

Perez regarded Chandler. *We?* Now she had an ally, someone she could work with together to bring justice to Peggy Scott Tuttle.

🐦 Chapter 26 - The Dark Rift

"I just work weekends," Freddy Monk said, "but there was this one guy who came in a few times. Peggy said he gave her the creeps."

"How so?" Perez asked. They were sitting in the gas station storeroom that also doubled as a staff room.

"She reckoned every time he came in, he would browse the aisles just so he could stare at her. He'd buy nothing, just the gas."

Perez made a note. She liked Freddy. He was just a typical hormonal teenager with a lopsided grin who sniggered a lot. There were no grins or sniggers today. Freddy's face was one of disbelief when Perez had told him Peggy Scott Tuttle might have been missing for the last six months. Freddy was managing the gas station today and had put a junior out on the register so they could talk in private. He still was a good kid, a little immature for his age, but he didn't get mixed up in anything with the local cops. "Did you ever see him?" Perez asked. "This man that was watching her. Have you seen anyone like that since she left?"

Freddy shook his head, took a swig from a bottle of Jones Black Cherry soda. "No." His mouth twitched. "And we get a lot of creepy people coming in." Perez could see he was struggling with the news. "That was more than six months ago…I can't believe she's gone missing, and that someone may have taken her." As a distraction, Freddy started peeling the label from the soda bottle, depositing little torn pieces of paper in a neat pile on the table.

"I don't know if someone has taken her, Freddy," Perez said. "I just wanted to know if you've seen or heard from her in the last six months."

Freddy shook his head. "Like I said, she just didn't turn up for her shift six months ago. I haven't seen her around town or anything. But, like I said, outside of work, I never saw her."

"Her mother said she had moved to LA, to get into acting," Perez said.

"LA?" Freddy's head shot up, his eyes like saucers. "She said nothing about that."

"She never mentioned about becoming an actress. Moving to LA?"

Freddy shook his head vigorously. "No." He seemed more disappointed than surprised that Peggy may have not shared this with him.

"She never mentioned any of her plans with you about her future?"

"She told me a lot of things. We were friends only at work. We didn't date or anything." He peeled some more of the label, obviously downtrodden that he would have liked to date her. "I don't know who her friends really are." He rubbed harder on a stubborn corner of the soda bottle label, his brow furrowed. "She has a lot of boyfriends too. She mainly spoke about them, you know, at work. Problems she was having with them, how many she was dating at once."

"So, she never mentioned about quitting her job here? Saying that she was unhappy?" Perez wanted to make certain.

"No." Freddy kept working the label off the bottle. "She just…"

"What?" Perez asked.

Freddy puffed out his cheeks. "She just sent a text to the boss. Said she was quitting. Didn't show up for her shift." Freddy scrunched his face. "I remember when I last saw her. She was leaving after her day shift; I was coming in to do the night shift over the weekend. She was supposed to be in the next day. She even said, 'I'll see you tomorrow,' and then she walked out the door."

"And that was the last time you saw her?"

Freddy nodded. "Yeah. It was like she was coming back the next day. But she didn't show."

"And you never ran into her afterwards? Never once around town?"

Freddy shook his head. "If I had, I would of told you. Like I said, outside of work, I never hung out with her. Didn't know what she got up to other than what she told me when she was working here."

Freddy was starting to sound defensive. "Hey, Freddy, it's okay," Perez said, softening her tone. "I'm just trying to figure out if anyone has seen her lately." To Perez, her line of questioning seemed hollow, meaningless, because in her mind, it *was* Peggy Scott Tuttle who was lying on a slab in Baltimore. But until the DNA results came back, she had to go through the motions, treat her as a likely missing person. "And she never texted you?"

"No. It was the owner who told me she wasn't coming back."

Perez made another note, another blot of familiar dread spreading out in her gut like it had when Vera, Peggy's mom, had said the same thing. No voice calls. No human interaction. Just text messages. "What can you tell me about her boyfriends?" Perez asked. "Did she talk about any of them harming her? Being rough with her?"

Freddy glanced up almost in alarm. "She never said anything

like that. Doesn't mean nothing happened, I suppose. She certainly didn't come to work with bruises or anything. She was the kind of girl that was probably the opposite."

"The opposite?" Perez stopped writing.

"Yeah," Freddy said, a bit more cheerful now. "She would often get into fights. Especially with guys. Beat up on them, too, so I heard."

"Did you see her get violent with anyone?"

"No."

"So how do you know she would beat up on guys?"

"You know." Freddy went back to peeling the label. "Rumors, people saying stuff around town about her."

"So, she had a few boyfriends and got into fights with guys?"

"It's a free world." Freddy shrugged. "But, yeah, there're rumors about that."

Perez made another note. If Peggy Scott Tuttle was getting into fights with men, physically that is, then it was plausible someone sought retribution, got their revenge, and killed her. Perhaps it was a group of men who hadn't taken too kindly to her. However, her cause of death—freezing her then resuscitating her just for fun—did seem a little elaborate, uncommon for someone wanting to take their angst out on her.

Perez needed to check out Peggy's ex-boyfriends. From what her mom had said, and now from what Freddy Monk had corroborated, the list could be extensive. They likely wouldn't be willing to come forward, and tell the truth, especially once they learned she'd been murdered.

"I'll need to see the security camera footage for the shifts that Peggy worked," Perez asked.

Freddy took another swig of soda. "No can do," he said, stifling a belch.

"I can come back with a warrant if you'd like. See the owner."

"That's not what I meant," Freddy said. "The recordings are erased after six months. Standard procedure. It's automatic."

Perez's hopes were suddenly quashed. "You mean there is no security footage at all prior to six months ago?" There goes any chance of identifying Peggy Scott Tuttle's stalker.

Freddy shrugged. "What can I tell you? It's company policy."

Six months. Peggy Scott Tuttle had been on ice for six months. Was it just coincidence? Or did someone know that the gas station security footage would automatically be erased after six months? And was that someone the same creepy person who came into the store to watch her?

Perez closed her notebook. While Freddy Monk had provided some useful information, which might turn out to be just plain rumor and small-town gossip, she knew she wouldn't get anything else useful out of the young man. "Your mother mentioned you thought someone was following you through Kenley Lane the other day?"

Freddy gave a shrug. "Just some guy."

"But you never actually saw the person's face? How do you know it was a guy?"

"Just a feeling I got. The way they walked. They were hunched over, hands in their pockets. I could tell it was a guy."

"Well, try and keep clear of that laneway, if you can," Perez warned. She made a mental note of the person Freddy had described, stood, and gave him her card. "Call me if you think of anything else. Especially if some creepy guy comes in and asks about Peggy." Either way, Perez needed to eliminate Peggy's supposed stalker just as much as elevating him to a person of interest.

"Like I said, we get a lot of creepy guys in here," Freddy said, taking the card, then smiling at it, as though he'd just scored a supermodel's cell phone number.

Seeing his expression, Perez shook her head. Teenage boys and their hormones. "Only if he asks about Peggy in particular." Perez doubted if the man would show up. Peggy was missing for six months before she turned up dead. And she had been missing. Peggy Scott Tuttle did not get on a Greyhound, nor did she hitch a ride out of town to the land of broken dreams. The more she contemplated the young woman's life, the more Perez was convinced Peggy had been abducted six months ago, held, tortured, then murdered, kept in a freezer before being dumped up at the state park.

Pocketing the card, Freddy gave Perez a cheesy grin, all thoughts of Peggy Scott Tuttle pushed aside. "Maybe we can catch a pizza sometime?"

Perez gave him an equally cheesy smile. "Fat chance there, Freddy." Perez headed for the door.

"Oh, another thing about Peggy," Freddy said, causing Perez to halt.

"What?"

"It might not be important," Freddy said, looking up.

"Anything is important in finding what happened to Peggy."

"Peggy and a few of her friends would go up into the foothills outside of town, into the woods up there a lot. She'd talk about it. They'd drink, hang out, and make out with a few guys from around town."

To Perez this wasn't noteworthy. But she would talk to Peggy's friends if required. "So, what was so special about this particular place?"

"Nothing," Freddy said. "I've never been up there. Like I said, Peggy and I had different friends, you know?" Freddy frowned, as though trawling back through his limited memory. "About a month before she quit working here, she came in one morning and said the night before that she'd been up there with some friends, had a party in the woods, lit a bonfire, played music, and drank. She said they all got spooked at one point. She reckoned there was someone roaming around up there, in the darkness, watching them."

Perez turned. "Did she say if she got a good look at this person?"

"Nah," Freddy said.

"What's this place in the woods called?" Perez asked.

Freddy looked at Perez. "It's called the Dark Rift."

◆ Chapter 27 - Edith Plover

First, she searched the internet, typing in *Dark Rift*.

Nothing. The closest mention was something called the Great Rift, a dark dust cloud in astronomy. Then she narrowed the search by typing in *Dark Rift, Ravenwood*. No luck either.

Maryland? Nope.

Perez then spent the next thirty minutes visiting various historical and tourist websites in Maryland and searching their own databases. Still no success.

Looking up from her cubicle, she saw Nate Garland loitering at the coffee machine. As he sauntered back to his desk, he caught Perez watching him.

"What's up, Hotshot?" he said with a smirk. "No headline-worthy serial killers to catch today?" He slumped in his chair and pulled out his cell phone and began texting.

Perez got up and walked over to his desk.

Garland glanced up, leaned back in his chair, and gave Perez the once-over.

He was the oldest detective in the homicide squad, had lived in Ravenwood all his life. If anyone knew what The Dark Rift was, he certainly would. "I need your help," Perez said, not relishing having to seek his advice. Before he could shoot another smart-ass comment at her, she quickly continued. "Have you heard of a place called The Dark Rift?"

"Yeah," he said, his eyes going wide.

Perez felt a slither of excitement.

Garland rocked gently back in his chair. "It's a place I'd like to push my ex-wives and their lawyers into." He let out a laugh and slapped his thigh. "That's for damn sure!"

Perez sighed.

Garland held up his hand, noticing Perez's unimpressed glare. "What's up, Perez? You need a little humor in your life."

"Can you help me or not?"

"In all seriousness," he said. "No. I haven't heard of a place called that. What is it? A nightclub or something?"

Perez explained what Freddy Monk had told her, about it being a teenage hangout up in the foothills outside Ravenwood.

"Sounds like a cult-gathering place, Sherlock."

"Sherlock?"

Garland did a double take. "Sherlock Holmes, the famous British detective? James Moriarty, his archnemesis? Never heard of them?"

"I know who Sherlock Holmes is," she said impatiently, regretting ever getting out of her chair to ask Garland.

Garland shook his head. "Can't help you. Maybe a bit after my time when I was a teenager. Back then we just hung out at the local burger joint, not up in the woods in the middle of the night."

"You've never heard the term used by anyone else?" Perez asked, her hopes fading.

"Can't say that I have. But I'll tell you what, Perez, since I'm such a nice guy, and you've come to me for help..." He leaned forward, just a little too close for Perez's liking, but she stood her ground. He reeked of sweat, fried food, and sour breath. "You know who you should go and ask?"

"Who?" Perez said, wishing he would just hurry up so she could escape the smell.

"Edith Plover. She's the librarian over at the Ravenwood Library. She's been here since time began. She may be older than Moses, but she knows a thing or two about town history."

Perez checked her watch. If she hurried, she might make the library before closing time.

"No, my dear, I can't say that I've ever heard of a place like that around here. Or anywhere else, come to think of it."

Perez stood at the counter of the Ravenwood Library. It was near closing time, and there were only a few patrons browsing the shelves. Edith Plover peered thoughtfully at Perez, with owlish eyes, through a pair of round-wire spectacles. She was compact, wizen-faced, and wore her gray hair fashionably twisted into a tight bun pierced with an opposing pair of black lacquered chopsticks with a twisting golden dragon motif. "You said it was a place up in the foothills outside of town, in the woods?" she queried again.

"That's right."

She made a show of thinking before shaking her head slowly. "Sorry, that I can't help you. It doesn't ring a bell." She gave Perez's hand a gentle squeeze, which Perez found to be strangely comforting.

Despondent yet grateful for meeting Edith Plover for the first time, Perez closed her notebook. Another dead end. Maybe this Dark Rift was a secret meeting place known only by a select group of teenagers who went there and named it as such. Unlike other known historical landmarks in and around the township, the place was probably undocumented.

"Thanks, Mrs. Plover."

"Not so fast, dear," Edith said, a mischievous glint in her eye.

"I said that I wasn't able to help you. But I may know someone who might."

Perez wondered if she was on a fool's errand, like a scavenger hunt for something that didn't exist. She'd already wasted enough time today. She should really head back, see if she could track down any of Peggy Scott Tuttle's current, and past, boyfriends.

"Alfred Beckett," Edith said, a faraway look in her eyes and a flirtatious smile on her lips.

"Alfred Bucket?"

"Beckett," Edith corrected Perez. "He's an old recluse who lives up on Dawson's Ridge, overlooking the township. Been here longer than me. The town practically grew up around him." Edith broke her distant gaze and looked at Perez. "He would know."

Chapter 28 - Alfred Beckett

Early the next morning, after an unsuccessful evening of trying to locate Peggy Scott Tuttle's past boyfriends, Perez decided to call on Alfred Beckett before work.

Beckett's house was a carcass of recycled wood and tin sheeting on a base of stained cinder blocks. It was an assortment of building materials collected, scavenged, or borrowed but never returned, fashioned into a haphazard yet solid-looking structure with a spiral of smoke coming from a crooked chimney stack on the roof. Snowflakes drifted down, settling on Perez's head and jacket, which she pulled tighter. She passed an assortment of machinery, seized and rusted, topped with snow. They hunkered like dead animals around the house. A porch of raw lumber, dark with age, wrapped around one side of the house, sagging in places, and had no handrail. A set of old stairs led up to a collection of doors stacked against one wall that gave the illusion of an entrance, but there was none that Perez could see.

Cautiously, she climbed the steps, convinced that one of the unstable treads would collapse, and she would end up on her ass in the snow. "Hello? Mr. Beckett?" she called out, unsure where the front door was among the tapestry of overlaid planks and repurposed wood that ran the length of the porch.

"Mr. Beckett? It is Detective Perez. I wanted to ask you some questions about the Dark Rift."

A door hidden in the side wall opened, and an outstretched

skeletal hand, like a creepy coffin bank novelty toy, beckoned her within.

Unlike the outside, the inside of the house was a picture of order and meticulous care. Perez found herself in a large open room lined with floor-to-ceiling bookcases crammed full of books, file boxes, maps rolled into scrolls, old digging tools, and a collection of rocks scattered among brass instruments. A large steamer trunk stacked with magazines sat in the center of the room, sandwiched between two button-leather sofas, the hide rich and lustrous, lovingly rubbed and conditioned. The floor was sealed wood, covered with threadbare rugs, perfectly aligned at right angles. Against one wall, a fire raged in a large stone fireplace, its edges blackened and the mortar cracked from driving away the cold from countless winter days. The room was warm and cozy, the air thick with the smell of polished wood, old leather, and woodsmoke.

"Take a seat," Alfred Beckett said. He hobbled and sat down in a rocking chair, his face catching the glow of the flames as they danced in the hearth. He was all skin and bone, thin and wiry but hardened like a ranch fence post. His thin, gray hair and skin were parched and weathered from a lifetime spent outdoors in the sun, rain, and cold.

Perez sat down on one of the leather sofas opposite him.

Two sharp and vibrant eyes focused on her.

"I wanted to ask you about the Dark Rift," Perez said. "And other landmarks around the township. Edith Plover, from the library, suggested I talk to you as you're one of the oldest residents and know a lot about the history of Ravenwood."

"Edith Plover..." Beckett's voice petered out, his face softened, and his eyes seemed to twinkle in the firelight, giving Perez the same expression Edith Plover had when she mentioned his name. The two seemed inextricably linked through some past romantic liaison. "Should have parked my boat in that harbor when I had the chance years ago." He chuckled. "You know I used to be a surveyor," Beckett said. "Traveled a lot, been all over the world when I was younger. South America, Australia, Canada, Russia."

Perez just nodded, letting the man reminisce. It would be a lonely existence up here on the ridge, hardly any visitors, she imagined.

"I'm retired now, bought all this land up here when the town was just one street and a few stores. Now look at the place. Built this house, too, with my own two hands."

"So, you've lived here for a while?" Perez asked.

"Sure have." Beckett's eyes suddenly frosted over. "The Dark Rift, you say?"

"I was wondering what you could tell me about the place. Where it is, and what's there?"

Beckett eased out of his rocking chair and went to the bookcase. After much deliberation, he chose a rolled-up scroll and motioned to Perez toward a large, high table with a brass banker's lamp on it. He unrolled the survey map and pinned down the edges with rock samples and a large magnifying glass. "When I was a lot younger, I used to hike up through the foothills and the forests around the town. Been nearly everywhere around here."

Perez stared at the map. It was yellowed and cracked with age, like parchment, but it was a thing of exquisite beauty, and the detail was amazing. It was crammed full of notations, carefully drawn lines, arrows, measurements, directions, and detailed field notes, all meticulously written in neat copperplate script. Pencil, ruler, and ink nib had only ever been allowed to grace the map.

"Beautiful handwriting, Mr. Beckett," Perez said.

"All keystrokes and thumbs today, your generation is," he scoffed. "We've lost the art of handwriting. Now, let's see what we have here." He leaned over the map thoughtfully and ran his fingers like he was following an invisible groove in the map's surface. "Here we are." His finger stopped on the landmark of Dawson's Ridge. "This is us here." His finger continued across the surface and settled again on another spot. "This is the church." Beckett spread his fingers in an arc behind the landmark of the church, over an expanse of green marking the foothills and the start of the forest. A scatter of thin, spidery dash lines marked trails, while thicker, full lines marked back roads. "It isn't marked on any map you can buy, but I know it's there," he finally said.

"What is there, Mr. Beckett? What's on the map?" Perez asked.

His eyes scanned the map, and he said without looking up, "I came across it maybe twenty years ago, when I was doing some prospecting."

"Prospecting?" Perez said.

"Mainly tin, some silver, if I was lucky. The foothills used to be riddled with mine shafts and boreholes back in the day, dug out or blasted out with dynamite by wildcat miners." He placed his finger on a spot. "Here."

Perez leaned down closer to the map and read the small inscription. *The Dark Rift*. "How come it isn't marked on any conventional map?"

"There's a lot of places in Ravenwood and the surrounding area you'll not find on any map," Beckett replied. His eyes crinkled into slits, making Perez feel like she was being scrutinized. "You're not a local, are you?"

"No. I have been here a few years. Plenty I don't know about the town and its history."

Beckett gave a chuckle. "This town has a hidden topography to it, other layers, like rock strata. The more you dig, the deeper you go, the more you will find hidden places buried from common eyes. Some by accident, some deliberate."

"I expect that's like any town or city, even large neighborhoods," Perez said.

Beckett shook his head solemnly. "Ravenwood is different. I have been here all my life, so have my parents before me, and my grandparents before them. There are strange things hidden in the woods, in the foothills, and in the waters of the rivers and creeks that even I don't know about. Places deep in the woods where you shouldn't set foot. There is more than one layer to this town, and to the people who live here. Take the bookstore, for example. You take a book off the shelf only to find another shelf hidden behind it with books that you're not supposed to see, not meant to read. Under the wooden floor in Jessop's Hardware, I've heard things are under there, secret passageways and hidden rooms."

"Just town gossip," Perez said, knowing full well that the rumor mill worked overtime in a place like Ravenwood—and thinking that maybe Alfred Beckett had spent too long up here on his own.

"It's not gossip," Beckett countered, raising a defiant eyebrow at Perez. "I've spent years researching this town, its history. It does have a dark and ugly past to it that folks in town prefer not to discuss, want to cover up." He turned his attention back to the map and tapped it with his bony finger. "The Dark Rift. It is deep in the forest. Nothing much up there, though, but thick woods and huge boulders. In my day, some kids used to go up there, hang out, smoke pot, and learn about the birds and the bees."

Perez looked wider around the spot where Beckett had placed

his finger. "What's this?" she said, pointing to a small, hand-drawn structure.

Beckett squinted at the map. "That's the old slaughterhouse and tannery. Was owned by the Cullen family back in the day. Been in their family for generations, going back as far as the eighteenth century. Was closed down in the nineteen fifties, something about chemicals leaching into the soil and ending up in the creeks."

"I can't recall hearing about such a place, and it's not on any map," Perez questioned, looking closer at the map. The slaughterhouse looked like it was in the middle of nowhere, perhaps five miles or so out of town. The nearest landmark Perez did recognize was Martha's End Elementary School two miles to the south.

"Oh, it is there, all right," Beckett said. "All the buildings are still standing. I guess it's a part of history people around here want to forget."

"How so?"

Beckett cast a suspicious eye over Perez. "Back then, before the Civil War, Maryland was a plantation colony, used plenty of slaves to work the tobacco crops." Beckett leaned in, his voice low. "I've done some historical research on the Cullen family and how they treated black folks back then. Let us just say cattle wasn't the only thing they used to hang from meat hooks in their slaughterhouse."

Perez felt her stomach churn with disgust and shame. She turned her attention back to the Dark Rift. "So, why is this particular spot called a rift?"

"Because also up there is an old borehole, one of the largest I've seen, drilled out by miners back in the nineteen sixties. The hills up there are littered with them, not as big as this one, though. Some were sealed off, plenty were not. Dynamite was used to blast the hole shut; instead, it sheared the surrounding hillside, wrenching a wide, jagged rent across the bore, turning it into a wide, deep rift, hence the name, the Dark Rift. That entire hillside is now a labyrinth of deep crevices, narrow trenches, bottomless sinkholes, and rocky fault lines. The original borehole now looks like a wide, gaping, open wound, black and as dark as the devil."

"And you've been up there recently?"

"Not recently," Beckett replied. His voice had grown empty, detached. "It was near on twenty years ago, maybe, when I was last up there. I stood on the edge of that rift, looking down into it. It had a deep, endless blackness to it that I've never seen in all my days, and I could have sworn I heard screams echoing up from the darkness below." Beckett shivered, seeming to break out of his trancelike state. He turned back to Perez. "Probably nothing, really, what I heard. Just trapped wind, deep underground, moving through the fissures and channels under the crust." He paused, then his face went cold. "But I ain't never going back up there." The glow of the fire rippled across the deep grooves and lines on his face, plunging part of it into shadow. "And I suggest that you stay well clear of that place too."

🐦 Chapter 29 - Halfway

After arriving back at the station, Perez began trawling through what records she could access of Peggy Scott Tuttle.

There wasn't much on her social media account. A few selfies, random pictures of cats, and the odd sunset. Not the usual plethora of photos that young people tend to post, documenting every waking, breathing, moment of their lives. And certainly, no activity for over the last six months.

It was the same with her bank account. Vera Tuttle had a stack of unopened bank statements belonging to Peggy that had arrived in the mail over the past months and had given them to Perez when she had asked. They covered the period from a few weeks before she supposedly left Ravenwood, to the most recent, being two weeks ago. There were just a few transactions on the day she walked out of the Sheetz gas station, then nothing. The account didn't move. And certainly no transactions in California. There was just over five hundred dollars in the account.

Marvin Richards had always told Perez to stick to the basics, the fundamentals. Walk in your victim's footsteps on the last day they were seen. Do this even before you talk to family, friends, ex-boyfriends, wives, husbands, lovers, past and present. You need to see the world through your victim's eyes just before they vanished and were last seen alive.

So, with Marvin Richards' sage words of advice in her head, Perez filled up her coffee cup and sat down at her desk. Then she called up the bank transaction records and slipped on Peggy Scott Tuttle's virtual shoes and went for a Google Maps walk, without leaving the comfort of her cubicle inside the homicide squad room.

With a population of ten thousand, the community of Halfway was aptly named after the fact that it was literally halfway between Hagerstown and Williamsport. It was there where Perez had started her journey following in the footsteps of what she knew was a dead person. A lot can be revealed by a person's spending habits, their personality, their friends and acquaintances, places they visited, what they purchased, and more importantly, bank records, leaving a digital trail, like footsteps, of where they went.

Peggy's shift at the gas station had ended at 3:00 p.m. on that last day. Her bank statement showed a purchase for $21.15 from Ross Dress for Less at Crosspoint Shopping Central. From there, Peggy had headed north five hundred yards, cutting across Cole Road before entering the Valley Mall where she next made a purchase at Tacos Carlitos for $7.61 in total. Whether she was just being thorough, or plain curious, Perez called up the online menu and did the math. Allowing for sales tax, Peggy Scott Tuttle had bought two Baja California tacos, $3.59 each. No drink. It was probably the closest Peggy ever got to California before she vanished.

Perez kept walking. Three minutes and a hundred and eighty yards later, she found herself at Victoria's Secret. There Peggy had made a purchase of $100.24 in total. Looking at the online catalog gave Perez a headache. The permutations and combinations were endless. Bras, panties, lingerie, sleepwear in a myriad of styles, not to mention beauty products and accessories. Perez was content with speculating that Peggy had wanted to purchase something special. If she wanted quality and affordable undergarments, she could have just picked up something while she was at Ross Dress for Less or Target next door, especially for a young woman who worked at a gas station and whose family was struggling.

No. She had been out to impress someone.

Perez checked the next purchase on the bank statement, the last one for the day, the last transaction ever for Peggy Scott Tuttle before she'd stepped off the face of the earth, only to appear six months later, dead.

From Victoria's Secret, Peggy Scott Tuttle had turned right, headed east through the mall, passing a Yankee Candle store on her right, Auntie Anne's on her left, before turning right again at Hibbett Sports and continuing past the Hagerstown Community College Valley Mall Campus. From there she had exited the mall, turning left, then walked another hundred yards before entering JCPenney and purchasing something to the tune of $40 from the Perfume Hut located inside.

Perez looked at the map on the screen, following the line of tiny blue dots representing Peggy Scott Tuttle's last movements, the footsteps of a ghost.

Victoria's Secret and perfume. Not extravagant purchases, but for Peggy they were. If she'd intended to turn up for her shift the next morning, as Freddy Monk had assumed when she turned and said to him, "I'll see you tomorrow," before walking out the door, then she was meeting someone that night, someone who justified Victoria's Secret undergarments and designer perfume. It was a special occasion, with a special person, not the usual "rough and tumble" guys she had perhaps dated in the past. Maybe someone new, maybe a cut above the other men she had known, perhaps having sex for the first time with him. She wanted to make it memorable.

Perez sat back in her chair, swiveling it slowly side to side, thinking, studying the progression of blue dots on the screen, before they abruptly ended. In her mind, she tried to imagine the rest of the day and into the night for Peggy. When did she realize that the person she was meeting, the person she had trusted, was going to take her, torture her, then kill her? Who was this person? How and where did she first meet him? Slowly, Perez began to form a progression, so typical in such cases.

Stranger, acquaintance, friend, boyfriend, lover, abductor, torturer, and finally…killer.

🐦 Chapter 30 - A New Body

It was one thing to follow virtual footsteps on a computer screen.

It was another thing entirely to walk in the shoes of the dead, to touch, smell, see, and feel what they did, but with your own eyes.

So Haley Perez decided to see for herself what Peggy Scott Tuttle had experienced, right up to the moment she vanished.

What should have taken a straight thirty-minute round trip—walking slowly, taking in the sights and sounds, starting at Ross Dress for Less at Crosspoint Shopping Central, crossing Cole Road, then going through the Valley Mall to Peggy's final destination, the Perfume Hut inside JCPenney—took over an hour. And all to no avail. Perez didn't expect to find some new revelation, some case-breaking clue. During her reconnaissance, she had taken in everything, and more, that Peggy Scott Tuttle might have seen, even straying from the trail of Google Maps' blue dots in her head, expecting the young woman to have done the same, wandering along, browsing the storefronts without buying.

Now Perez stood outside, under a low sky the color of sharkskin, her hair and face buffeted by a crisp, dry breeze, in the southern parking lot of the Valley Mall. Snow was piled in clumps. Trees, spindly and bare, sat like skeletal hands. She would need a warrant to requisition the mall's security camera footage, which was her next move. Maybe Peggy didn't walk alone. Maybe she had a traveling companion. Did she eat both tacos or split them with someone else? All these questions and more buzzed inside her head as she set off again toward her car. Perez glanced up at a large building on her right that ran the entire length of the southern parking lot. When she first arrived and started her walk, Perez hadn't noticed the A-frame sign on the footpath near the building's entrance. It was small and insignificant compared to the huge, blue-and-fiery-orange sign that adorned the building's frontage. *Energize Wellness.*

A tinge of excitement sparked inside her as she walked over and read the wording on the A-frame: *Whole Body Cryotherapy. Free first session. Totally Safe.*

The young woman standing behind the counter looked up as Perez entered the wellness center, which looked, smelled, and felt remarkably like any other large gym she had visited. She paused and looked around. Modern, industrial chic, with gleaming, polished metal, and recycled air that was artificially scented like a Nordic pine forest to disguise the bland scent of sweat, exertion, and the sickly stench of commercial rubber flooring. All of this was accompanied by the dull, repetitive thump of a three-note hip-hop soundtrack, punctuated by the occasional jarring clang of iron being dropped, and the grunts of men who sounded like they were giving birth.

In a millisecond, the woman behind the counter reshaped her face, transforming it from the bored look of cured concrete to one full of energy, excitement, and overt cheerfulness. She threw a dazzling-white smile at Perez. "Hi, my name is Rhianna!" She had raven-black hair cut into a short bob, a narrow face with sharp features, and was of average height, with a lean and lithe body. *Obviously.*

"I'd like to know about your cryotherapy sessions," Perez said, leaving her badge firmly in her pocket.

The woman's smile got even whiter and brighter before she spoke rapidly. "You saw our sign on the footpath? Sure. Is it just for yourself?"

Perez nodded.

"It is wonderful." Rhianna's eyes rolled up in their sockets, as though she was having a stand-up orgasm. She then launched into a rapid explanation of all the benefits, such as improving your overall well-being, accelerating cell regeneration, easing muscle soreness and inflammation, and increasing the body's immunity defenses.

To Perez, it equated to stripping off butt-naked, then jumping into a freezer for a few minutes, causing all your blood to be drawn away from your bodily extremities. When it came to her own body, Perez had a simple mantra: do not mess with Mother Nature.

Rhianna pulled out a brochure. "When would you like to book in for your free session?"

"Is it possible to first have a look at one of these"—Perez looked down at the brochure—"cryopods? Perhaps you can give me a tour?" Perez did not want to commit to anything, certainly not stepping into some freezer box and getting blasted with whatever it was they blasted you with. She knew a little about cryotherapy. It seemed all the craze among the West Coast rich and famous. She wasn't a movie star or a celebrity. She just wanted to chase down any lead, no matter how small, on how Peggy Scott Tuttle may have been frozen. It was a long shot, and Peggy may not have been there.

"If I'm happy, then I'll do a full session," Perez lied, taking the brochure, and balling it up in her jacket pocket.

Rhianna's smile grew even brighter, and Perez could have sworn she saw her eyeballs rotate with dollar signs like a Vegas slot machine. The woman was obviously on commission, encouraged to sign up as many new members and sell other ancillary services to the public as she could.

Unclipping a walkie-talkie from her belt, Rhianna spoke into it, and moments later, an equally fit-looking young man with a radiant smile appeared and greeted Perez.

"Brady here will look after the counter while I show you the cryo chamber," Rhianna said.

Cryo chamber? It sounded ominous, as though Perez was about to step into a vault, be frozen and then be thawed out in one hundred years from now. Maybe world hunger would have been solved by then.

Perez followed Rhianna as they made their way down a narrow, tunnel-like corridor of subdued overhead lighting and plush carpet, leaving behind the din of banging, clanging, and thumping music in their wake.

Despite being warm inside the gym, Perez gave a shiver. There was no way someone was going to put her in a freezer and turn her into a human ice cube. The corridor ended at what actually looked like a bank vault door, complete with a heavy lever handle and electronic keypad.

Rhianna turned to Perez, raised her hand to shield one side of her mouth, as though she were sharing a secret with her, in a room full of people, despite it being only the two of them standing there. "It's just for effect," she confessed. "Makes people think they're entering some futuristic laboratory." She punched a code into the keypad. "Usually, I'm expected to put on a white lab coat, but we'll drop the ceremony on this occasion."

Disneyland indeed, Perez thought.

The door gave an audible hiss, and Rhianna pulled it open with the lever handle.

Beyond, a rectangle of pure darkness yawned wide, and there was nothing fake or theatrical about the wall of frigid air that hit Perez in the face.

Rhianna gestured with her hand. "After you."

The darkness beyond was impenetrable. Perez took a tentative step forward, then another, and crossed the threshold.

🐦 Chapter 31 - The Chamber

The star-covered heavens lit up, bathing the inside of the room in a celestial light, from hundreds of fiber-optic strands hidden in the ceiling above Perez's head.

A row of three gleaming, polished metal cylinders, each ringed with a halo of lights above, stood upright in the middle of the room. The smooth sides of each cylinder were dotted with lines of twinkling lights, and a tendril of mist seeped from the base, completing the mystical, supernatural effect.

Perez walked up to the first cylinder and placed her hand on its cold surface. She turned back to Rhianna. "Impressive. Can you explain how they work?"

"I can give you a free session now if you'd like." She gestured toward a door on the opposite side of the room. "You'll find a robe, slippers, and gloves in the changerooms."

"Gloves?"

"To wear when you step into the pod. Just as a precaution from the gas vapor. You'll only be inside for three minutes, and you'll feel like you've been given a completely new body when you emerge."

I'm happy with my current body, Perez thought, turning back to the pod. It looked like some futuristic, upright coffin, a pharaoh's sarcophagus, harboring some bandaged-wrapped mummy inside. "Three minutes, my ass," Perez murmured.

"Sorry, what was that?" Rhianna came up behind Perez and peeked over her shoulder.

Perez quickly turned, not realizing she had spoken her thoughts aloud. "Sorry, I said 'What kind of gas?'"

"Oh, nitrogen." The woman shuffled around, grabbed the handle on the side of the cylinder, and pulled. The cylinder split in half, revealing a padded interior, a seat for the occupant, and not much else.

Yes, Perez thought, *it definitely looks like a coffin, even has the padded interior.*

"These are single-person cryogenic pods," Rhianna explained with an extravagant wave of one hand toward the interior. "They use a liquid nitrogen vapor, with a temperature range between negative one hundred degrees Celsius and negative one hundred sixty degrees Celsius. You simply step inside, and let the nitrogen vapor envelop you for up to three minutes." She gestured toward Perez again. "Are you sure you won't give it a try?"

Perez gave a forced smile but firmly stood her ground. "Maybe some other time." She walked slowly around the pod. There were no external tubes or pipes. Everything must be built into the machine. Returning to the front of the pod, she saw an electronic panel displaying a glowing, semitransparent skeletal shape of the human body, with a web of red and blue vessels and capillaries. "And an operator is present at all times?" she asked.

"Yes."

"And are these all of the pods you have in this location?" Perez asked, subtly trying to interrogate the woman while also appearing to be a fastidious potential customer.

"Just three at the moment, but they're so popular, we've ordered another six."

"Six? Are there any other places around here that have these?"

"There are a few other health and wellness centers. But we have the most advanced cryopods in the state."

Another sales pitch, Perez thought. "And can they be bought privately?"

At first the woman seemed confused. "I guess you could buy one, keep it in your home. Come to think of it, I have never really thought about it. A lot of our members are simply happy to come here on a regular basis. I imagine they're awfully expensive."

Perez could tell the woman was getting a little suspicious of her line of questioning. Her face had lost its helpful, cheerful glaze. "So, if I come for a full course of sessions," Perez asked, "will it be you personally supervising? I want to make sure I get qualified care."

The eagerness returned to Rhianna's face. "But of course. There are only two qualified consultants. Me, and another woman called Amber."

Perez looked at the pod again, imagining Peggy Scott Tuttle trapped inside, the dial—or whatever the damn thing used—turned up full. "Is there any chance of someone being frozen inside one of these…pods?"

The brilliant smile immediately slid from Rhianna's face, replaced with a look of abject horror. She shook her head vigorously, as though Perez had suggested she cut off her own arm and give it to her as a Halloween back scratcher. "Definitely not!" the woman exclaimed, appalled at the mere possibility of such a thing.

"Accidentally, I mean," Perez qualified, trying to appease the woman's distress at the sheer audacity of even suggesting that something that looked like a large household freezer could be used to freeze a person alive.

"There are numerous fail-safes," Rhianna said, sounding offended. "It simply could not happen. It is only the vapor that reaches those low temperatures, and you are inside for only a few minutes. To the occupant it feels like you have just stepped into a cold room for a few moments, then you get out."

Perez stepped forward, secretly enjoying antagonizing the woman, putting her on the spot, asking her questions that no one else might have. "But you could still freeze someone inside of one of these? Couldn't you? If you wanted to? Slowly freeze them alive?"

"I...guess...if they stayed inside long enough, and if you altered the controls and the safety override." She gave the machine a troubled look, as though seeing its capability in a new, horrifying light. She turned toward Perez, her face plagued with doubt. "But why would you want to do that to someone?"

Before Perez could respond, her cell phone rang.

She watched the screen pulse with the incoming call—but let it ring. And ring. She must have heard her ringtone about a million times before. But when a phone call becomes the messenger of bad news, really bad news, you hear the ringing differently. It sounds different. It feels different. Like how a phone ringing at 2:00 a.m. sounds and feels different than a phone ringing at 2:00 p.m., as if by telepathy, the bad news travels ahead of the radio waves that carry the voice, and reaches your brain before the words reach your ear.

Perez answered the call.

◆ Chapter 32 - Plans

Despite believing she had driven enough distance from Ravenwood not to be recognized, as an added precaution, she wore her hair up, tucked underneath a Ravens ball cap.

The surgical face mask, while not mandatory at the store, was an added bonus. This particular superstore had a dedicated baby section, and she spent a full, nauseating ten minutes browsing the aisles. There were huge packs of disposable diapers, diaper bags, changing tables, breastfeeding bottles, stacked cans of baby formula, standard strollers, lightweight strollers, and jogging strollers. Bouncers, rockers, baby walkers, and swings. Finally, she found what she was looking for and chose the cheapest one possible, carrying it to the checkout where she paid cash.

The checkout cashier handed her a voucher along with her change.

"What's this for?"

The young girl smiled. "If you go online, enter your details, and use this redemption code, then you'll get an extra twelve-month warranty with this particular brand."

"That's okay," Sabine Miller said. "I don't need it. I only plan on using it once."

Ignoring the perplexed look from the cashier, Sabine Miller lifted the infant car seat off the conveyor and walked quickly out the store.

Once back in her car, Sabine dialed a number on her cell. It was a phone number that had taken considerable time to track down. But time was what she had plenty of while in prison. The call went straight to voicemail. *Even better*, Sabine thought, and she began speaking. "Hi, I'd like to leave a message for Rachel Gideon. You don't know me, Rachel, and I'm not going to tell you my name." Sixty seconds later, Sabine ended the call, then smiled. Everything was going to plan.

"My God, this kitchen is huge!" Maggie said.

Becca, Paige, and Maggie stood in the partially completed kitchen of Becca's house.

"It is a lot for just one person," Paige said. The cabinets had been installed, so had the stove and sinks. Everything was still wrapped in protective plastic.

"I'm thinking more for resale value," Becca said.

"Surely, you're not thinking of selling after doing all this?" Paige looked at Becca questioningly.

"Some day," Becca said. "But I won't be going anywhere for a while."

"Good," Maggie said with a decisive nod. "There's only three of us now. Us gals need to stick together."

"What about Sabine?" Becca asked.

Maggie shook her head. "She's not part of this group anymore," she scoffed. "The bitch will be gone soon; you mark my words, and I can't wait."

"How about the two of you come by for lunch on Friday, and to see Mallory?" Paige asked, facing Becca and Maggie.

"I'd love to," Becca replied.

Maggie touched Paige's arm. "I'd love to, honey, but I've got a prior engagement."

"Such as a date with your new man?" Paige raised an eyebrow.

Maggie rolled her eyes. "I wish. No, nothing that exciting.

I've got to go into the city to see my lawyer, tie up some loose ends with the divorce."

"Well," Paige said, turning to Becca, "how about you come by early, spend the morning, and stay for lunch?"

"Sounds good. I need to get out of here for a few hours before I go stir-crazy."

"Say ten?"

Becca nodded. "Come on," she said to Paige and Maggie, "let me show you the rest of the place."

◆ Chapter 33 - Going Nowhere

Haley Perez wanted sole access first to Peggy Scott Tuttle's bedroom.

So while Vera Tuttle sat shattered and inconsolable downstairs, and while police set up a cordon in the street, and while a forensic team scoured the other parts of the family home, Perez sat upstairs alone on Peggy's bed. Even with the bedroom door closed, the screams and sobs still floated up to where Perez was.

On the now-defunct assumption that her daughter would be returning from Los Angeles at some point, Vera Tuttle had kept Peggy's bedroom clean and tidy, a picture of neatness and order, belying the chaotic mess Haley Perez would have expected.

Unfortunately, this meant Perez could not experience the room in situ, as intended, when Peggy had taken her last breath inside it, had thrown off her shoes, tossed her clothing on the floor, and slumped down on her unmade single bed. Not that all young women who lived at home with a doting mother would leave their room in such a constant state of cyclonic mayhem. Just most of them.

The small space was now denude of any clues of recent habitation. Every surface had been wiped clean, leaving a slight lemon scent. The carpet had been freshly vacuumed and smelled of lilacs. Like all good detectives, Perez had gotten down on her knees and inspected the pile with her fingers. All clothing had been washed, pressed, and neatly folded away. There was no graveyard of lost, unmatched socks or odd earrings or unused, discarded tampons under the bed. The trash can under the small writing desk, often a rich source of provocation and motive, was now empty, with a clean liner inserted. What did Perez expect to find in the trash? A used home-pregnancy test stick? A cruel handwritten note from her killer signed with his full name and social security number? A town map with a thick, red, squiggly line starting at the Tuttle family front door and ending at the killer's back door?

There was no secret diary hidden in the bedside drawer. No loose floorboards where secret love letters were concealed from prying motherly eyes. That didn't stop Perez, however, from methodically searching the room from top to bottom with gloved hands, consciously trying not to disturb anything, and returning to its rightful place whatever she had moved.

After thirty minutes of careful, respectful searching, under the smoldering gaze of Ian Somerhalder, who sat staring out at her from a photo frame perched on the small dresser, Perez concluded that nothing remarkable, nor anything scandalous, could be found to suggest Peggy Scott Tuttle lived some promiscuous double life, despite what her mother and what Freddy Monk had suggested. Unless, of course, all proof of that had been discreetly removed by Vera Tuttle, armed with spray bottle of all-purpose cleaner and a large trash bag.

Disheartened, Perez sat on the bed again and looked around the room.

A small walk-in closet beckoned.

Peggy liked pink and blue, and wore the typical assortment of tops, skirts, and jeans for someone her age—just a little brighter and a little more revealing than what Perez, who preferred darker, neutral colors, might have worn.

On a chrome rod under a long shelf, clothing was hung according to type. More interfering handiwork by Peggy's mother, no doubt. Again, Perez's attempts to capture a true sense of the young woman, of her personality, of what was important to her, were thwarted by her well-intentioned but still meddling mother, who had reframed the bedroom, Peggy's hallowed and private space, into what a mother thought it should be.

Peggy did not have an abundance of clothing, which was to be expected. Surprisingly, though, the clothes she did have were tasteful, carefully chosen to mix, match, and coordinate, to maximize the fashion mileage out of every hard-earned dollar spent. There were some quality garments, nothing too cheap or tacky and nothing too expensive. No brand labels there, though. Peggy worked hard for her money, and she spent it wisely. Her outward appearance was important, and she was frugal. Nothing slutty.

In a set of drawers under the hanging rail, Perez found undergarments folded neatly and separated into bras, bikinis, and a few boy shorts. Again, tasteful purchases, Gap and Target. But there were no purchases from Victoria's Secret. Nothing. Not so much as a single thong. Slipping out her cell phone, Perez dialed Annabel Chandler.

"Hey, Annabel. Can you check on the clothing inventory for the victim, see if she was wearing any garments from Victoria's Secret."

"No problem," replied Chandler. "I'll call Baltimore, see if I can get the clothing inventory. I'll call you back."

Perez ended the call, grateful that Chandler was discreet, wasn't intrusive to ask why Perez had made such a request.

Squatting down, Perez looked at the few shoes that were laid out in a neat row, almost as if a ruler had been used. Flats and sneakers, and a single pair of leather ankle boots. Again, simple, inexpensive, restrained. Not a pair of pumps in sight.

Standing on her tiptoes, Perez stretched up and looked along the deep shelf above the hanging rail—and everything changed.

Pushed at the very back of the shelf, were a pair of pink, limited-edition Converse high-tops that looked practically new, the sides unblemished. Next to the sneakers, was a blue Kate Spade backpack, still with its tags attached.

Grabbing them both, Perez snapped photos of the sneakers and the Kate Spade bag, with her cell phone, wondering where Peggy Scott Tuttle got the money from to buy such extravagant purchases. Then she held them, one in each hand, her eyes going from one to the other. Both items would easily be considered prized purchases by most young women; the bag itself probably cost two or three weeks' worth of wages from the Sheetz gas station where Peggy had worked. Both items were not the kind of fashion accessories you would leave behind if you were going to Hollywood, the fashion mecca of the West.

The items in the bedroom, in the drawers, and in the closet displayed all the signs of a young woman who was going nowhere, and certainly not leaving her mother, sister, and home in a hurry.

Once she returned the bag and sneakers to where she had found them, Perez's cell phone rang. It was Chandler. "Just got the clothing list from Baltimore. She wasn't wearing any underwear at all. Just a few base layers under her jacket and nothing under her jeans."

"You're certain?" Perez asked. She could understand not wearing a bra at times, but no underwear?

"Positive. No underwear is on the clothing inventory." Once again, Perez noted Chandler didn't ask about her line of questioning, but she did want her opinion. "Don't you think it is strange?" Cradling her cell between her ear and shoulder, Perez began searching the pockets of each of the hanging garments while she spoke.

"No bra, I can understand," Chandler said, confirming Perez's thoughts. "I guess that when he redressed her to dump her, he kept her underwear. I don't believe she wasn't wearing any by choice."

Perez thought the same. She kept searching through the clothes on hangers while Annabel Chandler waited patiently on the other end. "The injuries we spoke about, "Perez said, "about her being frozen, then thawed out repeatedly."

"Yes?"

"Could that have been done using a cryogenic freezer?" Perez moved along to the next hanging garment, a black jacket.

"Like the ones gyms and day spas have?"

"Yes. Apparently, it is good for your circulation, makes you feel younger." Nothing in the black jacket. Next was a pair of jeans.

"Look, I don't really know how those machines work, the mechanics of the process. I guess you could freeze someone like that. I imagine first you would have to rewire the machine, though, override the controls somehow, ramp down the temperature. Do you think one was used on her?"

Bingo! Perez's gloved hand hit something in the jeans pocket. "I'm not sure." She wriggled her hand in deeper. There was something scrunched up inside the pocket. It had the feel and texture of paper. Grasping the object with her fingers, she gently pulled it out. It was a small, folded piece of thin cardboard. With her cell phone still balanced between her ear and shoulder, Perez carefully unfolded the card.

"Hello? Haley? You still there?" Chandler spoke in her ear.

Perez looked at the card, and her heart skipped a beat. "I'll call you back." Perez quickly cut the call, slid her cell away, then held the card up.

It was a free guest pass to Energize Wellness.

🐦 Chapter 34 - The Killer is There

Perez pushed open the front doors of Energize Wellness with a little more force than intended, startling the woman, Rhianna, behind the counter.

"Oh, so you've changed your mind," Rhianna said. "I think we have a cryopod free for your session."

Reaching the counter, Perez held up the guest pass with one hand, in front of Rhianna's eager face, and her detective's badge in her other hand. "Did a woman named Peggy Scott Tuttle come in here as a guest to work out?"

A look of concern flashed across the Rhianna's face. "Oh my," she said, her eyes switching back and forth between the guest pass and the badge. "The name sounds familiar."

"Peggy…Scott…Tuttle," Perez slowly repeated, pocketing her badge.

"Was that the young woman found dead in the state park just recently?" Rhianna said, her voice wavering. "I thought I saw it mentioned on the news just before." She looked up and to her right.

Following her gaze, Perez saw high on the wall a flat-screen TV, the sound turned down. A reporter, Katie Kundy—according to the name on the screen—was holding a microphone, talking to the camera, snow falling gently around her. In the background, between the shuffle of police officers, Perez could clearly see the front porch and door of the Tuttle home. "Christ," Perez muttered. Between her leaving there and racing to get to the gym, the circus must have arrived at Vera Tuttle's house.

"You don't think she came here, do you?" Rhianna said, pulling Perez's attention back on her.

Perez placed the guest pass on the counter and slid it toward the woman. "Please just check your records. I need to know when she came in: dates and times." All during the drive back to the gym, Perez berated herself for not asking previously if Peggy Scott Tuttle was a member or had been registered as a visitor, using a free guest pass.

Rhianna shook her head. "All member records are private, confidential. I can't possibly give out that information to you." The woman seemed to take great pleasure in telling Perez this. "And if my memory serves me correctly, I believe she wasn't a member here or even a guest."

"So now you know the names of every member?" Perez said, drumming her fingers on the countertop.

Rhianna gave a smug look. "We like to give a very personalized experience to all our members. And I do know most of them on a first-name basis. The woman whose name you mentioned, I would recall if she was a visitor or one of our members."

Perez stopped drumming on the countertop, regarding Rhianna closely. The claim to know everyone that came through the door was fabrication, designed to stonewall Perez. Two could play at that game. "That's fine. I was just hoping to do this discreetly, you know?" Perez said breezily.

Rhianna's expression tensed slightly.

Perez continued her nonchalant tone. "I'd much prefer doing this quietly, not draw attention to your members or to the public." Perez pocketed the guest pass. "Which will happen when I return here with a court order compelling you to release the details of your gym membership, including details of all guest visitors."

"Wellness center," Rhianna replied defiantly, a cold look in her eyes. "As I have said before, we are not a gym. We are a wellness center."

Perez waved her hand dismissively, not interested in semantics. "Whatever." She took a step back from the counter, making to leave.

Rhianna let out an audible exhale and started typing on the computer keyboard, stabbing the keys as though they were to blame for every personal failing in her entire life. Moments later, a contemptuous smile creased her face as she scanned down the computer screen. "There you go." She glared up at Perez. "Like I said, I have no record in our system of the woman you're looking for ever being a member or being admitted as a guest."

Perez walked back to the counter. "Are you certain?" Another dead end. Perez couldn't believe it. *Perhaps it is too much of a stretch*, Perez thought. Maybe Peggy Scott Tuttle had never used the guest pass she had been given. She pulled out the small card again and looked at the terms and conditions on the back. It was valid for seven days use, full facilities except for the swimming pool. "Is it possible that she came in as a guest but was never registered into your system?"

Rhianna looked as though she had been slapped in the face. "We have strict policies and procedures here that all staff must adhere to, for legal as well as for health and safety reasons. No one is allowed to enter as a visitor or a guest without filling out a form. Even contractors must first register their full contact details and sign a waiver form here at the desk."

Definitely another dead end. Perez began tapping the guest

pass on the counter, her frustration growing. The trail, as quickly as it had appeared, was slowly fading. But Peggy was linked to this location. She had a guest pass. Maybe it was just one of those marketing handouts that are thrust at you by promotional staff as you walk through a mall. Peggy had taken the proffered free pass, shoved it into her jeans, and had forgotten about it.

Then Perez remembered something Marvin Richards had told her. When the victim's trail goes cold, stop and start looking at the movements of the killer. The victim is gone, is dead, or assumed dead, if you have no body. But the killer is still very much alive. Pursue their trail instead. The killer is there, with you, close by, maybe once breathing the same air as you are now. Had occupied the same space that you are now standing in. And why? Because the killer had done what you are now doing: following in the victim's footsteps as they had once stalked them, as you are now stalking the dead. Look around. The killer was there or had been there. What can you see?

Perez put away the guest pass. Perhaps Peggy Scott Tuttle's killer was a staff member there, worked at the gym. Perez knew she would be pushing her luck to get access to the employee records. No judge in their right mind would grant her such an order, especially when she had no real proof, no substantial connection that Peggy Scott Tuttle was ever there. And even if she had been there, taken a free session, what did that prove? All Perez had was a guest pass she had found in the young woman's bedroom, and the wild assumption that the victim could be placed at this location. Hardly solid evidence to grant a court order to access the private and confidential records of all members and employees. Perez needed more. She needed solid evidence connecting the victim and the killer, putting them in this same location. At this point she didn't even have a tenuous link. She had no link at all, just the barest of threads that was threatening to break under the weight of speculation and assumption.

Marvin Richards wouldn't approve. But then again he wasn't there, didn't feel what Perez was feeling right then. She turned and walked away from the counter, not even bothering to thank the woman.

Perez stopped dead in her tracks. *Of course!* Why didn't she see this before? She angled toward a cluster of sofas and soft furnishings near the entrance, Marvin Richards' advice ringing clear in her ears. "*Tell me what you see?*" There on the wall, a perfect row of self-assured smiles, gleaming white teeth, and faces full of belief and vitality. Perez had three times walked right past the row of picture frames of each of the fitness staff—or "wellness crew" as the signage above said—and yet it hadn't registered with her. Another oversight. She didn't need the employee records. Most of the information she wanted was there on display for the world to see. Below each framed photo was a small, laminated placard. Name, title, qualifications, and a glowing endorsement from a client.

Dismissing the woman, Perez started at one end of the row photos, pausing at each in turn, slowly scrutinizing each male face, as though conducting a police lineup of suspects. There were eight men in total, ranging from personal trainers to sports nutritionists, even a sports psychologist. She did two passes of the photos and found herself lingering more on one particular photo, drawn to one particular face that seemed to move the needle of cerebral curiosity in her. A feeling, hunch, impulse, that cops get when they first cast eyes on a stranger and instinctively know something is not entirely right about them.

Stepping closer to the particular photo, Perez placed her

hands on her hips and tilted her head. White male; dark wavy hair; hooded green eyes; thin, wedge-shaped face, with a smudge of stubble across his jaw. An attractive young man, maybe in his late twenties. However, there was just something about his piercing eyes that seemed to peel back Perez's clothing, leaving her with a sense of nakedness under his alluring gaze. It was as though she wasn't looking at a photograph at all, but rather, a living, breathing hologram, like he was standing right in front of her, giving her his full, unwavering attention.

The man definitely had an aura about him, a seductive, beguiling gaze. Unlike the other staff photos, his wasn't a staged, forced pose. No smile, just the slightest tilt at one corner of his mouth. Not a smirk, more like acute self-awareness. Perez imagined he drew his fair share of attention from women, both young and old, in the gym. Perez glanced down at the placard under the photo. Personal trainer, highly qualified. She read the glowing endorsement, obviously from one of his female clients. "Tyson is always attentive of my personal needs and goals. He's warm, considerate, and I always feel so special with the sessions I have with him."

"I bet he makes you feel special," Perez said. Maybe it was another leap of faith by her. He could just be a "gym shark," a fitness predator, as they are known in the industry; a flirtatious staff person showering attention and overt praise on female members, attention and praise they probably would never receive from their husbands or boyfriends.

Perez studied the face a moment longer, then snapped it with her cell, and walked out.

🐦 Chapter 35 - Speeding

According to DMV records, Tyson Kotter lived at a property along Mountain Laurel Road, a two-minute drive east of Ravenwood.

Aerial photos showed a quarter-acre block backing onto Greenbrier State Park, along with a farmhouse and barn. The location was isolated, and perfect.

Parking her SUV on the shoulder of the road, out of sight from the property, Perez climbed out and went the rest of the way on foot, using the forest trees on both sides of the road to shield her approach. She was unsure if Kotter lived alone, and there wasn't much background information about the man Perez could quickly find. He was twenty-eight years old, and his DMV photo was similar to his photo on the wall at the gym—except he was staring blankly at the camera. No seductive, beguiling gaze. No tilt at one corner of his mouth. His eyes, however, retained that drilling-into-your-skull feel to them. Registered to him was a 2010, white, single-cab Chevrolet Silverado.

The forest thinned, and the partial shape of a farmhouse filtered through the slash in the trees up ahead. Perez rested her hand on the trunk of a large oak and watched.

The house had a large wraparound porch with wooden siding, sash windows, and a tin roof. Large and airy, but in desperate need of attention. A chimney of worn brickwork ran up one side of the house. In its prime, the grand farmhouse would have been spectacular, but neglect, scorching summers, and bitter-cold Maryland winters had taken their toll.

A simple dirt road led to the property and split into two smaller, narrow tracks. One curved past the front steps, forming a circular driveway around a large cottonwood tree before rejoining the main dirt road. A second track angled to the right and led to a small red barn. The place looked deserted, and Perez couldn't see any obvious vehicle, but it could be parked at the rear of the property or in the barn itself. It did seem like a strange property for a young man, unless he specifically wanted solitude and to be away from the prying eyes of townsfolk.

Keeping hidden within the tree line, Perez slowly circled around to the rear of the house while keeping a distrustful eye on the barn as well as on the house, for any signs of movement. Reaching the back door, she peered through a side window and into an open kitchen. Once again, there were no signs of life, no dishes on the kitchen table or countertops, nothing on the cooktop. The kitchen looked neat and tidy—very neat and tidy. In fact, it made Perez question if someone actually lived there.

She tried the back-door handle. Locked.

Moving around to another side of the house, she found another door. Perhaps laundry or mudroom? She tried this door. Locked. Perez couldn't criticize someone for securing their property correctly, but that didn't ease the niggling frustration she felt. She spent a few moments performing a quick walk of the perimeter, seeing if there were any open windows or other ways to gain access, all the time keeping a watchful eye on the dirt road that led to the front of the property.

Perez came up empty handed. Undeterred, she next moved to the red barn, only to find a heavy chain threaded through the door handles with a padlock, and the windows boarded up.

Discouraged but not beaten, Perez headed back out along the dirt driveway toward the mailbox near the road. Maybe she could glean some information from Kotter's mail, if there was any to see.

Her cell phone rang. It was the Washington County Sheriff's Office. Before leaving, Perez had put a call into them, provided them with the DMV details and vehicle registration for Tyson Kotter's Chevy truck. The county sheriff's office was one of the jurisdictions responsible for speed enforcement. It was a long shot, but Perez wanted to know if Kotter had been picked up on any of the speed cameras installed in and around Ravenwood. The caller promptly told her that Kotter had been issued three speeding citations, all from the same camera location, the most recent, just a few days ago.

"Are you certain?" she said to the caller.

"Yes, Detective. The vehicle registered to Tyson Kotter was picked up on three separate occasions in the Martha's End Elementary School zone."

Martha's End? Where had Perez heard that name before? Then she remembered. She had seen it on Alfred Beckett's map. The elementary school was two miles south of the abandoned slaughterhouse that was once owned by the Cullen family.

A cloud glided overhead, blocking out the sun, and a cold breeze spun around Perez as she stood on the dirt driveway, looking back at the farmhouse, her cell pressed to her ear, her hair waving across her face. The caller said she would email Perez the details. Perez thanked her and hung up. Standing where she was, Perez suddenly felt exposed, out in the open, so she headed back to the tree line, her cell phone firmly in her hand.

Dark clouds were beginning to form in the west, bruised and swollen with rain, and musky earthiness rode the breeze. The atmosphere bristled with electricity. In the distance, a bolt of lightning, jagged and blinding, cut down from the darkening sky and seemed to pierce the earth. Moments later came a deep roll of thunder that seemed to reverberate the ground itself. As she approached her SUV, the first fat drops of rain began to pepper the ground around her.

Her cell pinged and safely inside her SUV, Perez scrolled through the three speeding citations that had been sent to her. The oldest was six months ago. The next was five weeks ago, and the most recent was… The windshield exploded.

Startled, Perez looked up as a deluge of heavy raindrops stitched across the glass as though she were taking automatic gunfire while a million tiny hammers began beating on the roof and hood.

Returning to her cell phone, she peered at the screen, at the time and date of the most recent speeding citation: 2:12 a.m. on the morning when Peggy Scott Tuttle's body had been discovered.

🐦 Chapter 36 - Slaughterhouse

It was dark by the time Perez had left Alfred Beckett's house for a second time.

If she hadn't been told what to specifically look for by Beckett, who had also drawn a rough map for her, she would never have found the entrance to the back road, and would have certainly driven right past it. It was hidden among the wild and disheveled undergrowth that had grown across the narrow opening, choking it off from the outside world. She almost missed the turn, passing it before realizing, hitting the brakes, and backing up. She turned in and nudged the police SUV slowly forward, pushing aside the thick undergrowth, ignoring the grating sound as low branches clawed at the front fenders and dragged along the sides.

Fifty yards in, she found herself under a canopy of twisted branches and drooping vines. She imagined long ago, the large trucks that must have passed through there, back and forth, delivering live cattle while refrigerated trucks drove away, carrying the carcasses of freshly butchered animals. Back then, the size and width of each truck was enough to keep at bay the encroaching forest. Now, after the rumble of trucks had long since faded, it seemed as though the forest had captured the opportunity and crept silently back, reclaiming the narrow road once again, closing over it like the skin of a healing wound.

Perez checked the speedometer. The old slaughterhouse had

to be close. She glanced down at the hand-drawn map on the passenger seat. According to Beckett's measurements, it should be less than two miles up ahead. Perez pressed on the gas a little more, and when the speedometer dial clicked over one point five miles, she stopped, turned off the lights, killed the engine, and climbed out.

Perez moved quickly along the unsealed blacktop, which soon transformed into a bed of coarse gravel. Then the forest on both sides pulled back, and the overhead canopy dropped away, revealing a wide expanse of open ground surrounded by a dark, tall wall of forest. Above was a vaulted ceiling of deep purple speckled with a billion stars, and the moon, huge and yellow, bathed the landscape in a watery gray. The storm had passed, leaving the night sky clear and bitterly cold.

The silhouette of a large structure loomed in front of her in the middle of the clearing.

Perez came off the dirt road, entered the forest, and then followed it around so she could approach the building from the safety of the trees. Under the ghostly wash of moonlight, she could just make out most of the building's features and the surrounding terrain. The main structure was encompassed by a tall fence, where a large set of gates at the front were drawn back. Scattered on the frozen ground outside the fence, near a road that seemed to surround the building, were the bones of disbanded machinery, piles of scrap metal heaped into conical anthills, and what looked like a large truck slumped on its side, the front cab buckled, the trailer twisted.

She continued skirting the edge of the forest, keeping a few rows back, hidden within the tree line while all the time keeping one eye on the dark, ominous shape of the building. There were no apparent signs of movement, no flare of a light, or the slightest beam of a flashlight. The place looked cold and dead, an edifice to industrial decline and abandonment. The perimeter fence had jagged gaps where the wire had been torn out. Over the decades, the place would have been ransacked, stripped of anything remotely valuable. Machinery left abandoned, metal wiring, copper pipe, electrical conduit, all pulled, wrenched, stripped, and stolen. What was left was the decaying carcass of a business long since closed. There were thousands of places, just like this one, scattered across the country. Usually at the end of some back road or buried deep in the scrub off the main highway or on the edge of a once populous and thriving town. Once-proud factories, serving the community, providing jobs, and sustaining families, now gone with just a desolate, barren wasteland in its place.

Once satisfied no one was watching her, Perez moved out of the safety of the forest and crossed the road. Out in the open, the temperature seemed to drop even further, and despite the layers of clothing under her thick, heavy police jacket, she'd never felt so cold in her entire life. Her face was numb, and a raw iciness seeped into her body, chilling her deep into her spine. Maybe this was what Peggy Scott Tuttle had felt in the early stages of being frozen alive.

She quickly scuttled through a large rent in the wire fence. The ground was hard and crusted with a brittle layer of ice that crunched underfoot as she made for a nearby hunk of rusted machinery, which was half buried among the frozen grass and weeds. Taking refuge behind the machinery, she took a moment to study the building up close. Parts of the exterior walls had toppled, leaving crumbled corners and jagged holes of brickwork. Not a single glass window remained. Instead, dark rectangular voids, like freshly dug graves, stared back at Perez.

On the move again, she felt her feet shuffle across the frozen ground, as though she were being pulled toward the building by the same fearful curiosity that one gets pulled toward a fairground haunted house. You know you should not go inside, yet your inquisitiveness for all things scary gets the better of you.

It was another hundred yards to the side of the building. There was a raised platform, a loading dock with a set of stairs that led to a large open-door entry. She paused again, half kneeling, watching the bare windows and vacant openings, expecting a ghoulish face to be looking out at her with a rictus grin. Instinctively, Perez reached for her gun on her hip, felt a reassuring surge of confidence as her hands wrapped around its butt. If Kotter was here, and he had killed Peggy Scott Tuttle, then he would bleed like anyone else. He wasn't some supernatural apparition or phantom. He was flesh and blood. And yet Perez felt the first stirrings of fear inside her.

Suddenly, the surrounding darkness, the morbid loneliness of the place, and the raw uncertainty she now felt, all seemed to converge into one massive wave of fear and doubt, smothering what little courage she had while sitting back in the safety of her vehicle. Maybe this was a bad idea, and she should come back in the daylight with a few patrol officers and search the building properly. And if they found nothing, what then? Embarrassment, humiliation, and a prolonged dose of ridicule that she would have to swallow for a long time, dished out by her peers, especially by a gleeful Nate Garland.

Perez closed her eyes and swallowed, steeling herself to go on, forcing herself to slow her breathing, which unknowingly had accelerated into short, shallow gulps in the last few moments. No. She needed to do this, follow her hunch, validate it before calling in the cavalry or suffer the indignation.

Her eyes sprang open, and she ran toward the loading dock stairs and entered the building.

Inside, Perez found herself in a cavernous interior. Large swathes of moonlight shone down in columns from above where entire sections of the ceiling metal were gone. The floor was a confused mass of twisted and scattered debris, piles of ice and snow, dead animals, and trash. Some walls were scorched by fire, others were covered in graffiti. The interior was coated in layers of grime, filth, and years of abuse. There were stairs leading up to a framework of raised gantries and offices on the sides. Meat hooks, curved and cruel, hung from a long conveyor system overhead, and Perez imagined livestock carcasses, big slabs of meat, dangling from the hooks as they were being pulled along. Parts of the cement floor under the conveyor were darkly blemished, stained from years of carnage and spilled blood, Perez imagined. She shuddered and kept moving deeper into the building, keeping her flashlight off, thankful for the moonlight guiding her way.

On the right, a set of descending stairs, framed by a tubular handrail, came into focus. Perez stood at the top of the stairs and looked down into the pool of blackness. The wave of fear and doubt returned, bringing with it a flare of panic that rose in her throat. She pulled out her cell phone, realizing it was still turned on. Inside the vaulted interior of the building, the ringer would be amplified, resonating off the walls like a bell tower at noon. Her fingers fumbled as she turned it off.

Taking a few deep breaths, she hung back in the shadows, forcing her galloping heart to slow down. Kotter was there. She could sense something malevolent below her, underneath her feet, in the substructure below, like she was standing directly over a mass grave. She glanced down the stairs again, her eyes unable to penetrate more than just a few steps.

There. She felt it again as she looked into the black hole of the stairwell, raw creeping fear slowly flooding her intestines, then seeping into her lungs, squeezing her chest, shortening inhales, her breath sounding ragged and labored, panting like a dog. Images exploded in Perez's head, light bulbs of pure dread, and unimaginable horror bursting in a building crescendo. Cattle, their huge shiny eyes wide with fear, nostrils flared, waiting their turn, warm sticky blood sheeting from the necks of those in front, those who had gone before, their hoofs coated red.

Perez felt her chest constrict some more, like she was having a seizure. Grabbing her breast, she squeezed her eyes shut, but still the fear found its way inside her inner eye. The darkness. She saw herself as a child, descending stone stairs, being swallowed up by an inky blackness. Then herself curled up in the damp darkness, her tiny fingers clasped tightly over her ears, trying to shut out the noise, the screaming. Huge, shiny, curved meat hooks floated into her mind, their barbed points digging deep into fetlocks. Cattle being hoisted high, moving with a morbid slowness along the conveyor, the sound of saws cutting through flesh and bone in the distance.

All the air seemed to have been sucked out of her lungs, and Perez collapsed to the floor, brought her knees up to her chest, and squeezed her eyes shut so hard it pained her. She couldn't breathe. There was no air. Peggy Scott Tuttle's warped and empty-eyed face floated toward her. The fetid stench of death preceded the young woman as her mouth yawed wide, seeming to want to swallow Perez whole, smothering her in a warm and sickly breath.

"No!" Perez gasped.

Then a sound, a low hum from below drifted up the stairwell. Gritting her teeth, Perez forced the ghostly apparitions aside, pushed back the images of carnage, and opened her eyes. Struggling to her feet, she stumbled toward the stairs, grasping the rusted handrail to steady herself.

She looked down into yawning, ominous depths.

She had no choice. It was a childhood fear she needed to overcome.

There. She heard it again. A low, mechanical hum coming from somewhere below. Her flashlight wasn't an option, but her handgun was. With her breathing returning to some semblance of normality, Perez gently eased her handgun from its holster, pointed the barrel down the stairs, and descended into the darkness.

She moved slowly down the cement steps, past one landing before spiraling around, then down again to the bottom, her handgun pointing at what her eyes were seeing, which was nothing except a soupy wall of black.

At the bottom, she paused, allowing her eyes to fully adjust. With painstaking slowness, hard edges and solid lines gradually materialized in front of her. The air was thick with the smell of rot and decay, heavy with dampness. There were puddles on the floor, the smell raw and offensive.

Perez edged forward, her gun sweeping left and right. There was a dim glow in the distance that added murky form to the passageway she was in. Drawn to the light, and the humming sound, she reached an open doorway, the door itself gone, the hinges buckled, the wooden frame splintered, a faint glow seeping out from the room beyond. Perez held her position just outside the room and listened. The humming was louder now, not a piercing drone, but a gentle murmur. It was then she saw blood on the floor, the outline of a boot, painting the rough concrete in a red, chunky tread.

Perez gritted her teeth, then pivoted into the room, her gun up, her eyes wide.

With its low ceiling, rough walls, and bare cement floor, the space looked more like an underground chamber, a dungeon. A chair sat in the middle. Someone was sitting slumped on the chair, their hands tied behind their back, a hood over their head, a battery-powered camping lantern on the floor next to their bound feet.

Dead or alive? Perez couldn't tell.

Looking past the person in the chair, her eyes were drawn to a soft wedge of light glowing in the far corner of the chamber.

Perez felt her sphincter tighten.

There it was, sitting like a giant honeybee hive, a power cable snaking away to a socket in the wall, fingers of mist spilling forth from its base. The cryopod pulsed in sync with an electric hum.

Someone was crouching at the base of the pod, their back turned to Perez, unaware she had entered the chamber of horrors.

Then movement from the person tied to the chair. Perez shifted her focus to the foreground. The head lolled. A paltry moan, the pitch enough for Perez to tell it was a woman.

The moan also drew the attention of the person crouching in front of the cryopod, their body partially in shadow. The person slowly rose to their feet and turned.

Perez brought her gun up and took aim right between the eyes of whom she thought was Tyson Kotter. "Tyson Kotter. Do not move."

Seeing the woman with the gun, Dylan Cobb stepped forward from the shadows and into the light, and looked right back into the eyes of Haley Perez. "There is no Tyson Kotter. Only me. And my name is Dylan Cobb."

🐦 Chapter 37 - Dylan Cobb

Dylan Cobb had been only three months old when his father walked out on him and his mother.

Not that it was an excuse for how Dylan turned out. His mother, Margaret Billingham, was solely responsible for that feat of evolutionary cruelty. Margaret, then single and penniless, took a very bitter interpretation of parenting after her husband left. She was an ambitious, hungry young woman. Born into abject poverty herself, she understood what it was like to beg, to borrow, to steal, and to go hungry. She also knew what it was like as a child to dress in hand-me-down clothes, to wear shoes that didn't fit. Her childhood predicament brought her pain, suffering, and bullying at school. However, it did fill her with a burning desire for a better adult life for herself, and herself alone. They say poverty forces you to be resourceful, inventive, and downright selfish just to survive. For Margaret Billingham, she excelled in learning those harsh but necessary lessons.

She had never wanted children, found them abhorrent and counterintuitive to her plans of attaining wealth and success through any means. So, she was shocked when she had discovered she was pregnant within the first few months of married life despite the precautions she had secretly taken.

Her first husband, a traveling insurance salesman, had wanted a child. He told her he would settle down, give up the road, get a regular nine-to-five job once they started a family. Turned out as soon as Dylan was born, his father decided very quickly that dirty diapers, sleepless nights, and a screaming newborn were not for him. He soon abandoned his fatherhood dream and ran back to his mistress, with whom he had been having a steady relationship with before Margaret became pregnant, to a town more than a thousand miles away.

So, all of Margaret's anger, bitterness, and resentment with the world, and with the lousy hand she'd been dealt, she directed at her own son, Dylan.

When Dylan reached an age of understanding, he could not comprehend what he had done wrong. In no uncertain terms his mother pointed out to him, repeatedly, that he was the byproduct of a failed marriage, the spawn of fertility miscalculation, and was now the noose around her neck.

Margaret had made a vow to herself when her first husband walked out the door that she would never trust a man again. While most mothers would see their progeny as part of their own flesh and blood, Margaret Billingham saw her son, Dylan, as the reason why everything was so wrong with her own life. Thus, she became an abusive and negligent mother who would beat, starve, and enthusiastically denigrate her son privately and publicly at every opportunity.

As a young boy, Dylan, with no father figure to guide him, had turned to the only adult he thought he could trust: his mother. And for countless years, she abused that trust.

Dylan Cobb, ironically, and as is the case with most adult misogynists, had grown to become the reflection of his mother's hatred of men. And thus, the seed of subconscious hatred of women was planted by his mother during Dylan's formative years, which made him what he was today.

For purely strategic reasons, Margaret had managed to lure, then marry, an extremely wealthy and much older man, Edward Brenner, who owned the company where she worked as a humble secretary. From that point onward, everything changed. Margaret Billingham became Margaret Brenner, and Dylan, at a very young age, was sent packing from the family estate on Long Island, first to boarding school, then to college. Ever since that first day he left home, Dylan Cobb never set foot back inside the grounds of the Brenner estate. This suited Margaret just fine. Her son had served her purpose, and Dylan, upon Margaret's insistence, was given a generous allowance and all his tuition was paid for by Edward Brenner.

Out from under his mother's crushing influence, and as an independent young man, Dylan Cobb had flourished. He actively pursued women as a sport, to be hunted, lured, trapped, and then physically and mentally destroyed. During his teenage years, he had numerous girlfriends, and like most misogynists, he was completely oblivious to his growing, festering hatred of the female species. He thought it was just a natural part of his behavior: the norm, not the exception, that all women should be treated like this.

In a woman's eyes, he would initially come across as confident, self-assured, supportive of women's ideology, their causes. Openly, he criticized sexual predators and rapists. Secretly, he idolized them. But as his relationships with women progressed, the once-charming and charismatic mask of Dylan Cobb would peel away, and the true face of a devout woman hater would be revealed. He would become controlling, condescending, rude, and sexually dominating, seeing women only as objects for his own sexual gratification and abuse. He sodomized a number of his girlfriends without their permission and continued to do so well into the relationship with scant regard for their objections or the physical injuries they suffered. The women were either too scared or too much influenced by his manipulative control to tell the police.

He'd sculpted his physique, spending many hours lifting weights and pounding the treadmill, even managing to get a part-time job as a personal trainer at a local gym. He didn't need the money; the Brenner allowance was more than enough. But being behind the counter of the local gym gave him something money could not buy, unfettered access to a fluid supply of female victims. He became obsessed with his appearance, dressed the part, and studied hard at college. At night he studied, too, but a different kind of curriculum. He would make a list of the women he had befriended at the gym—their names, physical traits, habits, what music they liked, where they worked, and where they lived. Having access to their membership details was one of the rewards of his job. He would follow them on Facebook, live with them day-by-day on Instagram, share in their special moments on Snapchat. All the while he was refining, culling, and adding to his list, accumulating not friends and acquaintances, but women he wanted to destroy.

Margaret Brenner had no idea the life her son had carved out for himself, even though it was she who had designed his adult blueprint when he was a child. She rarely saw him. Dylan much preferred to live his own life in another city where he studied and worked.

Then one day Margaret had received a phone call from the local police in the town where Dylan lived. It seemed that her son had been more than slightly overenthusiastic with one of his new girlfriends. The woman, a college sophomore, had called 9-1-1 after Dylan tried to strangle her during some weird sexual game. High-priced lawyers were secretly engaged by Margaret without Edward's knowledge. She'd told her husband she needed the money for a sick relative in Nebraska who required urgent, life-saving surgery.

The college sophomore had argued that it was sexual assault. Dylan's lawyers argued that it was asphyxiophilia, erotic asphyxiation, and that she consented to the act during intercourse. Depositions were sealed; a plea was made; compensation was paid, and all charges were eventually dropped.

After proceedings had concluded, Margaret sat down with her son at an exclusive restaurant two blocks from the courthouse—a son she hadn't seen in almost five years. And when she'd gazed deep into his eyes, she saw something that only a mother could see. She saw the seed that someone else had planted all those years ago. A seed that had first grown into a strong and determined sapling, but then, under her disfigured nurturing, had blossomed into the manipulative, sexual predator seated across from her.

🐦 Chapter 38 - Something Missing

Dylan Cobb was completely naked, not wearing a single shred of clothing.

His skin was pale as alabaster with every single muscle clearly defined. A body painstakingly built through years of disciplined exertion and vanity. He stood perfectly still, unblinking, his physique a living, breathing, flesh-and-blood rendition of a Gray's Anatomy diagram.

Perez's eyes drifted lower, down past his abdomen before abruptly stopping—at nothing. Despite his physical perfection, it took Perez a few moments to unpretzel the knot of confusion in her head, to reconcile what her eyes were seeing versus what her brain was telling her she should be seeing. There was a major flaw, an unnatural deletion to this sculpture that Michelangelo himself would have been proud of. Something was missing. Something pretty damn obvious now that she had noticed it. Where she had expected to see an appendage, the male organ, there was nothing, just an ugly scar fusing together the crude overlap of mismatched skin. Where the base of the penis would have joined with the perineum area, there was a just a small, moist opening, like a duct. There was no scrotum, no dangling balls, just the skin pulled under the pelvic bone, reminding Perez of what a life-sized, naked Ken doll would look like.

The woman on the chair moaned. She was coming awake from some unconscious stupor. Perez risked a quick glance at her, wrenching her eyes momentarily from Cobb. Then she smelled it, the rank, sour odor of urine, saw that the front of the woman's shirt was damp, a chest-high dark patch, and a puddle around the front legs of the chair. Perez cast her mind back to Peggy Scott Tuttle sitting against the stone monument. The same rank smell, the same dark patch on her clothing. Chandler had said, that in a cruel, demeaning act, someone had urinated on Peggy Scott Tuttle's body.

Bringing her eyes back to Cobb, Perez squeezed the grip of the handgun harder. She wanted to kill him, kill this vile filth of a creature that was standing naked in front of her.

Cobb still hadn't moved. Hadn't flinched. Hadn't made a single sound. No words. No questions.

"I don't care what your name is. Untie the woman," Perez hissed through gritted teeth.

Finally, movement. Cobb tilted his head. "Or what, Detective Perez?"

For Perez, the revelation wasn't surprising. It was him who had been following her, who had left the black rose on her windshield, and had sent her the bouquet with the narcissistic note. And yet as she stood there, pointing the gun at his head, she couldn't help but feel that something was amiss, not right—apart from the fact that he had no penis or balls. He certainly was a lot younger than Garrett Mason. If Mason was Dylan Cobb's student, his apprentice in crime, then Cobb must have lived a full, horrific life so far with a litany of victims to his credit that no one knew about in order to have attained the role of teacher not student. Of master not apprentice.

Cobb stepped forward, and Perez snapped out of her thoughts.

"What are you going to do exactly, Detective Perez? Or can I call you Haley."

Perez began to slowly apply pressure to the trigger of her gun. "Don't move," she said, forcing herself to ignore the morbid curiosity of staring again at his groin area. "Or I'll shoot." It was a hollow threat, and she knew it.

Apparently so, too, did Cobb. "No, you won't," he said, an arrogant, goading smile spreading across his face. "You can't shoot me; you won't shoot me." He raised his hands. "As you can see, I am unarmed." He took another step forward. "You don't have the balls."

A retort flashed into Perez's mind, but she let it fade. He was indeed unarmed and being butt naked emphasized that fact. If she shot him, even just to injure him, how could it be justified? He had no weapon. Unless he was concealing something, was about to pull a weapon out of his ass. Not even Penn & Teller could achieve that feat of misdirection. This placed him at a distinct advantage despite Perez being the one holding the gun.

Cobb edged forward some more, his hands still raised, his mouth now shaped into a heinous grin. "Do it," he whispered, his eyes a hypnotic spiral.

Perez could feel her anxiety rise, her breath shortening. Her handcuffs were clipped at the back of her belt under her jacket. It would require two hands to cuff him, and that meant she would have to holster her gun to use both hands. This wasn't playing out well.

Another step forward.

Distress flared in Perez. She could feel her heart beating against the inside of her rib cage. "I said don't move, or I will shoot."

"If you do," he said, "then how will you explain shooting an unarmed man?" He stretched his arms out like a human crucifix, and slowly did a one-eighty, coming back to face Perez again.

"As you can see, I'm hiding nothing." Then he lowered his arms. "You want to kill me, don't you?"

Taking one hand off the gun, Perez fumbled with her fingers in the pocket of her jacket. She pulled out her cell and stole a glance at the screen. No signal. She looked around the walls of the room, then pocketed the phone.

Her breathing grew shallow. The end of the gun barrel started to waver. Her mind screamed. Why did she feel like this? Like he was in control? She was the one with the gun!

"I can see it in your eyes," Cobb said, his voice a soothing, hypnotic whisper, "your slow creeping fear. You are all alone. No backup. Just you and me."

He was playing mind games with her, trying to get inside her head. She just needed to block him out.

Another step forward. "You want to kill me because you know what I did to Peggy Scott Tuttle." He nodded to the woman in the chair. "And you can guess what I'm going to do to her as well, can't you?"

Abruptly, Cobb turned his back on Perez and began walking away from her and toward a small utility cart that sat next to the cryopod. "I'm gonna help you out, Haley," he said over his shoulder, his soothing voice echoing inside the chamber. "I'm going to make it easier for you to kill me. I'm going to give you the perfect excuse to use justifiable, lethal force."

"Wait!" Perez yelled, her aim wavering some more.

Ignoring her, he reached the cart. "Now, what do we have here?" His voice was now light, almost comical. He began sorting through tools on the cart. "Nope. Nope. Nope. Ah…what about this?" He kept rummaging. "Nope. Don't worry, Haley." He glanced at her over his shoulder. "You will still have a distinct advantage. I don't have a gun, whereas you do." Moments later, he pulled something off the cart, held it up to admire it. "Yes. This will do very nicely." Cobb turned and began walking back toward Perez.

In his hand she could see something long and shiny.

"You have a gun, with what…maybe fifteen rounds in it?" He stopped. "Whereas, I only have this." He held up a long knife so she could see it. "This is a German-made brain-sectioning knife. Twelve inches of molybdenum stainless steel with a nonslip handle." He looked at the blade lovingly. "Beautiful, isn't it." His eyes snapped back to Perez. "No reason for you to panic." He began walking toward her again. "I'm sure you're a good shot. You just have to kill me before I cut off your pretty head!"

Perez slowed her breathing, readjusted her grip on the gun. "Drop the weapon, or I will use lethal force."

Still Cobb continued forward. "Good. Make it sound official, like how you have been trained. Now you can say it was self-defense, that you feared for your life, that you believed you were in immediate mortal danger."

"Drop the weapon, or I will shoot."

Cobb stopped but kept hold of the knife.

The distance between them was about twenty feet. She couldn't miss.

"May I make a suggestion, however?" He gave a flick of his head toward Perez. "May I suggest that you lower your aim slightly. Aim for center mass. A headshot will make it look like you intended to execute me, that you had murderous intent. A judge may look harshly on that."

Perez faltered. If he came any closer, she would shoot him. She had given him enough warnings to drop the weapon. Why was he doing this? Why did he pick up a weapon so casually, giving her a reason to shoot him? Did he have a death wish? It didn't make sense.

Then by the time Perez realized her fatal error, it was too late.

With lightning speed, Cobb leapt sideways, toward the woman tied to the chair, hunching down behind her. Using the woman as a shield, he reached around, brought the knife up and under her chin. The jovial smile vanished from his face, replaced with a sinister, evil snarl. "Put the gun down, Haley, or I'll give you this woman's severed head as a memento of this special occasion."

Chapter 39 - Stand Off

A clear shot was out of the question, a feat requiring superhuman handgun marksmanship not even Dirty Harry would attempt, let alone pull off without killing the hostage.

As Perez moved, slowly circling to open up the angle to shoot, so did Cobb, in the opposite direction. Tilting the chair on one leg with his other hand, he pivoted the woman slowly around with him while remaining hunkered behind her, the blade of the knife never leaving her throat.

"What's the matter, Haley?" he taunted, one focused eye poking out from behind the woman's right ear. "Surely this whore's life shouldn't stop you from killing me?"

They were locked together in parallel orbits, Perez holding her aim, Cobb holding his knife. "Take the shot, Haley. Let us see how good you are with that gun." Cobb gave a mocking laugh. "I've seen you at the shooting range too. You need to practice more, Haley. You keep anticipating the recoil. That's why your shots fly up and to the left."

This had to be a lie, Perez thought as she continued circling. There was no way he had watched her at the gun range where she trained. He was bluffing, trying to get under her skin. "Let the woman go. Take me instead."

The chair stopped. Cobb tilted his head, seeming to contemplate the offer. "Would you then allow me to do what I was going to do to this whore?" He pressed the knife harder, drawing a line of red across the woman's skin. She was still drowsy, not lucid enough to know what was happening to her.

"Will you gladly sacrifice yourself for a complete stranger?"

Cobb didn't budge from behind the woman, still using her as a human shield. "I'll kill both of you in the most painful of ways if you're lying to me."

Perez began to slowly lower her handgun, her aim dropping one centimeter at a time from his head. "You can do to me whatever you want. Just let her go." There was no way she had a clear shot. She could only just make out the barest slither of his skull, one eye pulsing at her, and his right forearm, which was pressed against the top of the woman's right shoulder, with his hand holding the blade against her throat.

Cobb nodded. "That's good. Drop your gun so we can play."

Perez made a split-second decision. She held her breath, slowing her heartbeat, and watched as the front sight of her handgun traversed downward, then stopped just below the right collarbone of the woman. She pulled the trigger.

In the enclosed space, the gun's report crashed and bounced off the walls, amplifying the sound tenfold.

Even before she thought she saw blood spurt from the top of the woman's shoulder, Perez was on the move, leaping to her left, opening the angle on Cobb's torso some more.

Instantly, he dropped the knife as his right side jerked back, exposing more of his flank to Perez. The bullet had passed through the woman's shoulder, at a downward angle, and into his chest.

The chair with the woman toppled sideways.

Cobb stood and stumbled backward, one hand clutching his chest, blood seeping through his fingers. He looked up at Perez, wild eyes the size of saucers, lips drawn in a rabid snarl of teeth and spittle. "You fucking cun—"

Perez pulled the trigger again, shot him diagonally across his flank, under his armpit. She stepped in, shot him a third time—in the groin.

And when all her fear and anxiety had all but gone, she stood over him where he lay dying, and watched as his breathing slowed. From his mouth came a wet, gurgling sound, riding on a ripple of pink, frothy saliva that spilled from the corners of his mouth.

He gazed up at her, his eyes cloudy and unfocused.

Perez raised her gun again, aimed it at his forehead, dead center, a killing shot.

"Do it," he rasped through blood-stained teeth.

A gush of steamy, bloody-yellow liquid poured out from his ravaged groin and began pooling under him.

With bittersweet irony, Perez thought otherwise and lowered her gun, then watched as he urinated on himself.

🐦 Chapter 40 - Tequila

"I had a panic attack," Perez said, her voice echoing in the large, almost empty room. "Plain and simple."

"There is nothing wrong with that. You have nothing to apologize for," Annabel Chandler replied, a consoling look on her face.

While she appreciated Chandler's vote of confidence, it didn't make Perez feel any better about what had happened—how, while standing in the darkness at the top of the stairwell in the slaughterhouse, she'd been overcome by pure, raw fear. In the days afterward, she had admonished herself for being vulnerable, weak, a total failure. She had never experienced a panic attack of such intensity before. Then again, she hadn't found herself in such a terrifying situation like that before. And, yes, she had been terrified. She wouldn't be human if she wasn't in that situation.

"It's okay if you want to talk about it," Chandler continued. "Or, if you don't want to talk about it, that's perfectly fine too."

Perez gave Chandler an awkward smile. "I feel like such a fool."

Chandler held up a hand. "Like I said, you don't have to apologize for anything. And you certainly shouldn't feel foolish. It must have been hell what you went through."

"Nothing compared to what his victims went through."

"*Victims?*" Chandler asked, a curious look on her face. "There are more?"

Perez hadn't told Chandler what she had subsequently

discovered about Tyson Kotter's true identity, about his monstrous past. That part of the investigation had just started, although she had told Chandler about what they had found at Cullen's Slaughterhouse—as it pertained to the Peggy Scott Tuttle case—where Cobb had built his dungeon to torture and kill more victims. Cobb wasn't "experimenting" on anyone. What he was doing with the cryopod was using torture as a precursor to murder. They had also found Peggy's purse and cell phone—minus the SIM card—and three burner phones, one of which he'd probably used to text Vera Tuttle, pretending to be Peggy. It was becoming all the more apparent to Perez that the voice mail Vera had received from her daughter shortly after she had disappeared, telling her mother that she had left town and was moving to LA, was actually Peggy's own voice made under duress, scripted and recorded by Cobb, making the illusion seem all the more real. Perez couldn't imagine the horror Peggy would have felt, after saying those words, knowing that she was never going to see her mother and sister or anyone else ever again.

Cobb had also managed to get one of the old, abandoned forklifts working, had used it to move his cryopod, which had been delivered from a supplier in California. A team of investigators were right now searching the farmhouse he was renting and accessing his bank records. Plastered on the walls of Cobb's dungeon were strange, demonic images he'd apparently downloaded from the internet. While waiting for the paramedics to arrive, Perez had snapped photos of them with her cell phone and sent them to Marvin Richards, seeking his guidance. She had also found a box containing miniature spy cameras. Police were checking Energize Wellness in case he had installed them in the female changerooms. Perez's own apartment was also being swept for surveillance devices.

Cobb's hostage was another vulnerable, young woman from an impoverished community, lured by lies and aspirational promises. The bullet had passed clean through the gap between her collarbone and shoulder blade. She was expected make a full recovery in the hospital and was forever thankful to Perez for freeing her from Cobb's dungeon of horrors.

In hindsight, Perez had realized that her own selfish urge to kill Cobb had affected her professional judgment. She had been fooled so effortlessly by his distractive ploy, such that the woman could have easily been killed. So she lied on her full report to Kershaw, said that the knife was already in his hand and that Cobb was standing next to the woman, about to kill her when Perez had entered the chamber. As they say, the closer to the truth the lie is, the more convincing you sound when telling it.

"I'm a coward. I'm not the strong person that everyone makes me out to be," Perez said. "Deep down, I'm scared. Really scared." Perez could feel tears welling in her eyes. Another sign of weakness. *Don't cry. Don't you dare start crying.*

Chandler reached forward and squeezed Perez's knee. "You're not a coward. I couldn't possibly do what you do, and you wouldn't be human if you weren't scared at times." Chandler shrugged. "Hell, I would have pissed my pants if I had to go into that hellhole." She laughed.

Perez laughed as she met Chandler's gaze, wondering if she should tell Chandler about her past, about the true source of her crippling fear? About how she was so scared of the dark, had been ever since she was a little girl and had experienced what she had, under the stairs of her parents' house? Should she tell Chandler about how she lied on her police academy questionnaire? There was a specific question about phobias such as claustrophobia, fear of heights, and fear of the dark. In pressure situations, police officers aren't supposed to collapse and curl up on the floor in the fetal position. That was exactly what had happened to Perez at the slaughterhouse when she started to see ghostly visions of Peggy Scott Tuttle and wide-eyed cattle being butchered. It was her secret, that she had cheated, lied on her entrance exam because she so desperately wanted to get into the police academy, to become a police officer, and eventually, a detective. Nothing else mattered to her.

She thought she was strong, that she could go after Cobb on her own. Kershaw was right. She wasn't a team player. She was, and always had been, a loner. Was she willing to suffer the aftermath, the inner demons that she had now opened the door to in her mind, demons that she thought she had buried long ago? Apparently not. Cobb had manipulated her, played mind games, making her feel like one of his victims. Now she understood how Peggy Scott Tuttle, and many more like her, had been fooled by a Pied Piper of misogynists.

"Right," Chandler said, picking up Perez's empty coffee cup and standing. "I need to give you some of my special medicine."

Perez looked up at her. "What medicine?"

"Guaranteed to chase away the blues." And with that cryptic comment, Chandler disappeared into the kitchen.

Perez wiped her eyes and looked around. Chandler wasn't wrong when she'd said she hadn't unpacked. Bare walls, bare floor, and two packing boxes used as chairs, which they now sat on in the middle of the almost empty, cavernous living room. A pile of packing boxes was stacked in one corner. Bright sunshine poured in from the large floor-to-ceiling windows, making the space light and airy.

Chandler had given Perez a quick tour of the massive house when she had first arrived, and Perez had promised to help her carry the mattress out of the garage—which alone was bigger than Perez's entire apartment—and up to the main bedroom. Packing boxes were also crammed in the entrance foyer, turning it into a maze that Perez had to negotiate through to get into the main part of the house.

Chandler came back, but instead of carrying two coffee cups, she held two shot glasses with a clear liquid inside and a bottle under her arm. "We need something stronger," she said, handing one of the shot glasses to Perez before sitting down again on the packing box.

Perez sniffed the contents. "Tequila?"

"Yep."

Perez glanced at her watch. "It's just going on nine thirty."

"So?" Chandler replied. "You're suspended until further notice, and I'm not on call again until after the weekend."

"Reassigned to office duties," Perez said. "Not suspended. And I've taken a few days off."

Chandler made a distasteful face. "I would have told them to shove their job."

They clinked glasses and downed the liquid in one go.

Perez winced at the taste, and before she could protest, Chandler was already refilling her glass. "You unpacked a coffee machine and tequila before anything else?"

She clinked Perez's glass with her own and downed it, not waiting for Perez to do the same. "Gotta get your priorities straight, honey." She gasped before refilling her glass.

"You've got enough packing boxes for a family of five," Perez said.

Chandler gave a shrug. "I had some stuff in storage. I should have gotten rid of some things before I moved." She seemed to notice what Perez was looking at. "Don't make fun of me and my packing boxes," she said with a laugh. "Otherwise, I'll get you to come by and help me unpack all of it."

"I won't say another word." Perez liked Chandler even though she'd only known her for a short time. The last few days had been testing for Perez. It had been three days since the incident at the slaughterhouse where she apprehended who she thought was Tyson Kotter, shooting him three times. Turns out he was a resilient bastard, not just because he had survived but also what she later discovered about him, the research she had done on who he really was and his past. It had left her thinking of the kind of people living in and around Ravenwood, monsters hiding in plain sight, people you would never expect to find there. Marvin Richards was right about his theory. Maybe Ravenwood was a safe haven where killers were drawn to. First, Garrett Mason and now Dylan Cobb. She wondered what drew Cobb to Ravenwood in the first place.

She had also endured the wrath of her sergeant, Brandon Kershaw. Despite apprehending Cobb, and saving the woman's life, Kershaw had gone ballistic when he'd found out that Perez had gone after Cobb on her own. "You should have reported in where you were going! Should have called for backup!" he had hollered at her in his office, much to the amusement of Nate Garland and the other detectives, who could clearly hear the tirade despite Kershaw's door being closed. It made no difference to Kershaw when Perez had explained it was just a hunch she had about who may have abducted Peggy Scott Tuttle, and where he could be found, or the fact that there had been no cell phone signal at the slaughterhouse to call for backup.

"You're lucky I don't bounce your ass back to patrol duties," Kershaw threatened. "I'd rather have no detective on my team than a dead one!" So Perez had been reassigned to office duties—

case filing, typing up reports, and conducting interviews—until a full investigation was done, where she could face disciplinary action. By the time she returned to her desk after Kershaw's berating, a six-inch pile of reports ready for typing had already found their way into her in tray. And someone—Nate Garland, Perez suspected—had hung a Lone Ranger mask on her cubicle with a sticky note: *You glory-seeking dumb fuck!*

"He had no penis," Perez said.

Chandler was about to down her tequila. She paused, the glass almost to her lips. "You're kidding me."

Perez shook her head. "A few years back, he got into a fight. There was an incident in a place called Erin's Bay on Long Island. He was part of some college frat group of guys who were terrorizing the small town. Rape and murder were involved."

Chandler lowered her glass, listening intently.

"Apparently, he'd built another dungeon where he kept women in cages. A struggle ensued, and someone cut off his penis."

Chandler spontaneously raised her glass. "Well, I'll toast to whoever did that."

They clinked glasses, threw back the tequila, and Perez continued. "Surgeons couldn't reattach it. So, they grafted skin, did the best they could to give him a small duct to pee from. They removed his balls too."

Chandler slapped her knee. "Neutered, as all rapists should be!" She gave a sullen look. "The doctors should have fed him his balls, too, while they were at it." She downed her shot glass and shook her head with delight. "I guess that's why he urinated on his victims."

Perez agreed. "Without a penis to rape them, the act of urinating on them was the only thing he could do with his own body to denigrate them, to exert his power over them, make them feel violated."

"What a cunt," Chandler said before tossing back another shot.

Perez stared at Chandler, wide eyed, and aghast at her sudden turn of language.

"What?" Chandler said defensively. "Look, I hate the word, but I think it is appropriate in this case." Seeing that Perez was still not impressed, Chandler put on the face of a petulant child. "Sorry, I won't use that word ever again in your presence."

"Good," Perez said, trying her best not to laugh. She was really glad she had accepted Annabel Chandler's invitation to come up to her house despite vowing never to set foot on Mill Point Road ever again, if she could avoid it.

Perez stood. "I have to go, Annabel, sorry."

"So soon?"

"I've got to drop by and see an old friend." Perez needed to see Marvin Richards. "I'll talk to you later?" Perez said.

"Sure." Chandler refilled her glass and held it up to Perez. "Here's to new friends."

Outside, Perez caught a glimpse of Rebecca Cartwright. She was walking away from Perez along the footpath, past Maggie Vickerman's house. Perez watched as the woman then cut left up the path that led toward the front porch of Paige and Scott Hamill's house. She rang the doorbell, and moments later, Paige Hamill appeared. They embraced before both disappeared inside.

Perez started her car, then waited for a few moments. There was just something about Rebecca Cartwright, how she walked, her demeanor when she thought no one was watching her. It always reminded Perez of a guilty person walking free from court.

Opening the glove box, Perez took out her notebook and flipped to a page where she had written down Phil Benton's cell phone number. She stared at it for a few seconds. Given her reassignment of duties, she really had no cases to work on. Maybe she should call Benton, take his file, and read through it. No harm in that—*but definitely make him no promises either.*

She put the car in reverse and backed out of Chandler's driveway. First, however, she needed to see Marvin Richards. She had much to discuss with him, and no doubt their conversation would stray to the topic of trout fishing. She may have caught a truly evil, sick, and demented killer; however, Perez was convinced there was something else lurking in the periphery, something more evil, more cunning, and deceptive swimming among the people of Ravenwood.

🐦 Chapter 41 - Stood Up

As agreed, Becca arrived at Paige's front door at exactly ten.

"Where is Scott?" she asked as Paige led her through to the kitchen.

"Oh, he had to go out this morning," Paige replied with a dismissive wave. "Something about going into town to do some research for his book."

"And Mallory?" Becca had expected to see Mallory with Paige.

"She's upstairs asleep in the nursery. She is due to wake up in another twenty minutes for a feed. It's Paulo's day off, so I'll be doing it. Before then, I thought we would have some coffee, and I need to tell you something."

"Sounds ominous."

Two coffee cups were already set on the counter, together with a plate of muffins.

"You didn't have to go to any trouble, Paige," Becca said. But the muffins did smell wonderful.

"Nonsense," Paige said, pouring the coffee. "Try one, they're zucchini. I made them this morning."

Becca tried a muffin, and they were indeed delicious. "I wish I could cook," she said.

"Well, I expect some nice meals coming out of that massive new kitchen of yours," Paige said. They both settled on stools at the counter. Paige looked at Becca directly. "I need to show you something."

"Okay," Becca said, intrigued.

Paige slipped out her cell phone, thumbed the screen, and passed it to Becca.

Becca stared at the screen, confused. She looked up at Paige. "What's this?"

"That is what I found in my trash can outside this morning. A few days ago I made a batch of those zucchini muffins for our new neighbor at Number Ten. I thought I would do the neighborly thing, you know, make them feel welcome. So, I made the muffins, wrapped them in a nice cloth, and took them across there in a nice gift basket. I rang the bell, but there was no one home. So, I left the muffins on the porch with a note."

Becca looked at the photos again. "Nice neighbor." The basket of muffins looked like it had been stomped on, the muffins pulverized, the basket crushed, and sprinkled with tiny shreds of paper, like confetti, which Becca assumed was Paige's note she had written. "You should go and confront them," Becca said, handing back the phone.

"There never seems to be anyone there!" Paige said.

"Well, someone is there now," Becca replied.

Paige's face froze.

Becca took another muffin. "There's a car parked in the driveway. We can both go together if you would like. I'm curious to meet them, too, but first I want to see your lovely daughter."

Paige went to the refrigerator and pulled out a baby bottle. "You can feed her if you like."

Becca felt something tug at her heart in a way she had never experienced before. Embarrassed, she turned away so Paige couldn't see the tears forming in her eyes.

She was late, a fact that didn't surprise Scott Hamill.

He leaned on the hood of his car and checked his watch again. Twenty minutes late, to be exact. He could understand why Sabine had chosen the location: The Golden Mile Marketplace, twenty miles southwest of Ravenwood, and just off US-40 East. There was no chance of anyone recognizing the two of them there. But why was she late? She said it was important they meet, in person.

He looked around the parking lot again, certain this was the place she'd told him to meet when she had called him last night. Scott's eyes wandered across the old strip mall in front of him, stopping at a book and video store. Maybe he should go inside to see if they've got a copy of his book. He doubted it.

Scott checked his watch again, his impatience growing. Where the hell was she? Or was it all crap what she had told him? It had been a twenty-five-minute drive there, and Paige wasn't expecting him back for least a couple of hours. But he had better things to do than waste time like this.

He pulled out his cell phone and stabbed the screen keypad with the number Sabine had given him.

The call went straight to voicemail. "Damn it, Sabine! Where the hell are you?" Scott growled into the mouthpiece. "I've been waiting here for nearly half an hour. Are you coming or not? I don't like being stood up. You told me you had some new information, some specific details about what happened that night at Becca's house that I could use in my new book. You told me it was going to be a huge 'bombshell,' something that no one else knows about. If that is true, then call back, and tell me how far away you are!"

Scott ended the call.

🐦 Chapter 42 - Human Bait

Intuition was telling Haley Perez that Dylan Cobb wasn't the one who had sent her the bouquet of black roses and the note, claiming to be Garrett Mason's mentor.

Cobb may have been watching her, been the one who had placed the rose on her windshield outside Vera Tuttle's home, and had killed Peggy Scott Tuttle. However, to continue the analogy, Cobb, just like Mason, was a florist, arranging, then delivering death. Someone else was the grower, the one who was planting the seeds of evilness inside their heads, then cultivating and nurturing it to grow and flourish.

Dylan Cobb, from what Perez had subsequently uncovered about his background, seemed much worse than Garrett Mason, had more victims to his credit. But she guessed even the best athletes on the planet still had coaches and mentors to keep them at the top of their form. And were there more like Mason and Cobb out there? More minions to draw from to serve this cloaked mentor? She had answered her own question with another: were there more fish in the ocean?

Cobb's eagerness to play out his sadistic fantasies was traded for guidance, tutelage offered by a truly murderous mentor. That was a common thread that ran through the victimology. Cobb's two current victims—to which Perez believed there could have been a lot more—came from forgotten and decaying communities, impoverished places with high levels of welfare dependency. They belonged to what sociologists call an "underclass," underprivileged people living in an alternate universe that most people either never knew existed, or if they did, turned a blind eye for fear of catching sight of something distasteful that would disrupt the normality of their middle-class, safe, and insular lives.

For Perez, it was as sad as it was gut-wrenching and bewildering as to how someone could prey on the vulnerable and the damaged. That they were easy, malleable targets was the only conclusion. The lowest hanging fruits of crime often came from the lowest, socio-economic branches of the community. Perez could only imagine what the beguiling Dylan Cobb offered someone like Peggy Scott Tuttle in return for her attention: hope when all she had was hopelessness. The dream of a better life, when all she had experienced was the drudgery of being stuck in a small town, living below the poverty line. It was all a façade that Cobb had given her a glimpse of.

All this and more, Perez laid out for Marvin Richards in his cabin while they drank coffee, and a fire crackled and burned in the woodstove. And when she was finished, and a mournful silence descended upon them, Perez could still hear the wrenching screams of Peggy Scott Tuttle in her ears. She explained that everything about Tyson Kotter was a façade, a masked creation, an elaborately designed false wall that provided him with a deceptive outward appearance, hiding who he truly was: Dylan Cobb. Once his DNA was submitted by Perez, nearly every law enforcement database in the country lit up like the Chernobyl control room.

"His real name is Dylan Cobb," Perez said. "Tyson Kotter is an alias. He spent three years in Attica, the maximum-security prison in New York State, for torturing and killing women on Long Island, where he kept them in dog cages. "

"Just three years?" Richards asked. "How the hell did he get out?"

"As far as I can tell—and I'm still looking into it—there was a plea deal done after he was sent to prison, in exchange for turning evidence against his mother, a woman called Margaret Brenner. Kotter, I mean Cobb, claimed his mother was the real architect behind the murders. I believe she's now the one in jail. Apparently, Dylan Cobb's real father skipped out on them both when he was just a child. Margaret Billingham—her maiden name—remarried into money, an industrialist called Edward Brenner. There was also some issue about crucial evidence that was later overturned on appeal and ruled as inadmissible."

Richards shook his head in disgust. "Typical."

"The story of Dylan Cobb, and what he, and a group of misogynistic college students did in a small town called Erin's Bay, on Long Island, is really interesting," Perez added. "You should read it."

Richards waved Perez off. "If I spent all day reading about the all the crazies in the world, I'd get nothing done."

"Cobb got out of surgery this morning. State police have him under guard in an isolation ward at the county hospital," Perez said.

"And you'd put three rounds into him?"

Perez nodded. "Center mass." *Except for the groin shot*, Perez thought. That one was for Peggy, and now for the other victims of Cobb that she had subsequently discovered.

Richards gave a weary smile. "You should have aimed a little higher. Gone for the head."

Neither said anything for a while, content to drink coffee and watch the flames leap and dance.

Finally, Perez broke the silence. "So how do we find him?" Perez turned to Richards. "The person who is behind all this? The mastermind behind Garrett Mason and now Dylan Cobb.

He's not going to stop. He's going to keep recruiting his minions, his disciples, nurturing them before turning them loose on the world to do his sick, twisted bidding while he hides in the background."

Richards seemed lost in his thoughts, his head slowly nodding up and down, his eyes not focused on anything in particular. Then he spoke. "Like I said at the very beginning, to coax out this particular fish, we must first entice it with a particular bait it wants." Richards finally met Perez's gaze.

🐦 Chapter 43 - Gravity

Both Becca and Paige walked into Mallory's nursery—and abruptly stopped as though they had hit an invisible wall.

Leaning over the baby's crib was Sabine Miller. She turned and glared at both women, her face warped, her mouth twisted with utter contempt.

"Get away from her, you bitch!" Paige snarled, her hands immediately balling into tight fists.

Sabine quickly whipped up the baby into her arms, turned, and then held her protectively against her body like a shield. Mallory, still dozy from a nap, didn't resist.

"You come near me, and I'll kill her." A manic smile spread across Sabine's face. "It would be so easy to drop her on her fucking head." There was an unhinged quality in Sabine's grin, like a drug addict desperate for another hit, slowly unraveling. Her facial muscle rippled and contorted under her skin, like there was a second face underneath trying to squeeze through.

Sabine gave a childish giggle. "Who knows, she may even survive the fall, but brain damaged for the rest of her life." She stroked the baby's head. "Their skulls are so soft, not fully formed yet." She glared at Paige. "How would you and Scott feel about that?" Sabine gave a choking laugh, obviously relishing in the torment. "I guess, then, you'll always have a baby on your hands; even as a fully grown adult, you'll be still feeding it and wiping its bottom."

The child started wriggling in Sabine's arm, coming out of her slumber. Mallory scrunched her eyes and gave a lazy yawn.

Paige held up her hands. "Anything you want, Sabine. Money, anything, just don't harm her."

Sabine tilted her head and gave a disconnected, vague stare, as though now talking to herself. "Oh…now it's you who wants something from me, is it? Now you're begging me."

"Just give me the baby, Sabine," Paige said, taking a step forward. "You can have me."

Shaking her head vigorously, Sabine took a step back, not realizing she was backing herself into the corner. Becca and Paige stood between her and the nursery door.

"You destroyed my life!" Sabine spat. Mallory began squirming uncomfortably. "You took everything that was precious to me." She gestured to Mallory in her arms, almost holding the baby up as an exhibit. "Now I'm going to take what's precious to you."

Paige took another step forward. "Just give me the baby. You can go free. I can give you anything you want: money, overseas plane tickets, safe passage away from here. No police. Nothing. I'll set you up where no one can ever find you."

"I don't want your stinking money!" Sabine screamed, spittle flying from her lips. "It was you who stuck the feds on us. You told them about Mark's investment company. You betrayed us. You told your father. He's got the connections."

Becca glanced at Paige.

"It was you that got him killed," Sabine continued.

Mallory began crying, her face turning as red as a beetroot.

Paige took another step forward. "You so much as harm a single hair on her head, and I will kill you," Paige said, her voice low, guttural, animalistic.

Upon seeing Mallory in distress, Paige felt a spike of maternal rage. How did Sabine get into the house? How could this be happening? Then she felt her heart ripping apart by the claws of betrayal. Paulo? Of course.

Sabine smiled as though sensing Paige had figured it out. "That's right, you bitch, your nanny: Paulo. I planted him inside your home. He is with me. I had a lot of time while in prison to think about this exact moment, to plan my revenge. I knew the only way I could hurt you wasn't financially, or through your dim-witted husband, Scott." Sabine gave a hideous little laugh. "I've been fucking him for years now, right behind your back, in your house, even in your bed!" Sabine held up Mallory again. "He's not even her father. Did you know that?" Sabine gave another manic laugh. "He had a fucking vasectomy for Christ's sake! He told me himself. He doesn't want kids, never has. But you forced him to fuck you day in and day out, to put a child in your self-entitled womb! A child that only you wanted. So, he went behind your back, got the procedure done, and then lied to your face, pretended that he wanted a family just as much as you did."

Paige felt as though she had been knifed in the gut. Her breath faltered, her mind flashing back to all those moments, intimate conversations with her husband, Scott, when he told her, more than anything, he wanted to be a father.

"You're pathetic," Sabine spat. "Nothing more than a desperate, privileged, rich girl getting adult welfare from your rich fucking parents. Everything that I had, I earned the hard way. I did the work, paid my dues." Sabine shook her head in disgust. "And then you come along and destroy all that with your rich daddy's help."

Paige could feel the room pressing in on her, the corners blurring at the edges.

"And you!" Sabine turned on Becca. "That night I was in

your home, in your closet, I saw the letters. I read them. I had lost part of my memory, that was the truth, when I got stabbed by Garrett Mason. But over time, while I was rotting in a prison cell, no thanks to Paige, my memory started coming back to me. I had a lot of time to think. Then I did some digging into your background, Becca, into your past. You're not as innocent as you claim. In fact, you are a murderous little liar." Sabine turned back to Paige. "I'm sure your friend's past will make a nice addition to Scott's next book, the sequel to *Mill Point Road* he's writing now."

Becca slid forward, toward Sabine.

"I pieced everything together." Sabine nodded at Becca. "Your marriage was over. Michael was fucking another woman." Sabine made a look of thinking. "Rachel… That was her name, I believe. You found out about the two of them, so you decided to k—"

It wasn't Paige who acted first; it was Becca. In a split second, she covered the ground between her and Sabine. With one fluid motion she clamped her right hand down on Mallory's dangling arm while at the same time brought her clenched left fist up into a wide arc and drove it into the side of Sabine's temple.

Sabine loosened her grip on Mallory and staggered backward.

Becca pivoted, wrenched the child out of Sabine's arms, then peeled away.

Paige poured forth a torrent of pure, venomous rage. Like a freight train at full speed, she barreled headlong into Sabine, both hands up, her fingers twisted like talons, clawing at Sabine's face, slicing, gouging, tearing at the woman who tried to take her baby away from her.

"I'm going to kill you, you fucking bitch!" Paige screamed, her talons turning to fists as she rained blows down on Sabine's head, battering the woman into the corner of the room. "I've always wanted to kill you ever since I found out you were fucking Scott, and now I'm going to!"

Both women scuffled together in a whirling, screaming torrent of clawing fingers, wild eyes, snarling teeth, elbows, fists, spit, and tears.

Sabine grabbed a fistful of Paige's hair, and jerked her head violently sideways, knocking her off-balance. They went at each other, like two feral animals fighting in a cage over a scrap of meat. Paige slid her hands up on either side of Sabine's head. Grabbing her ears, she started wrenching Sabine's head back and forth violently. "I'm…going…to…kill…you!" she shrieked, banging Sabine's head into the wall, punching an indent into the drywall with the back of Sabine's skull.

Together, they lurched sideways, crashing into a small bookcase. Nursery books, plush teddy bears, and a pink unicorn all toppled to the floor. In a murderous dance, they waltzed around the small room together, crashing into a rocking chair, then into a chest of drawers, then back against the wall.

Holding Mallory protectively to her chest, Becca watched on. Mallory had stopped crying, her big wondrous eyes watching in curious fascination as her mother spun, screamed, and raged.

Sabine brought her knee up and drove it into Paige's stomach.

Paige doubled over, breath-stealing nausea blooming inside her. She collapsed to her knees, clutching her stomach, gasping for air.

Wiping blood from her lips, Sabine looked down at Paige. "You pathetic little whore," she hissed.

"No!" Becca screamed. She watched as Sabine stepped in and kicked Paige in the side of her head.

Paige slumped lifelessly as Sabine turned, staggered past Becca and out the door.

Calmly, Becca placed Mallory back into her crib before dashing out after Sabine.

Sabine only made it to the top of the sweeping stairs when Becca caught up with her.

Grabbing a handful of hair, Becca yanked Sabine's head, pulling the woman back as though she were tethered to an invisible rope that had suddenly drawn taut.

"Not so fast," Becca said, catching her, then dragging her away from the edge of the steps.

Sabine pivoted in toward Becca, who began pushing her toward the railing. Sabine hit the railing with her lower back and let out a grunt, then began to arch backward as Becca drove her farther up and out. Sabine was taller than Becca by a good foot, which meant that her center of gravity was higher. Bending her knees and grabbing both of Sabine's breasts, Becca hoisted her farther up and back.

Sabine arched precariously over the railing. Panicking, she grabbed at Becca's forearms, but Becca shrugged her off, pushing her backward even harder.

Sabine glanced sideways and down—at the hard tiled floor of the atrium twenty feet below. "Nooo!" she hissed. "Please!"

Ignoring her pleas, Becca continued pushing Sabine's upper torso. Sabine's feet lifted off the ground, her arms whirred and her body tilted like a teeter-totter. With her face twisted in fear, Sabine finally slid over the balcony rail and disappeared from view.

And when the sound came a split second later, it wasn't a

sickening, bone-cracking smack. To Becca's ears, it was more like the sound of sweet relief. Becca stood at the rail and looked down. "Not this time," she whispered.

Below, Sabine lay, wide eyed, with her neck and limbs grotesquely twisted and buckled. Becca continued staring down at Sabine's lifeless body, didn't avert her gaze, even when Paige, groggy and clutching her head, slid up next to her.

Paige looked down and then nodded.

The two women stood in silence for a full minute, gazing down at Sabine, watching as a dark, crimson puddle edged out from under her head.

Paige wiped the blood from her nose and straightened her chaotic hair with her fingers. She took a deep breath, then said, "I have a plan."

◢ Chapter 44 - Tartarus

Despite sitting next to the wood-burning stove, their discussion in the last half hour had left Haley Perez feeling like she had stepped through a hidden portal into a cold, murderous world filled with dark, mythical monsters.

The conversation had shifted away from Dylan Cobb and to finding the person behind him and Garrett Mason. Richards believed the clues lay in the demonic pictures Perez had sent him.

A book on Greek mythology lay open on the table, displaying a picture of a huge demonic beast with horns and bulging muscles, straddling a torrent of fire and brimstone that rose from a deep rift in the Earth's crust. Bodies, blazing like torches, lay strewn on either side of the wide rift, the entire scene a maelstrom of unearthly horror and carnage. The picture looked very similar to the ones Cobb had plastered on the walls of his dungeon chamber.

Richards swiveled the book so Perez could see the picture better. "In Greek mythology, Tartarus was said to be an abyss, a place used as a dungeon where the sinful were imprisoned, condemned only to an eternity of torment and suffering."

"Splendid," Perez murmured, wondering if maybe Richards had spent too much time alone in his log cabin.

"Let me explain more. The name Tartarus also refers to a deity, the physical monstrosity with razor-sharp talons, whose face has been replaced by an inward spiral of darkness."

"And you find reading up on this"—Perez paused, trying not to offend her mentor—"interesting, a hobby?"

Richards offered a smile, more out of amusement. He indicated toward the rows of books choking the shelves behind him. "Not a hobby. Studying mythology, philosophy, and the classics can tell you a lot about modern-day killers."

"When I find a killer with horns and razors for hands, I'll be sure to let you know," Perez said, eyeballing the image in the book.

Richards settled back in his chair. "Over the years, I've seen similarities between characters in mythology and the most heinous murderers in society, and the crimes they commit. Mythology, folklore, urban legend, even scary stories told to children at night by their parents to keep them in bed, whatever you wish to call it, all have themes firmly rooted in the battle of good versus evil, in human suffering, in the paradox of life and death. Just watch the news each night, and soon you'll see the reality of it all."

Perez deliberately chose a "low-news diet," not trusting what tended to be reported in the daily media.

"Stories about people being stolen by some mythical monster living in a cave or a lair are not as mythical as you may think," Richards continued. "Marcus Kemp is an example of someone displaying what we would consider traditional monster traits."

"Marcus Kemp?" Perez asked, taking out her notebook.

"Sociology PhD student at Yale. He was in the news recently, part of a group of Ivy League college students who devised a game to kill innocent people at famous New York landmarks."

"A game?" Perez asked. The world was getting sicker by the second.

"The game had an online tally board, so players could keep score," Richards explained. "When police raided his parents' Brooklyn brownstone, where he was living, they found in the basement a dungeon hidden behind a false wall where he kept women in dog cages." Richards leaned in. "Sound familiar?"

"Dylan Cobb," Perez said, making notes, including to never trust a man with more dog leashes than dogs.

"Exactly. You should look up Kemp," Richards said. "It makes for fascinating reading."

"But not monsters hiding under children's beds," Perez countered. "Those are just made-up stories." Unlike most children, Perez didn't need scary bedtime stories to keep her in her room at night when she was a child. Her father roaming the house was enough.

"Do you know who Milford Brooks is?" Richards asked.

Perez stopped writing and looked up. Now it was starting to make sense. "The Night Crawler," she whispered, trying to think back to what she had read about him.

"The serial killer from Pennsylvania who broke into people's homes during the day while they were at work," Richards nodded, seemingly impressed.

"He would lay in wait for them under their beds," Perez said, remembering now.

"Once they were asleep, he would crawl out from under the bed and strangle them." Richards tapped the picture in the open book. "Marcus Kemp, and Milford Brooks were no mystical creatures. They, and many others like them, such as Dylan Cobb, are flesh and blood monsters of the humankind, and perhaps far worse than any bedtime story."

Perez made a mental note to check under her bed when she got home tonight—and every night, from now on.

"Like I said, monsters of the humankind exist, and the world is full of stories, myths, folklore about monsters," Richards said. "But I believe mingled in with all the myths are actual factual accounts of serial killers and murderers who were never caught. They eventually died, but their stories live on. They become labeled as a myth or scary folklore."

"And those who get caught," Perez said, "become famous, like celebrities."

Richards smiled like a proud teacher. "Books are written about them. Film, television shows, and podcasts are made based on their gruesome exploits."

"They become glorified."

"By us," Richards added. "Take the case of Robin Hood, the winter serial killer who was terrorizing the Midwestern states a few years back."

Perez knew the case well, had read about it extensively. Robin Hood, a name that the media had given him, would hunt, then kill, his victims using a crossbow, pinning them to a tree while they were still alive. He was eventually caught by an ex-FBI agent, a woman, in a town called Willow Falls, Iowa. She nearly died trying to apprehend him.

"The media just adds fuel to the fire," Richards said. "The version of Robin Hood we've come to know as the heroic outlaw of English folklore never really existed. But the winter serial killer, Robin Hood—a name given to him by the media—did."

"It fueled his ego, I imagine," Perez said, "being given that name." But there was nothing heroic about his exploits. Was it ten or fifteen people he had hunted and killed? Perez couldn't recall the exact number.

"Killers crave attention, and the media crave ratings," Richards continued. "It's a match made in hell, a macabre trade in murder and suffering. It sells newspapers and puts eyeballs on screens."

"So how do I catch him?" Perez asked, wanting to get back

on topic. "The person who sent me the black roses with the note?"

"He thinks he is a god, or certainly godlike." Richards paused as though waiting for Perez to follow his thinking.

"He believes he is impervious, immortal, can't be stopped, is far more superior than everyone else around him," Perez said, seeing the clues Richards was giving her, wanting her to arrive at the solution herself, take ownership.

"Like the man with wings who flew too close to the sun," Richards prompted.

"Icarus," Perez said.

Richards smiled. "So, you do know some mythology."

"A little, from high school."

"Good."

"Icarus thought he was invincible. He thought he was a god."

"And what does his story tell us?"

Perez thought for a moment. "Man has limitations, and when he overreaches, he is in danger of failing." Her heart skipped with excitement. "Vanity is what gets most serial killers caught. They think they're invincible, immortal."

"It's no different than the person who sent you those black roses, with the accompanying note."

"He wants me to know how clever he is," Perez said.

"Almost." Richards raised his eyebrows.

"How much *cleverer* he is?"

"Correct," Richards replied. "He wants you to know that he is better than The Eden Killer because he taught him everything. And that he's better than you or any police."

Perez took a few moments of quiet reflection to assess what they had covered. Garrett Mason thought he was a god, built his own Garden of Eden in his basement, filled it with Adams, no

Eves. It was his own interpretation of the biblical story. Another myth? Another story?

Richards tapped the side of his head. "And inside here is where the worst monsters imaginable hide."

"But Ravenwood is such a small town. I can't believe we would have so many 'monsters' living here." Perez thought about Peggy Scott Tuttle, about her being experimented on, and the parallels to Frankenstein, another monster.

"Small towns tend to attract the worst villains," Richards said. "There's less chance of them getting caught."

"Smaller police force," Perez said thoughtfully.

"Less resources. In some small towns, you can get away with murder, and never be caught. You know my theory on this." He smiled at Perez. "So, you opened the box and read the files?"

"All eighteen of them."

"There could be more," Richards said.

"Made to look like missing persons or staged to look like they had legitimately gone away, like how Adam Vickerman and Peggy Scott Tuttle were made to look as though they had decided to leave town," Perez added.

"Correct," Richards agreed. "My theory is proving to be more than just a theory. Both Garrett Mason and Dylan Cobb were drawn to Ravenwood and the surrounding area because, statistically, the chances of them being caught are a lot less than other places they could have chosen to live."

A spark of shock ignited inside Perez. Her eyes went wide. "He contacted them."

Richards nodded. "He reached out to Mason and Cobb, told them to come here, offered them support, and mentoring, and told them the odds were in their favor."

She looked down again at the picture of Tartarus. Now she knew where she had to go to catch him—directly into the lair of the monster itself. Just then, Perez's cell rang.

It was Kershaw. He would have another meltdown if he'd found out she was meeting with Marvin Richards to discuss current and past cases.

"Perez, where are you?" he said loudly.

Perez held her cell away from her ear. "I'm on leave for a few days. You suggested it. Remember?" Perez could sense the agitation in Kershaw's voice.

"Well, cancel it. I need you back on deck. A woman has died up on Mill Point Road, in that gated community. Garland is up there now and will be tied up for a few hours with the forensics team. We're short of detectives at the moment, and I need you back here to conduct interviews."

Perez's heart constricted in her chest, thinking about Annabel Chandler. She tried not to sound anxious when she next asked, "Who is the dead woman?"

"Sabine Miller."

Perez's heart relaxed slightly but was still pumping fast. She couldn't believe what Kershaw was telling her. She was just up there this morning. "So, who am I interviewing?"

"Two women. Rebecca Cartwright and Paige Hamill."

A cold needle of shock slid into the front of Perez's neck and into her throat, making her tongue feel numb, and as though all the saliva had evaporated from her mouth.

"I believe you know them, so I thought you'd be the best person to conduct the formal interviews. Garland will join you when he's finished up there."

She ended the call to see Richards giving her a knowing smile. He had heard the entire conversation.

"Those women," he said, shaking his head, "are another prime example of what I've been saying to you for the last few hours."

🐦 Chapter 45 - Too Trusting

Three days would pass before Rebecca Cartwright and Paige Hamill would finally come into the Hagerstown police station and give their formal statements.

Paige Hamill spent two days in the hospital under observation for a concussion she had suffered, while Rebecca Cartwright had been bedridden—on strict doctor's orders—for a sudden bout of the flu. To say that Haley Perez was a little more than dubious when she later discovered both women had the same medical physician, would be an understatement.

Strangely enough, Nate Garland had also taken sick and still hadn't returned to work by the time Rebecca Cartwright and Paige Hamill appeared. Rumor had it that Garland was indeed lying low, not for medical reasons. Allegedly, Garland had a large debt owed to an Albanian bookie who was out looking for him. With other detectives snowed under with their own cases, Sergeant Kershaw had no choice but to allow Perez to conduct the interviews herself on what initially looked like an apparent accident.

The three-day delay did, however, allow the autopsy of Sabine Miller to be concluded and gave Perez enough time to make some initial inquiries of her own for the case, and to do some digging on another resident of Mill Point Road. The newest.

"Why did Sabine Miller want to steal your baby, Mrs. Hamill?" Perez said as they sat in one of the interview rooms.

Perez had already interviewed Rebecca Cartwright. If there was any collaboration between the two women as to what had transpired that led to Sabine Miller's death, then both women would've had plenty of time to set their story straight, given both were there when it had happened.

"She was obviously jealous," Paige said, "of the family Scott and I had."

Paige Hamill seemed willing to cooperate, wasn't guarded with her responses so far, like she wanted to tell her version of events. Also, to Perez's surprise, Paige had come to the interview without a high-priced lawyer in tow.

"She wanted to hurt me, hurt Mallory," Paige continued, her eyes growing glassy with tears. "After all, it was no secret among my neighbors and friends that Scott and I had been trying for ages to have a child. Perhaps Sabine was driven by extreme jealousy and rage."

"Rage?" Perez asked. "Why do you say Sabine had acted out of rage?"

Jealousy seemed slightly extreme to Perez as a valid motive for Sabine Miller to take such drastic action to kidnap or want to harm a baby. "What had you done to her to evoke such an...extreme response?" Perez asked. "Is the baby not yours?" To Perez, that seemed like a valid explanation to warrant someone grabbing another person's baby. Paige had already explained in intricate detail the vicious fight she and Sabine had after Rebecca had freed Mallory from Sabine's grasp.

"She is my child," Paige said, with coldness in her eyes.

"So why was Sabine Miller so enraged with you, Mrs. Hamill?"

"She'd fallen on hard times, had gone to prison," Paige replied. "Perhaps she thought that I was somehow to blame for that."

"And are you to blame for her going to prison?"

"If my memory serves me correctly," Paige said, continuing her glacial stare, "Sabine and Mark Miller had conned hundreds of investors out of their life savings." Paige offered a thin smile. "I think no one else is to blame for their misfortune other than themselves."

There was more to the story, but Perez could see she wasn't going to get anything more out of the stoic, statuesque woman sitting across from her. It frustrated Perez how they had clammed up, these women of Mill Point Road, closed ranks around each other as they had when she and Marvin Richards had interviewed them in the aftermath of catching The Eden Killer. What was it about these women? They came from different backgrounds, at times seemed to hate each other, yet through shared adversity, they clung to each other for moral or immoral support. All except Sabine Miller, who was now dead. "And what about Paulo Costa, the nanny you employed?" Perez asked. Paulo Costa had disappeared, but a warrant was out for his arrest.

"He obviously was in partnership with Sabine from the very start," Paige replied. "He came with impeccable references from an agency. But as you said, Detective, after you did some police checking that neither I nor the agency could, his credentials now appear to be false. We were all fooled. Sabine obviously had been plotting this for some time while in prison."

Perez pointed her pen at Paige. "Plotting against you specifically. No one else." Perez made a note. *Check on who else Sabine Miller made contact with while in prison!!!*

Paige leaned forward with a half smile. "As you well know, Detective, jealousy is one of the four motives to commit a crime. Love, lust, loathing, and greed." Paige leaned back and touched the corners of her mouth with her finger, as though fixing her lipstick, before casually adding. "She was also fucking my husband behind my back, for starters."

The air vent above went silent. Perez paused mid-stroke, her last train of thought completely slipping off the tracks.

"She wanted what I had." Paige waved one hand.

This certainly was a revelation. Finally, Perez was getting somewhere. Without looking up, she wrote and double-underlined, *Get Scott Hamill in for an interview.*

"Did this affair continue when she returned to Mill Point Road?"

Paige took a sip of water. "My husband and I have an understanding."

Perez looked up expectantly.

Paige's eyes narrowed. "That if he strays ever again…it will not end well for him."

Perez made another note. *Paige threatened husband. She is rich (rich parents). He is not. Keep it in your pants or the money train will end.*

"What about Sabine Miller?" Perez asked. "Did you also warn her to stay away from your husband?" Perez was angling for motive. Perhaps that was what the fight had really been about. Then again, she couldn't imagine anyone fighting over Scott Hamill, especially two obviously strong-minded, ambitious women. Perez had watched a television interview with Scott Hamill promoting his book. The man came across as an arrogant, shallow, sexist, douchebag. Maybe deep down he wasn't.

"I believe she did approach my husband when she returned," Paige said. "But he rebuffed her advances. Perhaps that just added fuel to her fire, being rejected by him, and thinking that she could just waltz back into town, back into our lives, and pick up where she had left off."

Perez thumbed through her notes. "You said that in the ensuing struggle, after Rebecca Cartwright had managed to grab Mallory from Sabine Miller, that Sabine Miller kicked you in the head, rendering you momentarily unconscious, then she fled the bedroom—"

"Nursery," Paige interrupted. "Mallory's nursery, not bedroom."

Perez pursed her lips. "Sabine Miller then fled the nursery, but Rebecca Cartwright didn't chase after her?"

"No," Paige said with an unblinking gaze. "Mallory was safe, and Becca came to my aid. I woke up and saw her kneeling over me."

"You said you were only unconscious for a few moments?"

"I guess so."

Perez returned to reading from her notes. "Then together, you both went outside the nursery, and it was then you discovered Sabine Miller lying at the bottom of the stairs?"

"Correct. Like I said before in my statement, in her haste, Sabine must have stumbled and fell down the stairs, hence the lethal injuries she suffered."

"Neither you nor Rebecca Cartwright chased Sabine Miller or pushed her?"

"No. She made a run for it. I didn't chase her. I was more concerned about the health and well-being of my child. Then when I came out of the nursery with Becca, we went to the top of the stairs, and were both completely horrified to see that Sabine had fallen. We then rushed down the stairs to see if we could provide any assistance, but it was too late. She was already dead. I then used my cell phone to call nine-one-one."

Perez held Paige's unflinching gaze for a few seconds. Both women were not telling the whole truth; Perez could feel it.

Rebecca Cartwright's statement and subsequent interview mirrored what Paige Hamill had said. Perhaps a little too closely. People witnessing the same event always had minor differences when describing it afterward, adding their own subtle interpretation. But not in this case. Rebecca Cartwright and Paige Hamill were like two peas in a cozy pod when it came to the death of Sabine Miller.

The county coroner had concluded that the fatal injuries suffered by Sabine Miller were consistent with someone tragically falling down such a grand, sweeping set of stairs before landing hard on the tile floor.

Paige Hamill had made some claims to Nate Garland while he was at the house, that Sabine Miller and the nanny, Paulo Costa, were colluding to abduct Mallory Hamill. During Perez's follow-up inquiries, it seemed clear that Sabine Miller was behind Paulo Costa posing as a nanny to infiltrate Paige and Scott Hamill's home. Costa's visa had expired more than twelve months ago, and there were large deposits, thirty grand in total, into his bank account starting three months before Sabine Miller was released from prison. Not bad for a guy who, according to his Hollywood agent, a year ago was attending CBS casting calls for *The Bold and the Beautiful* at Television City in Los Angeles while bussing tables in a restaurant at The Grove across the street. While in prison, Sabine Miller had also set up a secret email account, using it to communicate back and forth with Costa, who was providing her with almost daily updates of what was going on inside the household, his daily routine with Mallory, and security measures within the home. So far, they hadn't been able to find Paulo Costa. He had just simply vanished.

"And you weren't suspicious at all about Costa?" Perez asked.

Paige shook her head. "I had no idea that he was an impostor, least of all having been planted in my home by Sabine Miller. I'm just glad that no harm came to my daughter. She is the most precious thing to me on this planet."

Precious enough to kill for? Perez thought. "And you didn't know that Sabine Miller was inside your house while you and Rebecca Cartwright were downstairs?"

Paige shook her head. "I had no idea how she got inside. I can only assume that Costa gave her access. He had no keys of his own, though."

"We found a set of keys on Sabine Miller," Perez said. "They look like a copied set, not original. Who has a set of keys to your home?"

"Just me, Scott, and my parents. I'd say Costa may have taken a set, had them copied, and returned them without anyone knowing."

This was what Perez was thinking too. She doubted Costa would have taken Paige's keys, more likely her husband's copy. "What about security cameras, Mrs. Hamill? You would've installed some type of nanny cam or surveillance device in Mallory's…bedroom?" Perez couldn't resist. She needed to unsettle this woman with the Mona Lisa smile. Paige Hamill didn't seem like the kind of person not to take such precautions. Everything about her—from the razor-sharp way she dressed to her perfect posture, how she spoke, even the subtleties of how her lips rippled, the movement of her eyes, the coy inclination of her head—spoke volumes of a well-rehearsed, meticulous woman who had built a carefully curated persona.

Paige gave a patient smile. The restraint to correct Perez again so obvious on her face.

"Perhaps I am just too trusting," she replied.

♦ Chapter 46 - Sisters

"Sabine was trying to kidnap Mallory. You were simply a mother protecting her child," Becca said. "She would have killed her."

They sat at a table in the far corner of Olsen's.

"I'm not so sure," Paige replied. She sat, calm and composed, a picture of dignified menace. They were sisters now, bound by an unwritten pact. Next to Paige, sleeping soundly in her stroller, was Mallory.

"You know," Paige said, staring into her coffee cup, "while I was standing there, looking down at Sabine, I was actually glad she'd fallen to her death."

She looked up at Becca. "As you said, Mallory could have died because of her."

Becca squeezed Paige's hand. "The things she said, the damage she could have done to your family. Now it seems obvious it was her who tried to plant that spy camera in my home."

"Sabine?" Paige said. "Before, you said you didn't think it was her snooping around your house."

"In light of what she tried to do to you and Scott, who else could it have been?" Becca replied.

"Why would she want to spy on you?" Paige said. "It's me she hated. Always has been jealous of what Scott and I have. So, out of spite, she tried to destroy our lives by taking the most precious thing I have—Mallory." Paige regarded Becca for a moment. "Why do you now think it was Sabine roaming around your house that night?"

"It all makes sense," Becca said. "She returns to Ravenwood, slips back into her old house, and wants to keep tabs on everyone. She saw us as good friends and thought that my house, given its current state, was easier to get inside and install a camera." Becca took a sip of her coffee. "Maybe she thought that through me she could find out more information indirectly about you. She was just being thorough. She already had the nanny embedded in your house keeping an eye on you."

Paige gave a sigh. "I guess we all have secrets we want to protect."

"Did you know that Scott had had a vasectomy?" Becca asked.

"Not initially. But then I had a separate gynecologist run some tests on some semen of his I had collected after sex. I wanted a second opinion. The doctor said that I was perfectly fertile, but Scott's semen lacked any sperm whatsoever. I originally thought I was the problem." Paige looked forlorn, then she gathered herself. "Scott thinks he can hide secrets from me, but he's hopeless at it. I found a card in his desk for a local clinic where he'd gone to get the 'snip,' as they say." Paige gave a sneering laugh and then looked at Becca. "It truly takes a gift for a person to keep a secret well hidden. Women just happen to be better at it than men." Paige's jaw then tightened. "What really hurt, was when Sabine threw it in my face, that Scott had shared what he had done—with her, of all people!" Paige tilted her head back and closed her eyes. "It was like they were conspiring together behind my back to thwart my attempts to conceive." She lowered her head, and Becca could see tears in her eyes when she opened them. "I felt devastated when she said she knew, had probably known for years. It just made Scott's betrayal all the more vile."

In the aftermath, Becca did think it was strange how Paige

had never once asked Becca about the letters Sabine had mentioned, about what she had said about Michael, their marriage, and the affair he was having. Thankfully, Becca had silenced Sabine before she could reveal any more. Yet it made Becca feel more cautious about the woman who was now sitting across from her. Unlike Sabine—who was obsessed with dragging every little piece of information she could out of people, only to use it against them—Paige was different. Then again, perhaps she wasn't. Becca decided to take the initiative. "About the letters, Sabine mentioned—"

Paige held up her hand, halting Becca. "You don't have to tell me anything, Becca," she said. "Everything that came out of that wretched woman's mouth was a lie, except for the part about her sleeping with Scott for years, and him getting a vasectomy. Those, I know now to be true."

"What about Scott?" Becca asked. "Are you going to tell him you know?" The more obvious question on Becca's mind was who really was Mallory's father, if not Scott? However, as Paige hadn't pushed her about the letters, Becca thought, out of mutual respect, she would return the favor by not asking. It would be much better for Paige to broach the subject with her on her own accord.

"Leave him to me, Becca. He believes Mallory was a miracle baby anyway." Staring off into space, Paige let out a deep sigh, the stress of the last few days clearly etched on her face. "They say that if women didn't have a vagina, men wouldn't give us a second glance." She brought her gaze back to Becca, a devious smile now on her face. "But I say, if men didn't have a penis, the world would be a better, and safer place."

The comment made Becca laugh. Never a truer statement had been spoken.

"You're not concerned that Sabine died in your home?" Becca asked.

Paige gave a shrug. "Why should I be? We used plenty of bleach where she actually fell, and we steam-cleaned the tile before calling the police. They didn't find anything under the balcony. If they had, that young detective would have said something." Paige slipped out a compact and began needlessly touching up her makeup. "Also, it's a daily reminder every time I walk down those stairs," Paige said absentmindedly.

"What do you mean?" Becca asked.

Paige checked herself in the small mirror before slipping the compact away. She tilted her head at Becca as if to say she should already know the answer to her own question. "Not to fuck with me or my child."

Paige took out her purse, slipped a twenty under her coffee cup, then stood before glancing down at Becca. "Now we have our own little secret together, just between the two of us." Paige bent down and—to Becca's surprise—kissed her lightly on the lips, then pulled back. "It's like we are sisters." And with that, Paige walked out.

🐦 Chapter 47 - More Secrets

"So why did you lie to me?" Perez asked.

"I'm sorry," Annabel Chandler replied, tears forming in her eyes. "I guessed it was only going to be a matter of time before you discovered my past, found out about the truth."

"Did you kill her?"

"It was an accident. You must believe me; I didn't mean to kill her."

"You changed your name as well." Another lie that Perez had discovered.

"It was for the better. Chandler was my mother's maiden name. I prefer it."

Perez paced back and forth in Chandler's living room. She stopped, then cast an accusing glare back at Chandler. "At first I was thrown by the name. Then I made contact with the hospital in Boston where you claimed to have worked. Turns out they've never heard of you."

Sitting on the sofa, Chandler seemed to be withdrawing into herself, a shrinking *Alice in Wonderland*. Her shoulders sagging, her eyes looking down at her fidgeting hands in her lap, her chin drooping.

"Starting with your DMV records, I discovered you actually worked as a trauma surgeon in Los Angeles, and not in Boston, like you said. You've been lying to me all along."

"I had to," Chandler said, still not looking up, her voice

sounding like it was coming from the end of a long tunnel. "It was the only way I could move on."

"So, tell me, why all the lies? Why the charade?" Perez folded her arms across her chest.

Chandler looked up. Their eyes met. Fury and heat in one, tears and remorse in the other. "It was a simple choice. Either I didn't perform the surgery, and the girl dies, or I take the risk. I do the surgery, and the girl lives."

"So, what happened?"

Chandler sat a little straighter, her chin a little higher. "You've done the background checking on me," she replied, a slight sting in her voice. "You tell me what happened. You claim to know the whole story."

Perez didn't care if Chandler was getting angry. Perez felt like she'd been betrayed. It was only because Chandler had mentioned when they first had met that she had moved to Mill Point Road, that Perez took an interest in looking into her background. Past experience had told Perez that anyone living or connected to that place seemed to be hiding something or involved in no good.

"I did the surgery. I saved the girl's life," Chandler replied.

"So the girl lived?"

Chandler nodded. "At first. Then two hours later, she arrested. Massive internal bleeding. Turns out I had accidentally nicked an artery on the way out. At first, she seemed fine, then she began to hemorrhage. She died on the gurney on the way back into the ER."

"So, it was an accident?" Perez asked, slowly, still not entirely convinced. "It does happen. Things go wrong during surgeries all the time, I imagine."

"Not exactly," Chandler said, a little sheepishly.

Now Perez was confused.

"I was reported by a groveling, ambitious junior surgeon who was assisting me that night," Chandler continued. "They found out I was slightly intoxicated, with a scalpel in hand and both hands stuck in some eight-year-old's open chest. They had to act, go by the book. There was an investigation, and for my sins, I got struck off for malpractice, lost my job. Can't practice anywhere."

"You were drinking?" Perez asked.

"*Had* been drinking," Chandler corrected her. Chandler rubbed the side of the temple. "I was on call as the backup senior ER surgeon that night. I had two glasses of wine with dinner. I didn't think it was a big deal." Chandler glared at Perez. "And no, I don't have a drinking problem."

"So, what happened next?"

"Turns out it was a big deal. I get the call. The resident surgeon on duty can't do the surgery, has never done that particular procedure before. I had to go in." Chandler let out a breath. "I'm not making any excuses for it, but I don't believe the alcohol in my bloodstream affected my judgment or my ability to perform the operation. I was also the only surgeon who could perform that specific kind of operation, had done it plenty of times before. The girl would have definitely died if I hadn't gone in. The only other option was to fly in another, experienced surgeon from Austin, and that would've been a two-to-three-hour delay. She would have died well before then. So, I scrubbed up and did what I had to do."

"And how did this junior surgeon, who reported you, figure that you had been drinking?" Perez asked.

"I don't know. I gulped down so much coffee before going into the operating room, that my bladder felt like it was going to burst."

"But drinking coffee doesn't flush the alcohol from your system," Perez said. "It's a myth."

"I know," Chandler nodded. "Afterward, I agreed to a blood test, the traces of alcohol were minimal. I was perfectly legal to drive, was under the blood alcohol limit for California. But the hospital legal counsel had other ideas, policies, and fine print to adhere to."

"So, you went from the glitz and glamour of LA to the quiet obscurity of Ravenwood to hide?" Perez asked.

Chandler sat a little straighter, her eyes a little narrower, her jaw a little tighter. "I'm a damn good surgeon! And let me tell you, the shine and the glitz rubs off very quickly the longer you live in LA. And, from what I've seen so far from this town, it's hardly a quiet and tranquil place." She looked accusingly at Perez. "A lot of people seem to be drawn to this town, for whatever reason, to hide from one thing or another."

Perez felt the insinuation and ignored it. Her own past wasn't the subject of debate right now. "So now you're a part-time county forensics investigator."

"It's given me a new perspective on life, and death," Chandler said. "I know I'm more experienced than all of the permanent medical examiners in Baltimore, but I've been relegated to a lesser role. I accept my punishment. I simply weighed the pros and the cons: try and save the girl, or stand by and watch her die. It wasn't a choice based on vanity or ego. I had twenty years of training and surgical experience behind me to do that specific operation. In that precise moment, no one else could've done it. It was a judgment call."

Perez thought about it for a moment. Maybe she was being a little harsh. She wanted to trust Chandler so much.

"Do you miss being a surgeon?" Perez asked. Her tone had lost some of its bitter edge.

Chandler made a face. "Of course I do. But I have to go with the hand I've been dealt. I came to Ravenwood to make a fresh start, build a new life. A new town, new faces, new people. And I love it here, even though I've only been here a short time. It's very different from LA, in a good way. LA can grind you down, slowly, one brain cell at a time."

"Well, that's something we can both agree on," Perez replied, her mouth flirting with a smile, but then she thought otherwise.

"I like my job at the moment, deciphering how the dead have died," Chandler said.

Reluctantly, Perez sat down next to Chandler. During the short period of time she had known the woman, she had grown to really like her. She saw her not only as an ally, in a professional sense, but felt their relationship was growing into real friendship.

Just as Perez was berating herself for being too abrasive, Annabel Chandler dropped a bombshell right on top of her head.

"But I have killed someone before," Chandler said, her face cold and defiant. "And on that occasion, I really meant to."

🐦 Chapter 48 - Love Lost

Winter weeds sprouted in unruly, disheveled clumps from cracks in the cold earth.

Disrespectful feet had trodden the dead flowers others had left, leaving the petals crushed to a papery ash that had mixed in with the snow.

With Mallory clinging to her breast, Paige Hamill stared down at the headstone, its curved top covered with a layer of pure white. "This is your father. Your *real* father." She kissed the baby softly on the forehead, breathing in that sweet, clean, innocent smell of a life yet tainted by sin. "And let no one tell you any different."

In the distance, a groundskeeper worked the hard, frozen earth with a long shovel, his movements slow and silent.

Here, where Adam Teal lay, the ground was dappled in the shade, the sun high and bright in a cloudless morning sky. It was a poor person's grave riddled with neglect and apathy. Paige knew that Adam's mother tended the grave as best she could. But the woman was stretched financially. Paige had done her research and had looked into the family. The Teal family were living just barely above the poverty line with Adam's three other siblings, in a tiny house in Beaver Creek, a small community three miles north of Ravenwood. Paige had driven past the house a few times, slow and curious, then kept going.

Adam's poor mother, Valerie, obviously did the best she could. But the best she could, wasn't enough. That would soon change.

This was the first time Paige had visited, and the sight of the grave had given Paige such a sharp stab of sorrow in her heart. A young man, barely nineteen, a college freshman who had attended Hagerstown Community College, taken so early in life.

She smiled as her mind wandered back to warmer thoughts of lazy afternoons and clean sheets. Of summer breezes gently ruffling her bedroom curtains. Of an empty house, silent except for the sound of their lovemaking. Of Adam's gentle manner, always considerate of her needs, always giving, never taking, always slow, never rushed. His powerful, virile body coveting hers. The crush of his chest on her bare breasts, the depth and intensity of his prolonged release. His seed, searing and copious, flowing into her, filling her, breathing a new life into her, something that Scott had so cruelly and maliciously denied her.

So let the charade continue. Let Scott ponder Mallory's true origin while he wallows in his own silent torment. Did he have the courage to broach such a self-incriminating subject with her? She doubted it. His own selfish deception ranked far worse than her own infidelity. In her mind, Paige hadn't cheated on her husband. Rather, she had done what needed to be done to get what she wanted—a child. There was no harm in that. Scott had not only cheated on her with Sabine—and with other women, she was certain—but had also cheated Paige out of a child in such a callous and manipulative way.

Paige looked down at Mallory, felt her heart ache with motherly determination to protect her child, no matter what, and basked in knowing that not a single cell of Scott was in her.

Paige kissed her fingers before pressing them to the headstone, then began walking toward the groundskeeper.

Seeing Paige approach, the groundskeeper stopped, leaned back on his shovel, and wiped his brow. After introductions and pleasantries were exchanged, Paige asked, "How long have you been working here, Curtis?"

"Near on twenty years now," Curtis answered. "I imagine I'll be here for another twenty years too. I like my job. The pay could be better, but it's simple work, and I like being outdoors."

Juggling a dozing Mallory, Paige slipped out her purse and held out fifty-dollar bill to the man.

His eyes first brightened, then dulled with offence. "Don't need no charity."

"Good, because it is not." Paige gestured behind her, to where she had walked from. "I want you to maintain that grave over there." She told Curtis the name and plot number. "In winter, clear away snow, in summer, any dead flowers, and the weeds. Keep it nice and neat, and I'll pay you fifty dollars a month."

Curtis took the note, then looked at it hard for a moment as though Ulysses S. Grant was some long-lost brother he had just recognized.

Paige saw embarrassment flicker across Curtis's face.

"You're not in any trouble," she said. "I can see the place is hopelessly understaffed, and you're doing the best you can. However, I'd like you to pay special attention to that particular grave. I'll be coming back once a month to replace the flowers, and I'll pay each month then. Just keep the area around the grave neat and tidy and keep our little arrangement to yourself."

"That's all?" The man stared at Paige, bewildered.

"That's all."

The groundskeeper slipped the fifty into his overalls. "Was he a friend of yours?"

Paige hesitated. "Yes, he was. Someone very special, who I didn't appreciate enough until he was gone."

The man gave a knowing nod. "I hear you. Same with my

wife. She passed on just two years ago. We go through life not appreciating what we have until it's too late, and it's gone."

Paige thanked Curtis again and walked away, holding Mallory a little closer to her heart.

🐦 Chapter 49 - The Message

"Hi, I'd like to leave a message for Rachel Gideon. You don't know me, Rachel, and I'm not going to tell you my name. Also, please don't bother trying to trace this number or try and find me. But it's important that you listen to what I'm going to tell you.

"What I am going to tell you is a piece of information you may find useful. I live in a small town called Ravenwood, in Maryland. I believe you are familiar with a woman called Rebecca Cartwright. More importantly, I believe you were very familiar with her husband, Michael, who died.

"Rebecca, or Becca as she's known around town, told me that Michael died in a motorbike accident. This was a complete and utter lie. She basically confessed to me that she killed him, and made it look like an accident.

"I thought you would like to know this. I believe you and Michael had grown very fond of each other. That is entirely your choice, and I'm not judging you. However, Becca Cartwright is a murderer. She murdered her husband and is now hiding out in Ravenwood.

"Do what you want with this information. This will be the one and only time I will contact you. Again, please do not try and find me. My only motive for telling you this information is that I'm a firm believer that justice must be served. Bad people in this world deserve to get what's coming to them."

🐦 Chapter 50 - Burnt Offering

It was a group of school kids who first called it in.

While playing in a vacant industrial lot on the outskirts of Ravenwood, they'd seen, and smelled, the remnants of a fire on an adjacent lot. What had once been a tan-colored sedan, had been reduced to a smoldering, charred carcass of metal, melted plastic, and bubbling rubber. First on scene was Engine Tanker 8 from Station 8 out of Ravenwood. The shiny, bright-red fire truck carrying fifteen hundred gallons of water made short work of dousing the smoldering wreck.

Within the wreck, the fire crew soon discovered the blackened remains of a single occupant in the driver's seat, and police and EMS were called later. When fire investigators had concluded their work, they discovered that an accelerant had been used, and that the seat of the fire was the body itself. Also discovered inside of the vehicle were bundles of clothing, coated in melted plastic that was assumed to be the carry bags the clothing was stored in. A laptop computer lay on the passenger seat, its case melted and fused together from the intense heat, with no chance of retrieving information from the hard drive. The warped remains of a cell phone were found in the passenger footwell, and on the back seat were the remains of an inflatable vinyl air bed that had been reduced down to the look and texture of a puddle of deep-brown molasses. A large lump of sodden ash sat in the lap of the vehicle's occupant. The material would later be identified as a thick stack of papers in a cardboard file, the fire and water rendering the papers totally illegible, so badly burned was the body, that it fragmented into several pieces when attempts were made to remove it, and twenty-six separate evidence bags were required to transport all the pieces.

The Connecticut plates on the vehicle, although warped and distorted, could still be deciphered and were tracked back to the registered owner of the vehicle: Philip Benton from Connecticut. While Benton was the registered owner, the registration had since lapsed, and a payment default notice had been issued. Dental records would later confirm that the body was, in fact, Philip Benton.

However, the strangest discovery of all, and the one that alerted the homicide detectives of the Hagerstown Police Department, was the blackened remains of a set of handcuffs and bone fragments of a hand discovered in the driver's side footwell after forensic technicians had sifted through the debris.

Following painstaking analysis of the wreckage, of the body, and through extensive scene reconstruction, the county coroner, the county sheriff's office, and the homicide detectives of the Hagerstown Police Department all arrived at the same conclusion: the occupant, Philip Benton from Connecticut, had been handcuffed to the steering wheel, accelerant had been poured on him and on the stack of papers in his lap, and then set alight.

Philip Benton had been murdered, burned alive while sitting in his own vehicle.

🐦 Chapter 51 - The Next Chosen

The irony was not lost on him as he disembarked the Greyhound bus at the Washington County Transit Center in Hagerstown and glanced up across the street and saw the name on the building.

Under the shadow of the triple-peaked façade of the building, a man sat on the steps, his face buried in his hands in anguish.

Clutching a small duffel bag containing all his worldly possessions, he crossed West Franklin Street, and under the shadow of Christ's Reformed Church, he hailed a cab for the short twelve-minute ride to the Sheetz gas station out on the national turnpike. He certainly wasn't reformed after the last twelve months. In fact, the time he'd spent removed from society had only served to fuel the bitter, blinding desire for revenge that continued to fester deep inside him.

At the gas station, he poured a large cup of breakfast blend from one of the Bunn coffee dispensers, grabbed a prepackaged turkey on rye, dropped his duffel on the floor under one of the stools along the window counter of the dining area, sat down, and stared out at the cars and travelers in the forecourt. He took a sip of coffee and closed his eyes in pure ecstasy. *My God, the coffee, real coffee.* Not that watery, acidic swill they served on the inside. Unwrapping the sandwich, he took a tentative bite, then uttered a faint moan of delight. Even though it was prepackaged, the sandwich was fresh and made his taste buds awaken from hibernation. He thought he'd lost all sense of taste and smell. For a few minutes, he ate in joyful silence, savoring each mouthful and swallow, a smile on his face like a blind person seeing the sunrise for the first time, or the deaf hearing the first chords of "Sweet Child o' Mine."

There would be no phone call, no introductions, just a simple drop that had been arranged two months ago. As he waited, his mind drifted back over the previous twelve months he had endured. The pain, the suffering, the terrifying indignation, often at the hands of those bigger and stronger than him. Those more experienced at being in prison, who knew how to break you both physically and mentally. There were several trips to the infirmary to treat various bouts of concussion, a broken nose, a fractured cheekbone, and two missing teeth. Not to mention one eye-watering surgical procedure involving internal stitches for an anal tear.

He shifted momentarily on the hard seat before continuing his painful trip down resentment lane. He thought back to what his life had been, the taste of freedom that went with having money. He thought about the house he had lived in, the vacations down to Mexico he enjoyed so much. All that was gone now—the money, the self-respect, and his dignity as well. Not to mention his friends. They were the first to leave him, to run like filthy rats. None of it was his fault. Only one person was to blame for the destruction of his former life. He had tried killing her, and for his efforts he'd suffered a fractured skull. Now he was back, determined to do it properly, to not take any chances.

It would be different this time too—he had a new friend, an ally who patiently listened to his story, shared in his suffering, sympathized with his predicament, and understood his soul-grinding need for revenge. His friend was clever, intelligent, charming while at the same time he shared his taste for vengeful violence. More importantly, his friend wanted to help him, had reached out a guiding hand when all others had turned their backs on him. His friend said he'd heard of his plight, had read about it in the newspapers, said it was unjust how he'd been treated, how he'd been painted as the villain, whereas, in fact, it was he who was the victim. So he had taken the guiding hand that was offered, allowed it to pull him out of the deep well of despair and depression that no amount of medication could fix. Soon hopelessness turned to hope, hardship to comfort, failure into opportunity.

He finished his coffee and was contemplating another when the atmosphere around him changed. He tensed, resisting the urge to turn and look behind him. That would be bad, breaking the rules. So he continued staring straight ahead, out of the window, as instructed. A shadow passed momentarily across the countertop where his arms were resting, moving right to left. He remained perfectly still.

Someone sat down on the stool next to him, and it took every ounce of restraint not to turn and look at his savior.

His nostrils caught a faint scent of cologne: a warm layered blend of rich leather, spicy almond with a floral tinge, a welcome change from the reek of shit, piss, sour sweat, and menace he was so used to when someone invaded his personal space. In his peripheral vision, he saw the person slightly stoop and place something on the floor before pushing it with his foot toward him and up against the base of his own stool.

He could tell, like him, the person seated silently next to him was also looking straight ahead. But when he got up and passed behind again, the man uttered a fleeting whisper. "Happy hunting." Then he was gone.

Hank Vickerman closed his eyes, then counted to sixty, as he had been instructed.

He opened his eyes, breathed a sigh of relief, then glanced down. There was another duffel bag, slightly larger than his own, at his feet. Without needing to look inside the bag, Hank knew his friend, his ally, had provided him with all the tools he required to execute his plan, to help him on his next step toward retribution. And next to him on the counter was a set of car keys that weren't there before.

Reaching down, Hank gathered up both bags, noticing that the new addition was considerably heavier than his own duffel bag, and made for the exit.

Warm sunshine and fresh, sweet air greeted him outside. He felt his spirits surge as he walked with more purpose, with more confidence and determination.

He was going to kill her, kill her properly this time, like he should've done the first time. Maybe even kill a few others, too, her treacherous coconspirators, her inner circle of friends, who he was certain also had a hand in his downfall.

Ten minutes later, while he drove the rental car, a town sign grew through the windshield.

Ravenwood.

A raven perched on the sign, bobbed its head in approval as it watched Hank Vickerman drive past.

THE END.

Turn the page for a sneak peek of
The Sisterhood, Book #3 in the Ravenwood Series

Author Endnote

Please Read Before You Post a Review

Ravenwood is an ongoing series, and as such, there will be some unanswered questions at the end of each book. New characters will arrive in the town; old characters may depart, and some characters, no matter how hard I try, just can't seem to leave! This means that not everything is tied up in a nice, little neat bow at the end. Some of the smaller, unanswered questions will spill over and be answered in subsequent books. Some mysteries will be solved; new ones will manifest, and old ones will remain a mystery until reaching a satisfying conclusion in future books. I don't do this to trick or manipulate the reader into having to buy the next book by leaving deliberate cliffhangers at the end. It's all part of wanting to create a larger, ongoing story about the town, its history, and townsfolk, with some major plot threads running through several books. I simply can't build a much wider, expansive story, and still have everything neatly resolved at the end of each book. Reality is not like that. The "bad guy" doesn't always get caught. A suggested romance may never eventuate. Certainly, answers to some of the questions will be forthcoming, but then I will introduce new mysteries for you to ponder until the next book. I just think the ongoing story is more interesting, and entertaining, this way.

So, before you post an honest review, which I would be extremely grateful if you would, please understand that by leaving some "loose ends" at the end of each book is not a cheap ploy by me to get you to buy the next book for commercial reasons. It's simply because I'm building an ongoing series that I hope you will continue to immerse yourself in and enjoy. I don't know how many books I will write in the Ravenwood series. Hell, I wasn't even going to write a sequel to Mill Point Road until fans of the book practically demanded I did! However, my promise as the author, to you as the reader, is that I will make the books in the series as enthralling, page turning, and suspenseful as I can without ever taking you for granted.

Best Wishes,

JK Ellem

Turn the page for a sneak peek of
The Sisterhood, Book #3 in the Ravenwood Series

Chapter 1 - The Sisterhood

"I did kill someone," Annabel Chandler said, looking around at the faces gathered around her kitchen table.

There was no point in keeping it a secret any longer. After all, she had told Haley Perez almost three months ago, and Annabel thought it was only fair to tell these women, the same group of women who had so brazenly shared some of their own personal struggles with her during pervious coffee catchups. Not that she had attended many. She had when she wasn't working, and not brain-numbing tired.

At first, Annabel had been standoffish, undecided about these three so diverse, yet seemingly similar women who seemed bound by more than mere friendship or neighborly convenience. The past events on Mill Point Road had obviously created a strong bond between these three women, and Annabel still felt like an outsider.

Inclusion. That is what Annabel craved the most in her life right now, that and to "come clean," to share her past, to stop pretending. The more she saw Rebecca Cartwright, Paige Hamill, and Maggie Vickerman, the more Annabel was drawn to the three. She couldn't explain why. Other than living in the same exclusive enclave high up on a ridge overlooking the town of Ravenwood, she had nothing in common with "The Sisterhood."

The Sisterhood. That was what Annabel had silently labeled the three women. Maybe the fundamental human need for inclusion, for belonging, trumped the differences between the women. Maybe it was the fact they were different from one another that made them a cohesive group.

It was time to share something personal with the group, lay down on the table some secret currency to garner trust. The time for hiding was over.

"I killed my brother," Annabel said. It sounded so strange to hear her own words, words that up until now—with the exception of Haley Perez—had been locked away as only thoughts, hidden deep in the façade she had created, never to be uttered in idle conversation.

Annabel looked at everyone in turn, knowing that these women were strong like her but, collectively, had the potential to make her stronger.

Maggie paused, her outstretched hand hovering above the plate of wild-berry muffins. Becca sat perfectly still, then shifted her eyes sideways at Annabel.

Paige Hamill gave a devilish smile as though Annabel was about to share some sweat-sodden sexual encounter rather than a tale of the cold, harsh death of a sibling at the hands of another. "Do tell," Paige said as a glint of curiosity sparked in her green eyes. Paige seemed unfazed, Maggie shocked, Becca curious yet watchful of Annabel.

Maggie's hand retreated, and Becca now turned her full attention to Annabel, raising one eyebrow questioningly.

Annabel looked at Maggie. "It was only that you were just saying, Maggie, a few moments ago, about Sabine's death. Her funeral." They had all attended the service a few weeks back, yet the topic of Sabine Miller always seemed to creep into the conversation, like her death was a standing agenda item. Rebecca Cartwright, and Paige Hamill had been completely vindicated; Annabel had seen the autopsy report. Sabine Miller had died accidentally falling down Paige Hamill's staircase, breaking her neck in several places, and fracturing her skull.

"I have killed someone." Annabel shrugged. "My brother, stepbrother, I should say." God! Saying those words felt so good. Annabel could feel the atmosphere change in the room—in a good way. Despite not revealing anything further, Annabel could see shoulders visibly relax some more, eyes widened almost in admiration, and faces softened, taking on a glow of mutual respect. A warm, larva-like feeling began to bubble up in Annabel's stomach. A slow, spreading sense of place, as she looked at the three women. She could feel her eyes blur, her vision ripple. These women knew. They were perceptive enough to know what was coming next.

And as if to confirm Annabel's premonition, Becca leaned forward and touched Annabel's forearm, her expression filled with real, honest compassion and understanding. "I'm sure, Annabel, that you had a perfectly valid reason for killing your stepbrother."

Yes! They understood. They had the foresight. Annabel regarded Becca for a moment. It was true; she did have a perfectly valid reason for killing him. Medically, it was called sustaining a fractured cheek and jaw, a broken forearm, and countless bruises, cuts, grazes, sprained wrists, and a few bite marks thrown in for bad measure. Mentally, it was sustaining years of abuse because she had felt powerless, stupid, and utterly incapable of finding the courage to change. After explaining all this and more, the mood around the table descended into a somber silence. Yet, from the women's expressions, Annabel knew she had laid down the right amount of emotional currency in front of the three. She had gained their mutual respect and acceptance.

Finally, it was Becca who spoke. "From what you said, it was either be killed or defend yourself. A simple choice. End the suffering or become a fatal victim to it."

The casualness in Becca's statement made Annabel think there was something more than just words to her statement. A same trodden path, perhaps? "I was stupid," Annabel said. "I allowed Martin to abuse me, both physically and mentally, for so long. We lived in the same town, literally three blocks apart."

"You weren't stupid," Maggie said, reaching forward and squeezing Annabel's hand, then diverting her own hand and finally grabbing that muffin. "Look what happened with Hank. He tried once, and I almost killed him in self-defense. I'm not sure if it was a valid reason to almost killing my husband."

"I could think of several valid reasons to kill mine," Paige murmured into her coffee cup before taking a sip. "Women are just more optimistic than men." Paige turned to Annabel. "We're more hopeful that a relationship will change, that a person will change. Unfortunately, we are willing to sacrifice our own well-being by clinging on to that hope." Paige turned toward Maggie. "Still no signs of Hank?"

Maggie shook her head. "Like I've said before, he is probably miles from here, wouldn't dare show his face. I'd guess he's living in Mexico, shacked up with a few of those whores he liked to visit when we would go down there on holidays. I'd be surprised if he's within a thousand miles of Ravenwood."

Paige nodded before turning back to Annabel. "So how did you kill him?"

"Paige!" Maggie protested, her mouth full of muffin. "You can't ask the woman that."

"If you don't mind me asking, that is," Paige quickly added.

"Not at all," Annabel replied. It was good to talk to these women about this. It felt like the anvil she'd been carrying for so long was now being shared by willing, helping hands. It was a burden, a constant reminder of her past, that she knew she would never truly shrug off. But at least now, thanks to Becca, Paige, and Maggie, the burden seemed less heavy. "I stabbed him in the chest with a kitchen knife. We were in the kitchen, and he'd just thrown a pot of boiling water on me. I had threatened to tell my father about him."

"Who remarried?" Becca asked.

"My father did," Annabel replied. "My real mother passed from ovarian cancer when I was just sixteen. Martin and I were around the same age. The abuse was subtle at first, then escalated over the years."

"Stabbed," Paige echoed thoughtfully.

"Three times."

Maggie seemed to be having difficulty swallowing the last piece of her muffin, while Becca's slow, spreading smile was only eclipsed by Paige's sudden wide grin and even wider eyes. "Good for you, sister," Paige said.

Sister. Yes, Annabel thought. This was a hallowed sisterhood. She felt as though a secret door had opened, and she was being ushered through, to join a select little group: the women of Mill Point Road.

"Some say blood is thicker than water," Annabel said, looking at each face in turn, seeing the reflection of conquered adversity. "But not if that blood is your own, and you've seen enough of it on your own hands and face."

The Sisterhood, order your copy today on Amazon

Jack Ellem is the Amazon #1 Bestselling thriller author in the US and in the UK.

His crime, mystery and suspense books have rocketed to Number 1 globally in the categories of Crime Fiction, Thriller Fiction, Financial Thrillers, Heist Crime, Kidnapping Crime Fiction and Noir.

His cutting-edge stories are unpredictable, multi-layered with sub-plots, twists, and turns that readers cannot see coming and his books have garnered thousands of five-star reviews.

Jack splits his time between the US, the UK and Australia.

So, whether you like crime thrillers, mystery and suspense thrillers, psychological thrillers, domestic thrillers, or just enjoy an addictive read, then pick up one of his books today in e-book or in paperback.

But BE WARNED! You might just find yourself up until 4:00 a.m., reading them.

Printed in Great Britain
by Amazon